About the

Andrea Busfield was born in Warrington, England, and worked for UK national newspapers for 15 years before leaving for Afghanistan where she worked as a civilian editor for a NATO hearts-and-minds publication. Whilst in Kabul, she wrote her first novel, *Born Under a Million Shadows*, which was published in 2009 by Transworld and sold to 18 territories. Her second novel, *Aphrodite's War*, was published a year later, also by Transworld, and sold to five territories. She currently lives in Cyprus with five rescue dogs and a horse.

THE SILENCE
OF STONE

ANDREA BUSFIELD

CillianPress|

First published in Great Britain in 2016
by Cillian Press Limited. 83 Ducie Street, Manchester M1 2JQ
www.cillianpress.co.uk

British Library Cataloguing in Publication Data.
A catalogue record for this book is available from the British Library.

Paperback ISBN: 978-1-909776-18-0
eBook ISBN: 978-1-909776-19-7

Winter foggy morning on alpine meadow
© Olha Rohulya | Dreamstime.com
By Bering Land Bridge National Preserve
(Frozen Lake Cracks and Bubbles) [CC BY 2.0] via Wikimedia Commons

Published by Cillian Press
Manchester - United Kingdom - 2016
www.cillianpress.co.uk

For Lorenz

Chapter One

For a long time Traudi couldn't move. For how long she couldn't say exactly because she was only a child and she kept falling asleep, but it was a long time, longer than she could ever remember – and she had always been good at remembering.

"Memory is a gift, Traudi, make sure you cherish it because in the end that's all that remains."

This was the advice of her mama, issued a year earlier and not especially welcomed at the time. Eight years old and clutching a spelling test bearing a gold star, Traudi had been expecting sweets, and so she stared at the stick in her mother's hands, watching it stir clothes in a bathtub, waiting for an explanation. After a few moments, she turned her attention to Heini who was stood in the doorway holding onto their father's hunting rifle. She raised her palms in question and her brother raised his eyes to the heavens, confident in the knowledge that their mother wouldn't see. A mother's love for a son is blind, of course, but in this case their mama wasn't only blind to Heini, but also to Traudi, to the dog on the couch, to the dust dulling the lamplight and the birds gleefully crapping on their freshly-washed bed sheets. Their mother couldn't see. Her sight had abandoned her in early childhood never to return, and occasionally, whenever she thought she was alone, she could be heard crying for colours she could no longer recall.

"Mama, where are you? It's me, Traudi."

The plea left the child's lips in little more than a whisper, and it brought no reply. The house was empty. The air stood still. And after a while, Traudi drifted back into sleep.

It was sometime later when Traudi woke again. A sluggish dawn crept over the mountains, casting the walls in a bluish grey light. Ice flowers spread their petals upon the glass of the windows. Everywhere was quiet. Even the rowdy river stood still; the open vein of the valley sealed and silenced by the kiss of another long winter.

In her bed, Traudi shivered and tugged at the blanket, bringing it closer to her chin. Deep in the valley there was no escape from the cold, not for the river, nor for the trees, nor for the hungry deer or the birds. Winter fell like a curse, making life harder than it had any right to be. Even the town suffered. An hour's walk away, clear of the forest and further downhill, it gained little from the drop in elevation and the people trapped there would often stare in stunned envy across the lake – at the homes of their neighbours standing in the sunshine, shining like gold on the diamond white snow, whilst they, grey-faced and red-nosed, froze in the shadow of the Dachstein. Hallstatt was beautiful, it was a fact beyond dispute, but it was a town one had to be born to. With the mountain at its spine and the lake at its feet, the town was a flower pressed by giants. At its heart, towering houses were divided by narrow, cobbled lanes, their pastel shades only partially disguising the perpetual battle for light. During winter the days were so short it could send a man mad. Suffice to say then that had salt not been discovered in the rock that protected and imprisoned them it was highly unlikely that anyone would have thought to settle in such a remote, sun-shy corner of the world. But salt had been discovered, and the mountains – cruel as they were – sustained Hallstatt's fortunes.

"Man may live without gold, but not without salt," or so believed Traudi's father, who worked at the mine and was a frequent exponent of the company line. A solemn man with deep set eyes – possibly from a lifetime spent working underground – he effused the soft odour of tobacco and wet stone wherever he went. Though his words were few and his affection limited to gruff words and pinched cheeks, he was an honest man and strong with it, and as well as supplying the meat for the larder he also provided the salt.

"A family may live without kisses, but not without salt," their mother once quipped and Traudi had laughed heartily, gamely repeating the phrase right up unto the day that their father left for work never to return. After that it didn't seem appropriate.

It was a man from the mine who delivered the news. Arriving in the midst of a storm, he revealed in soft, serious tones, that his name was Herr Bittner. There had been an 'accident', he said, and when it became apparent that by 'accident' he meant 'death', their mother responded by grabbing her stomach and seeming to lose balance. Herr Bittner hurriedly pulled up a chair and urged her to sit before asking Heini to fetch a glass of water. Traudi stayed where she was, stood by the fire, watching the man's leather coat drip rain onto the floorboards.

Mr Bittner was clean-shaven, unlike the men of the valley, his eyes were hooded and weary, and when their mother had recovered enough to listen to what he had to say, he littered his apologies with talk of cables and shafts, of efforts frantic and sustained. Amidst her mother's tears and her brother's unvoiced shock, Traudi heard only one truth; that the mountain behind them, with its craggy stomach violated and empty, had swallowed her father, like a toad feasting on flies.

The light was receding when Traudi next awoke. The stubborn grip of sleep had loosened its hold, releasing her slowly, allowing her to fly, and for a moment she felt happy – until she opened her eyes to find herself lying on the floor.

Confused, Traudi glanced at her hands. Tangled around her fingers was the silver necklace her mother had given her. In her palm lay the bone angel carved by her brother. Heini had rarely been generous – not with his gifts nor with his time – which is why she treasured the angel, despite it coming after the most terrible fight, when the children had yet to come to terms with the loss of their father, or their new roles within the home.

"I am the man of the house and you must do as I say!" Barely nine years old, Heini had erupted with all the red-faced fury of a drill sergeant having had his authority challenged. Grabbing Traudi by the hair he forced her to the floor.

"Wash it."

"I will not."

"Wash it."

"I will not!"

"Wash it!"

"No! You can't make me, Heini! You are not my father!" And with no words to counter the argument, nor the experience to diffuse it, Heini hit Traudi full in the face; the back of his hand propelled by months of unshed tears that burst from his gut to erupt in blood upon his sister's split lip. For a moment, maybe more, neither of them moved, both too stunned to react to the violence. But then Traudi's face crumpled, breaking the spell, and as she sobbed her brother fled the house, his cheeks burning with shame.

It was many hours later that Heini resurfaced. By then their mother had returned from Hallstatt, aided by the long stick that detected the obstacles her eyes no longer saw, and she had been nothing more than curious when she arrived home to find her only son absent. Her lack of concern was partly due to a belief that it was in the nature of boys to sometimes go missing, and largely due to the fact that she couldn't see the state of her daughter's bruised face. In the half-light, Heini entered the room as quietly as his boots would allow, but their mother, blind as she was, had the ears of a bat.

"Where have you been, Heini?"

"Nowhere." As he spoke he glanced at his sister on the couch. Caressing the dog's rump with one hand, Traudi used the other to point to the cut on her lip, her eyes livid and threatening.

"*Nowhere* is no answer, Heinrich. I want to know where you've been," their mother insisted.

"Hunting, Mama. I've been out hunting, that's all."

"And did you catch anything?"

"Only a cold."

"Then I assume you'll want the soup that's been waiting for you."

"I guess."

After their mother left her seat to tap her way to the kitchen, Heini took off his boots, ran his fingers through his thick, blond hair and carefully approached his sister. Head bowed, and with his cheeks coloured by something more painful than cold, he knelt by the couch. Before raising his face he brought his hands to rest on the shin of Traudi's leg.

"I'm sorry," he mouthed. "I really am very, very sorry."

And because Heini was her brother, and his blue eyes shone with all the tears he had been fighting since the death of their father, Traudi nodded. A few days later, he handed her the small

11

angel he had carved from the antler of a deer. Though the wings were unbalanced and the face teetered on the wrong side of ugly, Traudi declared the angel to be the most beautiful thing to have fallen out of heaven's blue skies.

"I'll wear it always," she promised, and her brother helped her attach the figure to the silver necklace her mother had given her the birthday before their father died.

Now lying in her bedroom, the light gone and her back all but nailed to the hard floor, Traudi squeezed the angel between her fingers. The bone was cold.

"Heini, where are you?"

Chapter Two

The men switched off their tracking devices, hung up their ropes, changed their boots, stored their skis and debated the merits of emptying their sodden rucksacks before agreeing, almost unanimously, that this was a job that would be better executed after beer.

As everyone prepared to leave, Leo took a moment to place cool palms over his eyes in an effort to ease the burning sensation caused by hours spent in the blistering cold. He didn't need a mirror to know the whites would be red as hell, making him look like an insomniac or a drunk, or a combination of both – something that wasn't too far from the truth these days.

"What about him?"

Leo looked up to see Günter pointing to where Reinhardt was sat at the end of the room, propped against the climbing wall, chin on chest, lips slack and moist, dribbling spittle and whisky.

"Bring him too." Leo smiled. "I'm sure he could manage another drink."

Behind him, Harald swore loudly. "I'm telling you now that if I get dragged away from my wife and bed again in order to find this drunk dog I'm holding you responsible, Leo Hirsch."

"From what I've heard it's your wife who encourages the drunk dog to go missing in the first place," Leo responded.

Ignoring the laughter of the other men, Harald threw his wet socks into a rucksack. He then checked his watch, more out of habit than design.

"Come on, Harri, one little beer won't keep you," Leo urged.

"True, but what about the ten other 'little beers', eh?" Harald frowned and glanced at his watch again. Being three decades older than most of the team he felt the call of his bed more keenly than the other men, but resigned to his fate he quickly laced his boots and moved to the climbing wall where he proceeded to rifle through the pockets of their partly-comatose rescue.

"What are you looking for?" Leo asked.

"Money," Harald muttered. "If the drunk dog's coming with us he can sure as hell pay for his own beer."

Berni's bar was little more than a wooden shack clinging to the edge of the town. It was a sorry looking place mainly frequented by hunters, bachelors and men unable to cope with the modern fashion of having their women drink with them. Ancient deer heads lined the walls, their eyeless sockets boring into the souls of men whose ancestors had cut short their lives, and a wooden cudgel was strapped across the bar ready to be deployed in times of disorder, of which there were few. Only two beers were available, *Stiegl* and *Zipfer*, but there was a plentiful supply of schnapps, brewed locally and famous for their ferocity. Should someone ask for food they were advised to either drink more or leave. If they wanted music they were told to sing. In short, Berni's Hut was a place bereft of charm, comfort, and more often than not, hospitality – which proved quite popular with the men of the mountain.

Despite the late hour drinkers were still spilling from the door into the ice cold air when the rescue team arrived. Squeezing through the entrance, Leo's boots slipped on the floor, wet with slush and wasted beer, and he was forced to quell a number of colourful protests by reminding everyone of the team's heroic status within the community as they ejected one sleeping drunk from a chair so they might settle their own sleeping drunk in his place.

"Is he having a beer?" Berni asked, coming to clear the glasses from the table.

"Why else would he be here?" responded Leo.

Berni threw him a look that was the default setting of most landlords in the region. "You found him up the mountain?"

Leo nodded.

"And how many times would that be now?"

"Three in four years."

Berni sucked his teeth in response. "Bus drivers," he mumbled. "No sense of direction." He wiped a wet towel over the table and went to fetch a glass of beer which Leo subsequently pressed into the grip of Reinhardt's unconsciously malleable fingers. He then bent to whisper into the older man's ear.

"Enjoy your drink, Reinhardt. The next time you do this we'll charge you for our time."

As if in response, Reinhardt lurched forwards, his body reacting to the new environment it found itself in, and Leo took the spasm as a sign of acceptance. Despite the grumbles of some of the team no one thought the man an intentional nuisance. Reinhardt merely had a weakness for strong drink and long walks. But on this occasion he had been lucky; the weather had been fierce and the team had found him within two hours of the call out, sleeping on the old pass to Gosau, sheltering behind a boulder on the Strenhang slope, the snow having only partially buried him. Had the team discovered him an hour later he might have lost his fingers, longer than that and they might have been dragging his frozen corpse back down the valley.

Leo moved towards the bar and Günter promptly handed him a *Stiegl* before running a hand through the long curls of his hair, wet with sweat from the exertions of the mission and the sudden warmth of the bar.

"Busier than usual," Günter shouted.

Leo nodded, raising the bottle as he did so to avoid contact with a Gamsbart goat beard protruding from the cap of a passing hunter. Almost immediately there followed a hefty blow to his left shin. A quick look at the floor revealed an unscheduled descent by a teenager. Leo nudged the youngster with the heel of his boot and into the path of being someone else's problem. He then raised his bottle for a second time. "To the fear," he saluted.

"To the fear," Günter echoed with a laugh.

Every six years or so, the region suffered a spectacular winter. Blizzards blew in from the Atlantic to bury the landscape without mercy or respite. Overnight, ploughs became the only mode of transport and they worked around the clock whilst the country's troops moved in, laying down their guns to take up shovels in an effort to preserve civil order along with the region's homes, as roofs bowed under the weight of the snow. Roads were closed, electricity was lost and, inevitably, the snaking pass connecting Hallstatt to the rest of the world was buried by avalanches. As the lake had partially frozen the town was trapped – no one could get in, no one could leave – and as a consequence, a slow panic took a hold of the community, with the women fretting about food supplies and the men growing increasingly alarmed by the town's dwindling beer stocks. This was 'the fear', and if Hallstatt was to eventually run dry the men wanted to know they had at least played their fair share in the disaster.

"Have you heard from Lisa?" Leo shouted to Günter.

Adopting a pained expression his friend confirmed that he had. "Three dresses and counting."

Leo winced in mock sympathy. "Let's hope the road opens before she discovers handbags and shoes."

"She'll have a job," Günter laughed, "I've informed the bank that my credit card's been stolen."

Leo raised an eyebrow, expressing both surprise and admiration for his friend's unswerving devotion to his wallet. He also thought him insane. Leo had once dated Lisa, a few years before Günter took the brave decision to marry her, and he was almost certain she would batter him when she returned home. Of course, Hallstatt men were always at their bravest, or most foolhardy, when a wall of snow stood between them and their women. Two days ago Günter's wife had driven to Bad Ischl, the summer haunt of the old Kaiser, now popular with tourists and the region's more fashion conscious housewives. Unfortunately, an hour after her departure the mountain shook the weight from its shoulders to bury the road back under twelve metres of rock, snow, forest and whatever else was in its path. Mobilised by experience, the authorities had reacted quickly to the emergency by closing the only other route into the town, fearing a landslide on the road from Obertraun. Lisa had no way back in and though Bad Ischl was barely 20 kilometres away it could have been the other side of the world right now.

"She'll kill you," Leo predicted.

"I know," Günter admitted.

At the far end of the room a group of teenage boys broke into a rousing, if murderous, rendition of a Wolfgang Ambros song. After glancing warily over his shoulder, Günter leaned closer to Leo. His face was sober, his eyes a little less so.

"In all seriousness, Leopold, it's in times like these, when the fear comes around and you're cut off from all that you know, that you come to appreciate the opportunities life puts in your way."

"Fair enough, Lisa's a good woman," Leo responded with a nod, only recognising the error a second later.

"I was talking about the peace and the quiet, *du Flasche!*" Günter snorted, poking his friend in the chest to add pain to the insult.

Permitting a weary smile to cross his lips, Leo drained his bottle and lit a cigarette. In his defence he hadn't been sleeping well, not that this was any excuse – it was commonly acknowledged that mountain men only got emotional about their dogs. But things had changed for him recently, life had become complicated and he'd had a lot more to think about. Though he was doing his utmost to resist it his mind kept dragging him home – to rooms standing lightless and empty, and to a suitcase packed and waiting by the door. He glanced at the bottle in his hand.

"Ready for another small beer?" he asked.

By 4am, the hut, and the few diehards left in it, found space to breathe again as 'the fear' lost its hold in the face of mass insobriety. Leo lit the last cigarette in his packet and wondered whether this might be his signal to leave. Before the idea took hold he ordered one 'final little beer' for himself and Harald who had volunteered to keep him company after Günter declared that having a double bed to himself won over any loyalty to Leo.

"What about the bus driver?" Berni asked.

Leo looked over to where Reinhardt sat. By now his chin had slipped from his chest and his head was resting on the table, close to the hand cradling the glass given to him some three hours earlier. The sight was nothing short of pathetic and, as Harald noted, it was an appalling waste of good beer.

"I think Reinhardt will forego this round," Leo announced.

"I wasn't asking what he was drinking," the landlord responded flatly. "I want you to tell me that you're taking him with you when you leave."

"Leave?" Harald interjected, almost dropping the cigar from his lips.

Leo draped an arm around the older man's shoulder, partly for balance, but also to demonstrate some form of affection. Harri was in the sixth decade of his life and for all of his complaints, punctiliousness and age, he could still match any of the men on the team; mountain for mountain, beer for beer. He was the type of man, in fact, that Leo imagined he might one day become – a thought that both pleased and disturbed him.

Leo looked over to Reinhardt. "Don't fret," he assured Berni. "We wouldn't dream of leaving Reinhardt behind, after all we might need his bus to take us to the next bar once you've run out of beer."

"The day I run out of beer, friend, is the day I stop breathing."

Harald cast an eye over the debris around them, taking in the empty bottles and marinated flesh. "In that case, you might be due a check-up, Berni."

Before the landlord could reply the sound of glass smashing stole everyone's attention. At the table where they'd left him, Reinhardt had finally come round. Surprising them all, he had moved from his seat and was now on the floor, both arms raised above his head, as though expecting a heavy blow to render him unconscious again. A second later, he started to scream.

"Save me! For the love of God, someone save me!"

"Jesus!" Harald shouted back. "How many times does this fool want saving in one night?"

Leo laughed. He then ran his fingers through his short, dark hair before vigorously slapping his cheeks. Being the leader of the rescue team, and one of the few men left standing, he felt a certain sense of responsibility towards their charge so, after finishing his cigarette he went to calm the situation, taking his beer with him.

Crouching by Reinhardt's side, Leo took hold of the man's upraised arms, forcing them into a less defensive angle. "Take it easy, Reinhardt. You don't need saving. You're in Berni's."

"Berni's?"

"Yes, you're safe. Christine raised the alarm, we brought you from the mountain and in a minute we'll take you home."

"You'll take me home?"

"Yes," Leo confirmed. "We'll take you home."

Reinhardt slowly raised his head, pausing briefly to wince at the light. He looked around and though it took him a while to focus, when his eyes finally settled on Leo they were unexpectedly clear. More than that, they looked scared.

"I'm not mad, Leopold."

"No one said you were mad, Reinhardt."

"That's because I've not said anything yet."

Reinhardt dropped his face into his hands and Leo patted the man's shoulder, shamed by a belated sense of guilt. He should have taken Reinhardt home to his wife, or at least forced some coffee down his neck. There was also a pang of regret at having left it to the control room to inform Christine that her husband had been found safe and unharmed. Leo recognised he was an asshole at times and it was a realisation that gave him no joy.

"I'm sorry, Reinhardt. We shouldn't have brought you here," he admitted. But if Reinhardt heard he made no effort to show it. Instead he raised his head to stare into Leo's eyes, as though searching for a sign, and when he spoke his voice was hoarse with emotion.

"I saw things, Leo."

"You saw what things, Reinhardt?"

"Unspeakable things."

"Is that so…"

"Yes, really."

Leo took a deep breath and counted to three. "ok, Reinhardt. Where did you see these unspeakable things?"

"Up there!" Reinhardt jerked his head backwards, indicating the mountain before grabbing hold of Leo's jacket, pulling him closer. Though his hands trembled his grip was surprisingly strong and Leo had to prise the fingers from his arm, all the while keeping his voice calm, as though talking to a child.

"Easy, Reinhardt. Don't worry yourself. Just tell me what you think you saw."

"I'm not *thinking* I saw anything. *I saw* what I saw," the older man insisted, and to Leo's astonishment large tears welled in Reinhardt's eyes. "And I saw them all Leopold, as true as I see you crouched here; all of the men, all of the women, even the poor, tatty-clothed children. It's the truth, I swear it is, and it was dreadful, pure dreadful; their tiny hands, their screams, the grief… Believe what you like, but God help me Leo, I'm telling you that I walked with the dead this night."

Chapter Three

Traudi was six years old when her father died, her brother was eight. Their father's death was nothing short of a tragedy, everyone said so, and when he was laid to rest it seemed that the whole of Hallstatt came out to watch as six pallbearers wearing miners' helmets lowered his coffin into the ground. In the driving rain, words were spoken, but no tears were shed – it wasn't that kind of town – and a band played sombre tunes until everyone returned home. As the crowd dispersed, Herr Bittner shook their mother's hand and financial help was promised, and subsequently given, through the widows' fund. But in real terms, in all the small things that get taken for granted before a tragedy strikes, the family was on its own, and the burden of death had little to do with managing, it was about learning to live – with fewer plates on the table, no cough in the night, and an empty chair by the fire.

Since that most terrible of days three winters had blown through the valley and – given their mother's disability and Traudi's still tender years – only Heini managed to retain a clear vision of the man who had once played such an integral part in their lives. In short, the boy had worshipped his father whereas the women of the house had merely loved him.

Therefore, when the family's grief was still raw, there was nothing anyone could do and there was nothing anyone could say that would bring comfort or reason to the pain the boy suffered. Heini was devastated. His father had been the one to teach him to ski, the one with whom he had gone hunting, the one who had given him his first knife. Tied through blood and a shared sense of solitude, the two of them had spent countless happy hours sat in easy silence, deep within the forest, watching the sun rise, waiting for the sun to set. But it was his father, and not the sun, that Heini's world revolved around. And though he had never been a playful boy he had still been a child – unthinking at times, occasionally demanding, yet firm in the belief that all would be well once his father returned home. Now there was a hole in their lives where security once sat. And though no one expected it, Heini had become the man of the house because he understood there was no other choice.

"Poor Heini."

Traudi ran her fingers across the collection of knives that her brother kept on a small table by his bed. There were six in total; all of them sheathed, lying side-by-side, evenly spaced and arranged in order of size. In front of a cupboard stood four pairs of boots, all of them polished and facing the wall. On a desk she found pencils, collected in a jar, casting spiky shadows across sheets of loose paper stacked in piles according to their colour. Not a thing was out of place, not a book, not a knife, not even a sock. It was a bedroom rigid with discipline. And knowing she shouldn't be there, Traudi closed the door before moving downstairs.

In the hallway, at the bottom of the staircase, a little to the left of the front door, was the toilet. The door was open and – as it should be if the toilet door stands open – no one was inside. There had been times in the past when the door had stayed shut with her brother behind the lock doing God only knows what, but according to her mother this wasn't a topic for decent conversation.

"Everyone needs their privacy," she had said.

"You make it sound like he's up to something disgusting."

"It's a toilet," her mother retorted, and she had raised her hand to signal the end of the discussion.

Moving to the kitchen, Traudi found a fresh loaf of bread on the stove, covered by a muslin cloth. On the shelf, by the window, was a leg of ham. Tearing at the bread, Traudi thought of her brother, knowing he would have slapped her fingers for not using a knife.

"Not here though, are you?" she said aloud, albeit to no one but herself.

Wandering to the front room the floorboards creaked beneath Traudi's feet as the house responded to the pressure and the cold wind rising up from the cellar. It was the strains of weight and weather that her mother believed helped wooden houses to speak, whereas concrete was 'cold and unfeeling'.

"Never live inside bricks," she advised, "they don't care about you and they tell you nothing."

Naturally, Heini had scoffed at the very idea of talking houses and he had informed their mother she was living behind the moon. But Traudi understood that their mother heard more without eyes and so she found herself listening, picking out sounds as the wood reacted to the wind, searching for clues. But for all of its groans, its sudden creaks and cracks, the house told her nothing she didn't already know.

She was alone.

At the door leading to the sitting room, the earthy smell of the river caught Traudi by surprise, reminding her once again of their father, striding through the house in his dark overalls, wafting tobacco and wet stone. With all of her heart, Traudi wished she could recall his face, but in the years he had been gone the sharp lines had melted into a blur. All that remained was a memory of heavy boots on the landing, a shape cutting wood, and a back disappearing down the pathway never to return. Occasionally, Traudi forced herself to focus, concentrating hard to recapture the look of his eyes or the fleeting warmth of his smile, but his features always shifted, drifting into someone else – sometimes it was her grandfather, sometimes the butcher, on one occasion it was Herr Mayer who lived in the woods with his dog and fat pigs. Nothing worked. Despite her wishes and strongest prayers, Traudi's father was gone, he'd never be coming back, and her picture of him grew ever more indistinct with each passing year. As a consequence, and though it pained her to admit it, Heini had become the one person, other than her mother, that Traudi looked up to, the one she admired. Her brother was the twine that held their family together and now, with him nowhere to be found – not in his room, not in the kitchen, not even in the toilet doing the unspeakable – it made her uneasy, until she noticed the fireplace.

Little more than a dusty glow on the iron grate, the fire was moments from dying, but it could only mean one thing; that her brother was near or, at least, not so very far away. It was Heini's job to light the fire. It was his first task of the day whereas Traudi had to wash up. Naturally, this was a chore she abhorred, not only because the grease slipped under her nails and the water wrinkled her skin, but also because of the sheer banality of the task; it was a job that anyone could do, even the blind, and yet it was her cross to bear simply for the sin of being the youngest and of being a girl. Traudi hated it. She positively longed for the responsibility of tending the fire, but her mama wouldn't hear of it and she remained as adamant as Heini that this should be his role and his role alone, and the only time that Traudi found herself released from the hell of the kitchen sink was when she was sick, which she was. Yes, she was. She remembered that now. There was a hot bowl of soup and a cool pillow for her head followed by a long and difficult sleep in which she caught glimpses of her mother – sitting at her side, standing at the window, sometimes curled into a ball on the floor.

Unconsciously, Traudi raised her fingers to her forehead, finding her flesh cold and damp. Toads were cold and damp. The mountain was a man-eating toad. And it was clear that little girls should have nothing in common with either of those things. She was clearly unwell and as such she had every right to expect her family to be there – to bring soup and cool pillows and stories of fairies and angels – and because no one appeared to be present, and because she was left with no other choice but to cope on her own, Traudi began to itch with a familiar rebellion.

Inspecting the wicker basket standing to the right of the fire, Traudi grabbed two logs and a handful of kindling, reasoning that she had to tend the fire if she wasn't to freeze to death. Having watched her brother a thousand times or more she deftly copied the way he arranged the twigs on the fading embers, waiting for them to catch fire before adding a log. Once she was satisfied the flames would take hold, Traudi moved to the couch. As she lay down, her hand reached for the dog, only to remember he had died in the spring.

After their father's accident, which was really his death, there was a concern within the valley that a blind woman with two young children might not be able to cope without a man. It was a concern shared by their grandfather who spent many months sat in his lonely old house in Hallstatt dreaming up ways to convince his daughter to bring her two children to live with him. For *Opa* it was a concern that grew ever more pressing as that first winter approached, shortening the day until it turned the ground white.

"It seems that we can't be trusted on our own," their mother one day declared, her sightless eyes looking between Traudi and her brother rather than at them.

"So we're moving?" Traudi asked.

"If that's what you want. And that's what I'm asking you: do you want to live in our house, in the place you were born, or do you want to move in with your *Opa*?"

"Will you be coming too?"

"If that's what you want."

Pondering the question for longer than was possibly decent, Traudi enjoyed the brief weight of responsibility her answer might carry. On the one hand she loved *Opa*. Furthermore, Hallstatt had a sweetshop, the existence of which occupied much of her thoughts in the valley. But on the other hand she loved being out of the town. She loved their house. She loved her room. She loved the deer in the forest and the angry springtime river that screamed at the mountain after its winter confinement, obliterating all other sound. There was no possible way she could choose between the two worlds, and so she had looked for the answer in the blue eyes of her brother who appeared to be blessed with fewer conflicting interests.

"This is our house," Heini had responded, speaking so firmly it left no room for doubt that this was the answer Traudi ought to give.

Their mother had smiled in response, reinforcing her daughter's suspicions. "And what do you say, Traudi?"

For a second Traudi had paused, imagining *Opa's* smiling face and the taste of sugar on her lips, before bowing to pressure and echoing her brother's sentiments.

"Good, then this is where we'll stay," their mother agreed. And that's what they did – they carried on living in the valley instead of giving up and jumping into the grave of their father.

With the matter settled, a simple routine quickly developed that cemented the family's decision and worked to silence the worry mongers around them. Every morning, with or without the sun's help, Heini rose from his bed to chop the wood that would feed the fire that would keep their mother alive whilst they were at school. When he returned home he chopped the wood to feed the fire that would keep them all warm until bedtime. Of course, this wasn't the only chore of the day, there were many more, and they were shared between the children amid varying levels of protest whilst their mother did as much as she was able. In the evenings, sat in the glow of Heini's fire, Traudi would read from the Bible, cross-legged at her mother's feet, while her brother cleaned his gun or sharpened his knives pretending not to listen. Their mother loved the Bible because it kept her 'connected with the wonder of God', and she insisted that Traudi read to them each night because she said it set them apart from the Catholics who kept 'their book in their church' and 'followed the Beast of Revelation'. As there were a lot of Catholics living in Hallstatt Traudi often wondered whether this was the real reason her mother didn't want to move to the town – for fear that the Catholics' Beast of Revelation might get loose and pounce on her sweet Protestant bones. It might also explain why so many people went missing.

Of course, there were days when the family had no choice but to go into Hallstatt – Beast of Revelation or no Beast of

Revelation – and their mother usually reserved this ordeal for Saturdays when they would leave the valley to spend her widow's allowance on flour, cheese, barley and beans, poultry and ham. On the way home they would stop by *Opa's* house to swap news and eat stew and always, without fail, *Opa* would try to foist money into his daughter's hands as they left. Because she was 'prickly', according to *Opa*, their mother habitually refused the help offered which is why Heini always stepped forward to silently take the notes instead. Sometime in the evening he would then slip the money into their mother's purse. It was a charade that everyone accepted and liked to ignore, but Traudi found it annoying because she was given no role in the subterfuge. *Opa* certainly didn't have any such scruples when it came to her washing his dishes.

Depending on the weather, they would usually leave *Opa's* before the sun started its weary descent. More often than not, it was rarely an easy walk home, not with all the provisions that had to be carried, and the road only remained a road for as long as there were houses to line it; out of sight of the town, the asphalt degenerated into a broken track that ran parallel with the river, climbing gradually steeper as it rose to meet the skirts of the mountain. It was a hard walk, and tough on their legs, and Traudi would constantly glance upwards – expecting the ancient stones of the Dachstein to fall and bury them, so oppressive was the shadow it cast upon their path. But it was also a fear that added to the magic of the valley; that kept it alive in a way the town could never hope to be. There was mystery and colour – from the hard white of winter to the lush green of spring, to the blue skies of summer and the golden hues of autumn – no matter the time of year or the mood of the mountain there was always something to feel, or a noise to fear, or a marvel to wonder at and see. Unless, of course, you were blind.

"It's something you adjust to," their mother admitted when Traudi asked how it must be to never see a flower or a bumblebee or even a tree for that matter.

"I'd hate it. It must be awful," she declared.

"Well, yes and no," her mother replied. "But I'm more able in other ways. For instance, I hear more than I used to, like the call of the birds or the talk of the house. My sense of smell has also changed and I feel more than before. When I open the window I can tell when a storm is coming or when it might rain – long before you tell me there are cows lying in the fields. Even so, and though I don't mind being blind as I know there are people far worse off than me, I'd give anything, anything at all, if the Lord would give me back my eyes, if only for a few minutes, so I might one day see your faces."

"In that case I pray the Lord spares you," Heini shouted, walking ten steps ahead of them, like a scout searching for danger. "Traudi's uglier than a pig dog with ticks!"

"You're the pig dog!" Traudi screamed back in reply.

"You are."

"No, you are!"

"No, you are!"

And their mother had sighed, just as Traudi now sighed as she woke to find dusk falling and the fire once again gasping its last.

Hauling her body from the couch, feeling groggy and fed up, she added more twigs. When the flames took hold she threw on another log.

"Mama?" she asked, though she knew no answer would come. "Heini, are you here?"

With another sigh Traudi reached for the angel hanging once

again at her neck. Offering a brief prayer to God, she asked Him to bring back her family as soon as He was able, or to at least give her a clue as to where they had gone. Then, prompted by the hunger unsettling her stomach, she headed for the kitchen.

Standing on her toes, Traudi reached for the ham on the shelf by the window. Though she knew it was wrong, and she even glanced around to check no one was watching, she took a bite from the leg. As she chewed she hummed to herself and grinned, feeling like the most glorious heathen and imagining Heini's outraged face should he come walking through the door to see the wanton savagery his absence had caused. After licking the salt from her lips, Traudi moved to the larder, searching for milk. In the gloom her fingers fumbled over a number of jars holding pickles and jams before coming to rest on a bottle. Before she could pull it from the shelf a sharp crack thundered through the valley, causing Traudi's heart to thump under her tunic.

She couldn't be certain, but it had sounded like gunshot.

Chapter Four

Leo rubbed his face and rose from the couch. His mouth was dry and he could only imagine how bad his breath smelt. He pulled off his boots followed by his socks and headed to the window, seeking answers he didn't expect to find because the noise that had woken him had come either from a hunter's gun or the mountain. If it was the latter it might mean a call out. If it was a gun, well, it would be a job for the police – the hunting season ended six weeks ago.

Outside, Leo found the world much as he had left it that morning; a landscape of white with roads and pathways reduced to corridors of snow by ploughs and shovels fighting an endless battle with the elements. Barely into the afternoon and a number of windows revealed lights turned on inside the tall, narrow houses that rose like shards from the earth, belching smoke from their chimneys, giving the town a magical, fairytale air. Even Leo had to admit that Hallstatt was beautiful.

Inspecting the mass of rock that dwarfed everything in its shadow Leo saw no obvious signs of a disaster having taken place, and without wishing to, his thoughts turned to Ana, almost managing to smile as he recalled her face when part of the mountain fell away during one of their many walks through the valley.

"How amazing is that?" she had whispered. "Like a bone

cracking; almost painful."

"It's only painful if you get in the way," he had replied, and Ana had laughed, a great, throaty laugh, fat with warmth and affection. Naturally, this had been at the start of their relationship, when they used to go for walks and she still found him funny.

"Damn it," Leo muttered. He shook his head, managing to add nausea to its growing list of grievances. Turning from the window, he glanced around the room and picked up his socks, only to drop them again as the idea of juice took precedence over laundry.

Walking into the kitchen Leo paused before a stack of plates waiting to be washed, wondering whether it might be time to invite his mother for coffee. It was perhaps an ignoble thought, but infallibly practical – Austrian mothers were genetically programmed to clean up after their sons, although most agreed this was a contract of care best left unspoken. Women could be contrary, even mothers, and Leo thought once again of Ana, recalling her general aversion to housework. Much to his amusement, his mother had considered Ana's lack of domesticity an affront to every law of nature and though she blamed 'the girl's indolent Spanish blood' for this deficit in her character she also suspected Ana might be a feminist.

Opening the fridge door, Leo cast an eye over the contents inside; two frankfurters, a jar of gherkins, a tin of herrings and a carton of orange juice. He reached for the juice, already knowing the carton was empty, to tip what dregs were left into his open mouth.

"Damn it," he muttered again before aiming for the bin, which was, of course, far from being empty.

Retreating to the hallway, Leo almost recoiled at the sight of his reflection in the mirror. His black eyes were bloodshot and his dark hair had been pasted to his forehead by sweat and deep sleep. He took a step backwards realising that if he shaved the goatee, right now, with that hairstyle he would bear a passing resemblance to Hitler. Perhaps if Ana was there he might even have found the strength to joke about it, but she wasn't there of course, and even if she were she would have felt compelled to reprimand him, and then he would have told her to lighten up, and she would have responded by calling him a fascist. They probably wouldn't have spoken again until he admitted that jokes about Hitler were hard to get right and even harder to justify. If Ana had been suitably placated they might then have made love.

Leo rubbed vigorously at his scalp, recharging the roots of his hair. Stepping closer to the mirror he blinked hard, slapped his cheeks and considered himself as presentable as he was likely to get. His eyes then moved to the rucksack leaning against the front door, bulging with the sodden clothes of the previous night's rescue. Due to its size it almost hid the suitcase waiting by the stairs – almost, but not quite. Still, there was nothing he could do about that now. The day was gone, and so was she.

Grabbing the rucksack Leo returned to the front room where he emptied the contents onto the dining table – one waterproof jacket; one t-shirt; one pair of socks; two gloves; and one hat – all of them wet and faintly malodorous.

"Damn it."

Losing patience with himself, Leo threw the clothes over four chairs before moving to the bathroom, feeling a sudden urge to wash away the stench of stale beer currently seeping through his pores.

It was early evening when Leo returned to Berni's Hut. The brisk walk had brought back the colour to his cheeks, but though he felt more alive he knew he was in no condition to repeat the performance of his previous visit. He had merely come to settle the bill. Pulling the hat from his head and the gloves from his hands, he ordered a juice. To his credit, Berni didn't flinch at the request, but neither did he move.

"OK, a *Stiegl*," Leo relented.

"Right you are, friend."

In stark contrast to his last visit, the hut was quiet and pretty much empty. Only Sepp the butcher was present; sat at a table enjoying a quiet beer before heading home to his wife and six daughters. It was fair to say that few men in the town envied Sepp's life, but with pickings being slim in a population of roughly 900 some of the younger ones made an effort to keep on his good side. Realising that he too was fast running out of options, Leo vaguely considered buying the butcher a drink until an icy blast blew in from the doorway, saving him from an expense unlikely to accrue any reward. Sepp's eldest was only 18 and being a teacher by profession Leo had little patience for teenage girls.

Before approaching the bar, the man who had come in from the cold paused to hang his hat on a peg next to a deer head. Traditionally dressed, a tide mark on his lederhosen revealed a recent battle with the snow. The scars disfiguring the right side of his face spoke of another battle altogether.

"Bergmann," greeted Berni.

"Bergmann," echoed Leo.

"Berni, Leopold," the older man replied, then, with the formalities over, he took the pewter tankard that had been placed on the bar and went to sit in his usual spot by the window. On the way he nodded to the butcher, the butcher nodded back, and Berni watched the exchange before returning his attention to Leo.

"So how's Reinhardt today?"

"Feeling worse than me, I hope."

"I'm sure he is," replied Berni with a rare smile. "He spent the night walking with the dead, don't forget."

"Don't remind me. It's all he could talk about on the way home."

"Well, in fairness to the man, he'd not be the first to lose his mind on the mountain."

"I'm sure he'll find it again once he's sober."

Berni laughed, poured himself a beer and knocked the glass against Leo's. "Still, Reinhardt ought to be thankful that none of you were injured – it was quite a storm you men went into last night."

"Bah, it's what we do," replied Leo, conscious of the fact that he sounded suitably selfless, almost heroic. "Anyway, I doubt he'll go wandering up the mountain again. He's scared himself witless."

"Are you men talking about Reinhardt?" Sepp approached the bar to place his empty glass on the counter before reaching for his coat. Leo confirmed that they were indeed talking of the bus driver, and the butcher nodded thoughtfully.

"He was in the shop earlier today," he revealed, "beef shank and a pork shoulder. As he waited, he made mention of all this business – seeing the dead and all that – and though I realise he's well known for talking rubbish, I have to say this for him; he didn't sound like a man seeking attention."

"I never had you down as a believer in ghost stories," Berni teased.

"I'm not saying I do," Sepp replied easily. "But what I am saying is there are plenty of people who have gone up that mountain and not all of them have come down. You should know that better than anyone, Leo."

"True," Leo accepted. He raised his bottle in recognition of Sepp's sobering truth and the butcher patted him good-naturedly on the back. For a man who chopped carcasses for a living his touch was surprisingly gentle. Settling his bill, Sepp bid both men a good evening. As the door shut behind him, Leo finished his drink and pulled the woollen hat back onto his head.

"Are you off already?" Berni asked.

"Afraid so," Leo confirmed. "I'm no longer the man I used to be."

"Age comes to us all, friend, but it should never interfere with your beer."

"Maybe next time."

Buttoning his coat, Leo headed for the door. Before he could reach it, a chair was kicked into his path.

"Take a seat."

Leo looked at Bergmann and then at the chair, unable to make sense of the invitation. The last time the old hunter had offered him more than a cursory greeting was close to two decades ago. That occasion had been memorable for two reasons: one, it was short; and two, it had taken place in the outside urinal. "Give my regards to your mother," was all he had said. And when Leo dutifully relayed the message to his mother her eyes had widened a fraction. Of course he had to ask why Bergmann might feel the need to pass on his regards and his mother's reply when it came was equally memorable for its brevity. "I knew him once," she said, "and nothing good came of it."

Leo took hold of the chair blocking his path and spun it round so he might straddle the seat. Bergmann raised an eyebrow, white with age, heavy with derision. Leo couldn't blame him – he'd probably be the same with someone thirty years his junior. He placed his hands on the table, inviting the older man to speak. Bergmann looked at Leo's open palms. Once the moment verged on awkward, Leo withdrew his hands from the table, and Bergmann nodded.

"I want you to tell me what happened last night," he instructed.

"What, all of it?"

"The bit about Reinhardt."

Leo felt the frown creasing his forehead, revealing his irritation. In front of him Bergmann kept his face still, his ice-blue eyes wholly unreadable.

"Reinhardt was drunk," Leo said flatly. "He'd had a fight with his wife and he went up the Strenhang Slope. When Christine sounded the alarm the team brought him down."

"So I gather."

Bergmann leaned forward, clasping his hands on the table. The fingers were meaty, with several knuckles displaying the bulbous mark of arthritis. Even so there was nothing decrepit about the man and he remained a formidable presence. Even by local standards Bergmann was large, still broad at the shoulders and in fairly good shape. Only his face betrayed the harsh reality of a life lived in the mountains and though he might have once been considered handsome the long winters had left his skin harder than tanned leather with the proof of a past accident evident in the deep scars that ran the length of his right cheek.

Leo leaned back in his seat, holding onto the top rail of the chair, ill at ease and uncomfortably aware of the odour of stale beer still seeping from his pores. As Bergmann's eyes bored into him, a prickle of sweat formed on his upper lip. He knew it was the hangover kicking in, but it made him self-conscious, as though he might look fearful, which he wasn't – he was merely perplexed. In front of him, Bergmann stared without blinking, as though waiting for something Leo ought to be aware of. But for the life of him, Leo had no idea what the old man might be after. In the past Bergmann had given generously to the rescue team. Could that be his interest? Perhaps he wanted to know if his euros had been squandered on beer. Unlikely, of course, after all it was widely accepted that the rescue teams spent much of their lives in the pub. How else could they find men foolhardy enough to risk their lives for no money? At a loss, Leo raised his eyebrows hoping the gesture might trigger an explanation. Bergmann scratched at the hole of one nostril using the back of his thumb and when he finally deigned to speak he affected the low-voiced disappointment of a man tasked with interrogating an idiot.

"Reinhardt said he saw something, didn't he?"

"Oh that," Leo half-laughed, "he was rambling, that's all."

"I'm sure he was, Leopold, but I'm not after your professional opinion, now am I?"

Leo's mouth fell open. When he realised, he reached for his cigarettes, to fill the void and plug his annoyance. Bergmann nudged the ashtray in his direction and Leo took it without thanks, his patience having run thin.

"Reinhardt believes he saw things," Leo revealed. And though he felt a pang of betrayal, he went on to repeat everything he had been told – from the wind biting at Reinhardt's face, to the sudden blizzard that engulfed him, to the rock that offered him refuge, and the unexpected appearance of the dead emerging from the trees, their mouths gaping in silent screams, their hands outstretched, begging to be saved. Leo then sat back, expecting the old hunter to laugh or at least rearrange the gnarled mess of his face into a smirk. But Bergmann merely nodded. He then drained his tankard, rose from his seat and retrieved his hat, abandoning Leo at the table – still straddling a chair, nursing a hangover and feeling decidedly foolish.

Chapter Five

The sun was shining with uncustomary intensity – showing a real sense of purpose rather than a tired obligation – and it lit the room, amplifying the dust, warming the wood and causing the house to drip. From every window droplets slipped from the rooftop, their splashes creating an odd kind of music and Traudi swore that even in the house she could hear the call of the river as it sprang back to life, its pebbles and banks washed by the melting caps of the Dachstein. From her place on the couch, Traudi welcomed the sudden warmth on her face. Though having lived through nine winters, she was seasoned enough to appreciate the warmth would be a fleeting respite from the cold and that once the sun sank behind the mountain the heat would die, like water thrown on a fire, returning the world to ice, turning the melting snow hard, making it heavy as concrete and strong enough to walk on.

"Like Jesus on the water," Heini once joked, and their mother had scolded him horribly for the blasphemy.

Reluctantly, Traudi lifted her head from the couch, wondering how on earth it was that such a small movement could exact so much effort. She had lost control of her body, she was convinced of it. From being unable to move she now felt too loose, as though her limbs were incapable, or unwilling, to take the weight. She imagined she was floating whilst being pinned to a board. She needed to eat, that much was clear. Yet she could barely find the strength to get to the kitchen. She was seriously unwell and struggling to function, so where the hell was everyone?

Forcing herself upright, Traudi wondered whether it might be time to seek help, seeing as no one appeared to be in any hurry to come looking for her. It wouldn't be so hard, not once she reached the track that wound its way down to the asphalt road. Of course, after the heavy snowfall it was bound to be blocked, but even if the track was impassable she was certain she could drag herself to Herr Mayer's, and perhaps he and his pigs could look after her for a while. He had no family of his own, and he might even welcome the company. Traudi was certain Heini would be furious once he discovered where she was, but that was her brother all over – always furious about something. Their mother likened his temper to a 'stress valve', but Traudi was too young to appreciate the psychological implications of premature responsibility. She was only aware that Heini issued more rules to follow than the Bible had pages: she couldn't touch the fire; she had to be home by dusk; she couldn't play with his things; she had to stay out of his room; she had to hang out the washing; she must use a knife on the bread; and she had to pretend that everything was fine if anyone ever asked. Well, everything wasn't fine. In fact everything was very far from being fine. And if Heini was going to have a cow about a visit to the pig farmer then more fool him. She had already broken most of his commandments anyway: she had been in his room; she had touched his things; she had built the fire; and she had eaten with her fingers. If Heini wanted to take issue with any of that, he could damn well come and find her at Herr Mayer's house where she would be sat in front of a roaring fire eating hot pork.

Traudi kicked her legs over the couch and onto the floor. After pulling on her boots she stood up, steadied herself and stomped to the pantry to take a few pickled gherkins from a jar. Traudi then pulled her favourite coat from the row of pegs in the hallway. The coat was her favourite by merit of being blue – blue like the sky, unless the sky happened to be grey, in which case it was blue like the sky ought to be. But less and less of Traudi's life was how it ought to be, and before leaving the house her eyes fell upon a black shawl, hanging limply from another peg in the hallway. The shawl belonged to her mother. It wasn't one of her best and she wore it only at night, while she was sat in front of the fire brushing Traudi's blonde hair or listening to excerpts read from the Bible. It was the shawl she wore when she was comfortable at home, and stung by an immediate sense of loss Traudi embraced the knitted wool, burying her face within the folds. She breathed in deeply, desperately wanting more, but finding only disappointment and the smell of dry dust. Even so, it was enough to make her falter; to stop her reaching for the door because no matter how bad things were, no matter how hard life became, she was her mother's daughter and there was a responsibility that came with that love. This was something Heini had taught her, the summer after their father died. He had been sat on a boulder by the side of the river, holding a stick with a line of wire attached to the end, weighted and baited by three wriggling brown worms. Traudi had been watching him fish whilst moaning about chores, adamant that life was less burdensome when they were younger.

"We had our father then," Heini reminded her sternly. "Now he's gone and our mother needs us more than ever before. We have to grow up and do what we can to help her. You know she loves it here, just the three of us, living in our house away from the noses of others."

"But *Opa* loves Mama and Mama loves *Opa*. I don't see how it would be so bad if we went to live with him."

"But it would be bad. It would be like saying we can't manage, when we can, and no one has the right to say any different. You know our mother would move to *Opa's* if that's what we wanted, but it would be awful for her. She'd be like us in her father's house – just another kid – and you know she would hate it. Look Traudi, would you keep a bird in a cage just because you thought it would be safer than in the trees? No, you wouldn't. You'd want that bird to fly and live its proper life. Traudi, our mother is like that bird – to trap her wouldn't be fair."

Traudi had tried to picture their mother, sitting in a golden cage before flying like a bird, but it was an imagining beyond her ability and the only creature that sprang to mind was a mole. It didn't seem right to mention it.

"Yes, I guess it's true. I guess it wouldn't be fair," she said.

Heini lowered his worms into the water before leaning back against the rocks, the rod held casually in his hands. It was a hot, humid day and the sun danced upon his blond hair while the river's light bounced in his blue eyes. Traudi recognised her brother was handsome and she wondered whether she was handsome too. She was even about to ask for his opinion, despite knowing he would probably say 'no', but then he silenced her by continuing to talk.

"People think that because our mother is blind she can't do things," he said, his brow creasing with the effort of collecting his thoughts, "but the only thing she can't do is see. Every day our mother cooks; she cleans the house; she mends our clothes; and she helps us with our homework. If she had to cut the wood she could, and yes, maybe she can't do a few things, like climb onto the roof to fix the guttering or put on another tile, but she can do all the other things. She has her stick. She can find her own way to town. And really, the only reason we go with her, or *Opa* comes to help, is because of all the bags she has to carry home. But of course, people don't see any of that; they only see a blind woman, which makes them blind in a way. So you see, Traudi, if people think we can't manage, that we can't get by and survive on our own, well one day they might come to our house and force us to move – maybe into *Opa's*, maybe into a special home for the blind and their children – and if that ever happened, if that day ever came, it would be because of us. It would be our fault because it would mean that we hadn't done enough to help our own mother."

Traudi groaned into the shawl, rubbing its woollen threads into her face, somehow feeling her mother's presence through the dusty smell of the wool.

"I'm sorry," she whispered. "I won't let you down, Mama. I won't run for help, not until, not unless..."

Shaking her head, Traudi hugged the shawl tightly, unable to demonstrate her love in any other way. And for a moment she felt her mother's arms reach for her, wrapping her in wool, stroking her hair, whispering assurances that everything would be fine. But it was only a moment and once it had passed there was nothing but dust and quiet.

Traudi wiped her face dry, pulled herself free and returned to the front room.

Once again the fire was in its perpetual state of near death and Traudi hurriedly added more twigs to the embers followed by three halved logs. A quick inspection of the wicker basket revealed supplies were low with only a handful of kindling left. It seemed a terrible injustice, given her recent promise to stay, and Traudi sighed heavily as she walked to the front door, which was locked.

Traudi squinted in confusion. No one ever locked the door, there was never any need. It wasn't as if they lived in a city, somewhere frightening like Vienna where terrible things happened to people sitting in their homes. This was the valley, where nothing much happened to anyone and no one came by who didn't belong. Even Heini never bolted the door.

Knowing there had to be a reason, but unable to think what it might be, Traudi shrugged and walked back to the kitchen to fetch the spare key that was hung on a nail hammered into the wall next to the crockery cupboard.

"This place has gone mad," she muttered.

Outside, as far as the eye could see, the snow was thigh-high except along the pathway that led from the house to the gravel road that led to the real road that led to the town. Traudi assumed Heini had cleared the way before disappearing with their mother, and any snow that had fallen in the meantime had melted in the sun leaving shallow puddles on the slabs their father had laid another lifetime ago. Traudi inspected the snow around her, looking for fresh footprints, but there were none she could see other than the stick-like holes of the wandering deer and after buttoning her favourite coat, she followed them.

Although Traudi's objective had been as clear as the morning sky – to pick up as many twigs as she could find and then return home – the fresh air and the presence of the sun, with no wind to nip at her fingers, worked to lure her deeper into the woods, ever closer to the towering wall of the mountain, until she realised she was heading for the river. This was of little surprise when her mind caught up with her legs because she loved the river. She loved it in the winter when it was still as a carpet of ice; she loved it in the spring when it slowly came back to life, tickling the rocks in its wakening belly; and she loved it most of all when it was fat from the rain and melted snow from the mountain, when it crashed through the quiet of the forest, rendering her deaf to all other sounds.

"This river has sustained the valley and the people in it for centuries," her mother once told her. But Traudi had been young at the time, much younger than she was now, and she misunderstood how the river might work to maintain a community, imagining instead the river as a special kind of spirit, a force for good that ran through the valley keeping its families safe. But though she was older and therefore wiser now, she still felt the same way. Subconsciously she reached for the angel hanging at her neck recalling, as she did so, words from the Bible. *Fear not, for I am with you.* As the words echoed in her head she heard the voice of her mother.

Clambering over a fallen tree, wading knee-deep through the snow, Traudi pushed further into the heart of the forest where the warm sun was reduced to dappled winks through the thickening canopy of branches. Her heart responded to the low rumble of the waking river, beating its welcome in her chest. As she neared the bank she passed a shrine holding a small statue of the Mother Mary and an icon of *Sankt Antonius*, the patron saint of missing things and persons. She couldn't remember having seen the altar before, but the mountains were littered with shrines decorated with candles and rosaries, and dedicated to all manner of injuries and disasters. Most were erected along the trails that wound through the trees but occasionally she discovered new ones such as the wooden shrine further down the valley that was nailed to a huge moss-covered boulder. Heini told her the rock was once the football of giants – before the dinosaurs killed them. But when Traudi later asked her mother about this she was told there was no such thing as giants and that the boulders were most probably the product of an ancient landslide. Naturally, Traudi found this explanation somewhat disappointing, but she believed her mother far more than her brother – well, at least for as long as the sun shone. When the sun set different rules came into play and her brother's stories gained greater credibility the darker the sky grew. And according to Heini the mountains were teeming with monsters.

Having read the Bible from cover to cover, and pretty much back again, Traudi knew that within its pages there was clear confirmation of the existence of evil, of unclean spirits and of demons. Though the Good Book failed to mention Heini's witches, Alps or even the blood-sucking dwarves, Traudi reasoned that as Jesus lived far from Austria he might not have actually known about them. But Heini did, and the children at school did, and it was generally agreed that the woods after dark were not the best place to be. Apparently, within the trees were hundreds of dwarves waiting to munch on the bones of lost travellers. When people couldn't be found they would slap their empty bellies and join the other demons who desecrated the town's graves to feast on the bones of the dead. As Hallstatt also had a Beast of Revelation hiding in the Catholics' church, Traudi's visits to the cemetery had become a quietly traumatic experience.

As well as the dwarves and the dead-eating dead there were Alps in the mountains, creatures so unconscionably evil they could turn a man's hair white. According to Heini, the Alps mainly dressed as wizened old men wearing wide-brimmed hats.

Occasionally they came as cats or massive black dogs carrying fire in their eyes and entrails dripping from their fangs. But even worse than the Alps or the demons or the man-eating dwarves, were the witches. They lived in the network of caves higher up the mountain, at a place where the trees stopped growing and the glaciers creaked and cracked. It was the witches who caused the storms that terrorised the valley. Whenever they met, they flew around the mountain's peak, gathering like a great swarm of bees riding upon broomsticks, whipping up the wind so they could hurl it down the slopes.

We wrestle not against flesh and blood, but against the rulers of the darkness of this world, against spiritual wickedness in high places.

For Heini, this was all the proof his stories needed; God knew the dangers, he'd explained them in the Ephesians, and if people didn't get that 'wickedness in high places' meant witches circling the mountains then they had to be crazy. This was what Heini believed, and because Traudi trusted the Bible – and her brother was older and therefore more conversant with the evil that dwelt in the world – she believed he was right.

Suddenly shivering, Traudi moved faster through the snow, trying to ignore the deeper darkness of the forest for fear of glimpsing fire-burning eyes. By the time she reached her old friend the river her heart was thumping like a drum in her chest. Climbing down a rocky embankment, Traudi carefully balanced her feet between two sharp, raised rocks and leant towards the edge of one of the river's giant steps. Beautiful icicles, as long as her arms, clung to the ledge and between them she cupped the gently flowing water into her hands and drank. After splashing her face the hard cold helped to chase away some of the fears of the world, and Traudi clambered back up the slope. But a quick look up, through the needles of the evergreen trees, told her she needed to hurry. Though the sun continued to shine, darkness could fall in the mountains with the speed of candle being extinguished, and Traudi had no wish to find herself in the woods with all of its flesh-eating spirits and murderous goblins when the light went out. Hastily, she grabbed as many twigs as she could lay her hands on and after filling her pockets she ran as fast as the snow would allow her.

Arriving home, the house was much as Traudi had left it, which was empty. Burying her disappointment, she locked the front door – having decided there must be a reason for it being locked in the first place – and hung the key back on the nail by the crockery cupboard. She then grabbed a handful of bread and bit into the ham. With her cheeks full she wandered into the living room where she emptied her pockets to place the twigs on the hearth to dry them in front of the slowly dying fire. Returning to the kitchen, she ate a little more ham before drinking water from the tap.

After the cold of the woods, the house felt warmer than it had done before. But Traudi looked through the kitchen window to see the sun's reckless descent towards the jealous peaks of the Dachstein. Another day was coming to a premature end and she kept her coat on. Traudi always felt sad for the dying sun, even though its rays exposed all the scratches and dirt on the walls. Walking into the sitting room she traced her fingers along the dusty wooden panelling, vaguely wondering whether she should do something about it. On the one hand it would please her mama, but on the other she could see no benefit in doing chores when there was no one present to admire the effort they took. So in the end she simply ignored the need, knowing Heini would be all too eager to issue orders when he returned home.

Crawling onto the couch, Traudi curled into a ball to keep herself warm. Her last thought was of her mother, standing at the door, holding a parcel of hot sausages.

When Traudi woke it was almost dusk, the room was grey, the fire was in its habitual state of near death and she felt her heart hammering in her chest. Below the couch, the floor moaned and she heard the distant creak of a door. Traudi leapt to her feet, pausing only to steady herself as her head span and her limbs protested.

"Thank you, God. Oh, thank you, God."

Running to the window, eager to see the evidence of her family's return, her head anticipated the tap-tap of her mama's stick as she entered the room and the practised gruffness of her brother's voice. Though the familiar sounds were simply the product of her imagination, Traudi knew it was only a matter of time before reality caught up, and though she had to blink back tears of relief stinging her eyes, she felt immediately calmer. And yet, there was already a part of her getting annoyed.

Without doubt, her family should never have been gone so long. While Traudi half-expected such selfish behaviour from her brother, she was surprised by her mother. Mama could be insensitive at times and not always truthful – such as the time she said the dog had died in his sleep when in fact Heini had taken him to the woods and shot him in the head. Traudi had been livid when she overheard her mother asking if 'the death had been clean', not realising she was standing at the door. And despite her claim that the murder was 'an act of kindness', when Traudi asked whether her brother would next shoot *Opa* in the head, her mother had actually laughed. It was hardly the reassurance Traudi had been hoping for. In fact she had been quite shocked at the time and it had made her wonder whether her mother might be as unpredictable as her brother.

Traudi clenched her fists as indignation began a small fire in her belly. Then, almost immediately, she took a deep breath and told herself she needed to be reasonable. After all Mama and Heini must have had a reason for leaving her alone. And as she thought of all the possibilities she forgave them enough to move on and picture them all later that evening, sat by the fire, eating a hot barley stew, their faces glowing in the warm light, feeling happy and safe. Perhaps, after Mama had recounted the terrible misfortune that had kept them from home Traudi would reveal the story of her own survival and her brother would look up, revealing respect in his ice-blue eyes after hearing everything she had endured. Of course, Traudi probably wouldn't mention biting into the ham or snooping in his room, but she would most likely admit she had kept the fire burning. Heini might even respond that under the circumstances she had had no other choice, further suggesting that in future she might build the fire herself when he was busy. No doubt she would still have to wash up, but it would be a start to a better life. Oh yes, they would have the best night, Traudi was sure of it. Furthermore, she would be able to sleep in her own bed again because she no longer had to constantly feed a fire that was in a permanent state of exhaustion. But first of all – before all the good stuff – she needed to be a little strict. That would be the right course of action, at least initially, and it would be wholly justified given her mother's long period of absence when she needed her care. Therefore, having thought about it, Traudi didn't instantly run to unlock the front door, nor did she rush out to greet them. Instead, she stayed by the window and waited for her family to come to her. When after a few seconds there remained no sign of them, Traudi moved to another window that looked out onto the field rather than the pathway.

Peering outside, it took only a second to spot the fresh tracks disturbing the blanket of snow. They came from the woods, not from the road, and instead of veering left, towards the front door, they swerved right, in the direction of the cellar.

Traudi pressed her face against the glass; no longer confident she wasn't dreaming. From the window there seemed to be only one set of footprints, not two, and it was clear that a great weight had been dragged behind them.

More than that, the snow was streaked red.

Chapter Six

With only one day to go until the semester break was over Leo realised, with a fair degree of fatalism, that he had accomplished absolutely nothing. The admin for the rescue team lay untouched, as did the plates in the sink, and the suitcase – that persistent, pitiless reminder of all that had gone wrong – remained by the door. In fact the only development, if squatting could be called that, was the arrival of Günter who found himself homeless after the pass reopened and his furious wife failed to see the funny side of her humiliation in the shops of Bad Ischl.

Leo sipped his coffee and looked at Günter's pale limbs sprawled over the couch. The intrusion irritated him. The fact that Günter could sleep also annoyed him, as did the realisation that he had purloined one of Leo's few clean T-shirts in lieu of pyjamas. Despite everything they had endured over the years – the highs, the lows, the shared girlfriends and the three nights in Vegas they agreed should never be mentioned outside of Vegas – there wasn't a part of Leo that felt any sympathy for his friend. Günter was solely to blame for the situation he found himself in. He was cursed by a myopic outlook on life, and it was a condition dangerously worsened by beer.

Leo bent forwards, unable to stop himself from inspecting a bubble of spit playing on Günter's lips as he snored. The change of angle gave him an astonishing view of two cavernous nostrils, and though Leo was just as annoyed with Lisa he could only conclude that she had earned every cent of the money she had managed to spend before her husband deactivated their credit card.

Conscious of how it might look should Günter awake to find him staring at his face, Leo moved to the study – a somewhat grandiose title for a room with a table and one chair. Placing the rescue team's admin tray out of sight, he flipped open the pages of Benn & Evans' comprehensive work on *Glaciers & Glaciation*, resigned to the fact that he had better get some work done. Despite an almost pathological dislike of students, Leo had clocked up ten years as a teacher, a fact which both amazed and depressed him. Time was running away from him, fleeing the sinking ship of his life, along with everything else.

"Damn it," he muttered, feeling distraction hovering to take him. He shook his head and returned to his books.

Geography was Leo's subject, glaciers were his speciality and because he was in a bad mood he pondered the idea of blowing his Third Years' recalcitrant minds with a lesson on landsystems and megageomorphology. Hell, he might even take them to the final frontier – Extraterrestrial Glaciations. Granted, it would be a challenge – his students had yet to grasp the basic concept of glacier motion, not to mention meltwater or snow and ice for that matter. But it was a fascinating subject, worthy of exploration, because the Martian ice caps worked differently to those on Earth, the class's primary sphere of glacial study.

Leo glanced at the wall a little to his right, his eyes drawn to the collection of stills he'd pinned there many moons ago. Sadly, there were no Martian ice caps to marvel at, but the Earth's own glacier formations were other-worldly enough and his eyes lingered with affection on the blue lobes of Alaska's Malaspina Glacier, on the huge, jagged facade of Argentina's Perito Moreno, and the 62km long Baltoro Glacier that sliced through Pakistan's Karakoram mountain range. The pictures were professional, spectacular and awe-inspiring, yet Leo knew that no photograph on Earth could ever do justice to the impossible beauty of such giants. It was a knowledge that also caused him some measure of anguish. Over the years, modern man had trampled roughshod over the very world it sought to improve. Greenhouse gas emissions had warmed the planet to such an extent that glaciers were rapidly melting. Hard to believe, but a hundred years ago the Glacier National Park, that great ice giant of Montana, had proudly boasted 150 glaciers – now it had 27. It was a shocking story echoed throughout the length and breadth of the globe. In the Northern Hemisphere, thaws were coming a week earlier than they used to and the freeze was occurring a week later. If the pattern continued, photographs would be all that remained one day of some of nature's most dynamic creations.

Leo had spent a lifetime around mountains; climbing them; searching them; and simply experiencing them. Over the years he had scaled not only the glacial peaks of the Dachstein, but also the glaciers of Pasterze in the Eastern Alps, Les Bossons in France, the Zugspitze in Germany and Norway's Jostedalsbreen National Park. If fate smiled kindly, he hoped to one day visit China's Jade Dragon Snow Mountain, because with climate change causing the glacier to recede by some 150m in 16 years many experts were predicting it would be lost within 50 years – becoming a memory to some, a photograph to generations more.

"You're obsessed."

That had been Ana's considered, and forthright, opinion the first time she had set foot in his study. And to be fair, it was hard to argue the point when she was stood in front of a picture of the mummified remains of a man who had been preserved in ice for more than 5,000 years.

"That's Ötzi," Leo had said.

"You've given him a name?"

"Of course I've not given him a name! What do you take me for?"

Ana had thrown him a look that managed to be both provocative and wary, but because he couldn't help himself, and he was keen to make a good impression, Leo proceeded to give a lengthy explanation of how a newspaper – not him – had named the mummy after the Ötzal Alps in which it was found.

"Considering he's been dead for 5,000 years he appears to be in remarkable shape," Ana had commented. "He looks like polished oak, more like a beautiful carving than a man."

"Yes, he is remarkable," Leo had replied and, without meaning to – given that Ana already thought him obsessed – he told her how a couple had found the body in 1991 whilst hiking on the Niederjoch Glacier, a fraction inside the Italian border.

"It had been another hot summer and the glacier had retreated thereby exposing a body, face down in the melting ice. The Austrian police were called, as it was believed the body was on our side of the border, and they thought, at first, that it might be the body of a music professor who had disappeared in 1938. But it wasn't, it was Ötzi – Europe's oldest natural mummy."

"And what happened to him?"

"They initially thought he was caught in a snowstorm, but it was a blow to the head that killed him, maybe from a fight or an ambush."

"I actually meant the music professor."

"Oh," Leo paused, "I don't know. Perhaps the discovery of a 5,300-year-old ice man distracted them from that inquiry."

To his delight, Ana had smiled at that, her painted lips stretching with all the innocence of a panther on the prowl. "Well, men can be so easily distracted, don't you think?"

Excited, if startled, by the challenge, Leo had tried to think of a response, but his head swam with images of Ana's full lips, her coffee-coloured arms and the tight seat of her jeans. She was beautiful – the most exotic creature he had ever encountered in Hallstatt – and as a consequence he felt uncommonly boyish around her.

Ana had recently arrived in Hallstatt to teach sculpture at the technical college. She revealed she had left Spain to reclaim her Austrian heritage – her mother was from Valencia, her father from Salzburg and, by all accounts it had been a messy and somewhat acrimonious divorce. After a chance encounter at the Post Office she had been subtly diverted from her path of self-discovery by the lure of coffee with a fellow teacher who introduced himself as Leo Hirsch. A week later she was in his study and Leo could barely believe his luck.

"And what about these?" asked Ana.

Vaguely conscious of staring at her breasts, Leo raised his eyes in panic. To his relief he discovered Ana wasn't looking at him, but rather at a collection of photos of children tacked to the wall. They were all dead, of course.

"Ah yes, this one is Juanita, this one is La Doncella and this is the Prince of El Plomo: three Inca mummies – none of whom I named," he informed her, sounding more relaxed than he actually felt.

"How old are these?"

"About five hundred years."

Ana emitted a whistle of astonishment. "They've still got hair."

Moving to her side, Leo raised a finger to trace the braids on one of the children. "Prince of El Plomo," he said. "He was discovered in 1954 on Plomo el Cerro in Chile. They think he was eight years old. His hair was woven into more than two hundred braids."

"The poor thing looks like he's sleeping."

"He probably was when he died. The boy was a sacrifice and from the vomit on his clothing they think he must have drunk a corn-based beer called *chicha*. After tucking his knees under his chin, he settled down, went to sleep and froze to death." Leo waved a hand towards a picture of the mummy known as La Doncella. Her arms were folded on her stomach, her legs were crossed and her eyes were also shut as though she were sleeping. "La Doncella was among three children found at the same time," Leo continued. "The ice had so perfectly preserved them that when a team of researchers examined their corpses they found their hearts were still filled with blood. They also had air in their lungs and their brains were so perfect they could have died moments earlier. Quite fascinating."

"Fascinating or ghoulish."

"Do you think so?"

"Yes, I do."

Ana continued her leisurely circuit of the room and Leo watched with a creeping sense of trepidation – half-hoping she would grow bored, or better still find herself overcome by desire, anything, anything in fact that might tear her eyes away from the wall just for a moment before she saw... but no.

"What's all this about?" she asked, coming to stop in front of a list he'd pinned to a corkboard bought from IKEA.

Leo shifted uneasily in his boots. "Names of people."

"I can see that," Ana had laughed. She glanced over her shoulder to where he stood. Her eyes were playful and warm, and Leo took a deep breath. There was no easy way to say it.

"It's a list of the missing."

"The missing?"

"Presumed dead."

"In Chile?"

"No, from here."

"What all of them?" Ana's eyes widened, her forehead creased and Leo came to her side. He had to admit, the list was actually quite long. But in fairness only a few of the names belonged to those who had disappeared during his time with the rescue team, the rest he had retrieved from the archives.

"It's a tough area," he explained. "Occasionally people go up the mountain and they don't always come down. I keep a record of them all, just in case."

"In case of what?"

"In case they reappear."

"Like Ötzi?"

"Well, no – not like Ötzi – they wouldn't be mummified, at least not in my lifetime, but I guess they'd probably turn up dead… like Ötzi."

Ana stared at him for a second, communicating a disquiet for which he appeared to be solely responsible, she then returned her attention to the list and began reading.

"Andreas Riezinger, Albrecht Heschl, Bernd Meurers, Claudia Kimmes, Kurt Eisl, Waltraud Bergmann, Christian Suess, Rudolf Koller, Markus…" She paused for a second, halfway through Markus Hirsch. "Hey, isn't that your surname? Is Markus any relation?"

"No relation," Leo replied, "though you could say there's a tenuous connection – he went missing in 1978 when my father led the rescue team."

"So, it's your father's fault he's missing."

"You could look at it that way."

"And what about this guy, the one from three years ago according to the date – David Chamberlain – was he your fault?"

"If you like," Leo replied, smiling though he couldn't be sure she was teasing him. "Actually, Chamberlain is an interesting case. He was an Englishman who moved to Hallstatt three months before he disappeared. The police were contacted by a relative who had been trying to get hold of him for a week and when they broke into his house they found his wallet, his car keys, credit cards, everything he might ordinarily need, even his watch, all of them left on the kitchen table. When the police asked around, the last sighting was of him running up the mountain."

"Was he being chased?"

"I don't think so. He was wearing a tracksuit and trainers."

"Jogging, then."

"It would appear so."

"And what do you think happened to him?"

"I've honestly no idea. The mountain and dog teams both searched, but there was no sign of the man, not a trace. It was summer when he went missing so there were no tracks to follow, not even any circling birds, we just had the information that he had gone for a run."

"And he just vanished?"

"It would seem like it, not that that's so unusual in this region. The mountains are riddled with holes and full of people who went up and never came down – hikers, ramblers, climbers, suicides, policemen, teachers, jilted lovers – they're all here or there, or somewhere."

Leo ran a finger down the names, from the top to the bottom of the page.

"Nice list to have on your wall," Ana commented dryly.

"You're just being polite."

"No, I'm not. I think it's great – not macabre at all, very normal, in fact."

"Glad you see it like that."

"What normal person, wouldn't?"

"Exactly."

And they had both smiled, because a photo collection of frozen corpses on the wall and a roll call of the missing-presumed-dead in a house belonging to man who lived on his own in a sun-shy corner of the world didn't seem especially normal at all. And after smiling they seemed to collide a little before sharing their first kiss.

"I'm hungry."

Leo glanced at the doorway to find Günter standing there – tugging at the crotch of his pants.

"And what do you expect me to do about it?"

"There's nothing in the fridge."

"I know."

Günter looked around the room, searching for, Leo presumed, something to sit on. It gave him some perverse satisfaction that there was only one chair available and he was sat on it. Günter rubbed his face briskly.

"Nice wallpaper," he noted, leaning against the door, pointing to the print of the Prince of El Plomo.

"Get your pants on," Leo replied wearily. "We'll go to my mother's house. She's sure to have soup on the stove."

Günter's face lit up. "Your mother makes great soup."

"So does Lisa."

"True, but there's less likelihood of your mother pouring it over my head."

"I wouldn't be so sure," Leo replied.

Making their way along *Seestraße* neither Leo nor Günter felt the need to speak. The wind that swooped over the lake cut sharp as knives in their lungs, negating the warmth of the sun, and they were hungry. February was coming to an end but the winter had merely reached its seasonal stalemate; neither going forwards nor back. Since the night of the call out, no snow had come to clog the streets, but the temperature struggled to rise above freezing, making everyone tired and brittle. In a week or two the great thaw would begin, but the tug of war between winter and spring could last well into May. Though Günter and Leo were proud Hallstatt men – from their North Face beanies to their La Sportiva boots – even they missed the sensation of warmth on their skin from time to time.

Heading towards *Marktplatz*, the two men passed a group of floppy-fringed students from the technical college. Their presence reminded Leo that Monday morning was fast approaching and he raised an eyebrow at Günter, resigned to his fate and silently lamenting their own fast-fading youth. Günter shrugged yet neither man felt moved to speak, not until several pockets of wandering Chinese came into view carrying rucksacks and cameras.

"I don't get the Chinese," Günter remarked before deliberately walking in front of one of the tourists who was attempting to take a photo while wearing mittens.

"Well, I'm sure the feeling is mutual," Leo replied, pausing to allow the woman to take her shot of the lake.

"I don't mean it in a derogatory sense," Günter shouted over to him. "I mean, I don't get why they come here. How have they even heard of the place?"

Leo took a second to think before rattling off all the reasons why a person might want to fly 7,000 kilometres to visit a town with no nightclub. "We're a World Heritage Site, we're one of the oldest, continually habited settlements in the world, we offer great scenery, there's plenty of salt and we've a church packed with 1,200 painted skulls. What isn't there to like?"

"Wouldn't it be easier to go to the one in China?"

Leo laughed, recalling the report in the local Press of a replica Hallstatt opening in the southern province of Guangdong. "Not quite the same, I suspect," he said.

"Not so many Chinese there for a start," grumbled Günter.

Leo grinned and pulled the woollen hat he wore further down his head, feeling the pinch of the cold at his ears. A little in front of him a young Chinese girl swung her arms wildly, fighting to keep her balance upon the icy cobbles, now cleared of snow but far more treacherous without the right footwear. Leo sprinted towards her, caught her arm and pulled her vertical, much to the delight of her friends. Naturally, one of them then pointed to a camera, and who was he to refuse.

"It's tough being a hero 24/7," he quipped as he brought his arms around the women gathering at his side. Günter shook his head and pointed to his empty stomach.

After gamely inspecting the photo on the tourist's camera display Leo shook hands with the group and ran to catch up with Günter, who had by now turned into *Badergraben*. As Leo reached the corner he was surprised, and slightly embarrassed, to see Reinhardt standing in front of the *Grüner Baum* restaurant. It was the first time he had laid eyes on the bus driver since pulling him from the Strenhang slope and though Leo felt obliged to offer a word of greeting he didn't want Günter turning up at his parents' house unannounced and demanding soup. Besides, Reinhardt appeared to be in dispute with someone dressed in Lederhosen. Leo couldn't identify the man from the back of his hat, but the bus driver was clearly unhappy.

"I've told you everything. There is no more!" Reinhardt suddenly shouted, roughly extricating himself from the other man's grip as he did so, oblivious to the stares of the startled tourists around him. As he stomped away, burying his hands deep in his overcoat, he spotted Leo and his eyes widened a fraction, perhaps feeling the same element of surprise or embarrassment that Leo had so recently felt. Leo raised his eyebrows in acknowledgement before glancing away towards the cause of Reinhardt's unseemly tantrum. To his very real surprise he found Bergmann staring at him. Even from a distance Leo could see the scars running down the length of the old hunter's face, a livid purple in the cold air, and he flinched under the scrutiny of the man's icy blue eyes. Unsure of what to do under the circumstances, Leo raised a hand to wave, but Bergmann ignored the gesture. Instead he frowned, spat on the ground and headed off in the opposite direction to Reinhardt.

"Great soup, Frau Hirsch," Günter said admiringly. He placed his spoon on the table and Leo's mother immediately swooped to pick it up. If there was one thing she couldn't abide it was mess.

"When are you going back to your wife?" she demanded, and Leo grinned, charmed once again by his mother's lack of tact.

"When she apologises is when I'll go back," Günter answered easily, leaning back in the chair and slapping his belly. Leo's mother handed him a napkin which Günter promptly used to clean his nose. About to discard it on the table, Frau Hirsch gave him a stare that needed no interpreting and Günter rose from his seat to throw it into a bin under the sink.

Leo's father, being more tolerant of the failings of his species than his wife, patted Günter on the back as he retook his seat

64

and passed him a *Zipfer*. Leo waited a moment, to see what it might bring, before eventually leaving the table to fetch his own beer. The three men then agreed to relocate to the front room to sit by the open fire.

Removing his reading glasses, Leo's father placed them on the open beak of an *Auerhahn* pheasant he had shot in 1984. He looked tired, and as it was Sunday his chin was unshaven – a small, but personally significant revolt against his wife's insistence that he accompany her to church. As well as looking untidy, the stubble on his chin revealed how far age had crept up on him. Leo's mother on the other hand revealed no grey in her deep auburn hair, but this was a miracle largely credited to the monthly attentions of a hairdresser.

"I saw Bergmann and Reinhardt on the way here," Leo said matter-of-factly as he pointed his toes towards the fire.

"A slow news day is it?" his father responded, and Günter laughed loudly – far too loudly for the liking of Leo's mother who quickly walked into the room to look at their guest with something close to suspicion.

"There's no more food," she said.

"But I'm a homeless man," Günter protested.

"Then stop playing the fool and go and apologise to your wife," she replied tartly.

Günter played to the sleight, clutching a hand to his chest, feigning an invisible and intolerable pain. In response, Leo's mother slapped him about the head. However, it must have been harder than she had intended because Günter looked slightly stunned and Leo's mother immediately offered to fetch him some strudel.

"So what's so intriguing about Bergmann and Reinhardt passing the time of day?" Leo's father asked.

"I don't think they were chatting, it looked like an argument to me."

"About what?"

"I don't know."

"Did they come to blows?"

"Not that I saw."

Leo's father squinted. "Not much of an anecdote you've got there, Son."

Again Günter laughed, and Leo tried to ignore him.

"It just struck me as strange, that's all," he said.

"Well, Bergmann is strange, and Reinhardt's no better," his father conceded.

"Perhaps, but what's also strange is that Bergmann spoke to me for the first time in 20 years the other day, demanding to know about Reinhardt."

"Demanding?"

"That's what it felt like."

"And what did he want to know about Reinhardt?" Günter asked, taking the strudel from Leo's mother with a smile as she re-entered the room.

"He wanted to know what Reinhardt was saying when we brought him down from the mountain."

"And what was he saying?" Leo's father asked.

"Nothing important – he was pissed and talking shit."

A hand slapped Leo about the head and Günter smirked.

"Less of that language in this house," his mother warned. "You're not in Berni's now."

Leo apologised, while rubbing his scalp.

"So what shit was Reinhardt saying?" his father asked, glancing at his wife and grinning.

"All sorts," replied Leo. "He's convinced he saw ghosts. He

reckoned he 'walked with the dead' that night on the mountain."

"He wasn't doing much walking when we found him," Günter interjected, snorting at the memory of the bus driver shivering behind a rock, half asleep, chest deep in snow. Leo was about to respond – to offer a nugget in Reinhardt's defence – but he found himself distracted by the question that appeared in his father's eyes and the small, almost imperceptible shake of his mother's head. Before he could comment, his mother killed the conversation in the best way she knew how.

"Have you heard anything from the Spanish girl?"

Chapter Seven

The floor was dusty and Traudi felt the dirt sticking to her skin, fastened by a fear that seeped from her pores, smothering her slowly, making it difficult to breathe. Above her head the rusty coils of several bedsprings were visible through three large holes in the mattress. She had glimpsed them only briefly, catching sight of them as she slipped under the bed to slide herself into the furthest corner of the room. Once the cold wall hit her back, she stared straight ahead, her eyes trained on the foot of the door, praying it wouldn't open.

Fear was not unknown to Traudi, she had met it before, usually in the forest as the light began to fade and her imagination conjured up witches and Alps and blood-sucking midgets. But this was different – far worse than any imagining. It was dense and it was black and she could think of no way to escape it. In the woods there was always a way out: a light breaking through the trees that would lead to the open field where the sky would loom large and the horrors of the forest would stop their pursuit. But now, when she considered that same field – that open space that defied the forest and circled her home – it became something different, something uncertain. It was a thing unsafe, an area offering no sanctuary from the dark, but rather a place to be seen in, hunted down and killed in.

From the tracks in the snow, Traudi knew that whatever

menace had broken free of the woods had walked out of the trees and straight for her house, up to and into it. Whatever nightmare haunted the dark had broken free of its boundaries, and everything had changed. Nowhere was safe. Every place was exposed. And her mama must have known this.

Traudi thought of the front door and the surprise she felt at finding it locked. For as long as she could remember the door had remained open, no matter the time of day, no matter the weather, no matter who was inside or out. And though she had assumed there must be a reason it was bolted she had failed to think of it, until now. For Traudi, the locked door was the final proof that there was something terrible outside – something or someone – and whatever it was that had intruded on their lives it could only be a bad thing, a monstrous thing, and Traudi was scared.

"Our Father who art in heaven, hallowed be your name, your kingdom come, your will be done, on earth as it is in heaven. Give us this day our daily bread, and forgive us our trespasses as we forgive those who trespass against us. And lead us not into temptation, but deliver us from evil. PLEASE, PLEASE, DELIVER US FROM EVIL, LORD. For thine is the kingdom, and the power, and the glory, forever and ever. Amen."

Traudi reached for the angel hanging at her neck. Though her brother had carved it as an apology, his care had transformed it into a charm. The angel would work with God to keep her safe. She had believed it from the moment she felt the bone resting on her skin. As for her mother, she also had protection: she wore a cross, the symbol of Christ the Redeemer, who died so the world might be saved from their sins. But Heini, well, he never wore anything. He had no amulet to protect him. No cross, no angel, not even a lucky pig in his pocket. He had always relied on their father to keep him safe, and when their father had died he had relied solely on himself. Traudi gasped, gagging at the anguish pushing at her throat and the thought of her mother and brother and only one cross between them. Jesus was powerful, but there was only so much He could do, and people had to believe in Him. They had to have faith and they had to say their prayers. But Heini, no matter how much their mother scolded him, had hardly ever said his prayers, and he stopped altogether once their father died. He was a boy who had turned his back on his faith and Traudi couldn't see how he could therefore be saved.

Fighting the despair rushing up from her stomach Traudi screwed her eyes shut, forcing back the image that was forming in her mind, that of her mother and brother – all that she loved, all that she knew – lying together, not so very far away, out of the bedroom, down the cold stairs, under the floorboards and dead on the cellar floor.

"Dear Father in heaven, please protect my mother because she loves you very much and please do everything you can to help my brother because he is only a boy and he knows not what he does. Amen."

The prayer was offered quietly in little more than a breath. Even so, Traudi tensed, waiting for a response – not from God, not from Jesus or even the Blessed Virgin Mary – but from the faceless terror that lurked below or around, somewhere close by, surely near enough to hear her. Forcing her eyes open, Traudi stared at the door, too frightened to blink until her sight blurred with the effort. Her head lay on the floor, her ears twitching, searching for warnings, anticipating the sound of a heavy tread on the stairs. But there was nothing. No sound that didn't belong. The door remained shut, the house stood in its own form of silence, and the only unfamiliar noise she detected was that of her heart banging in her chest, and the blood coursing through her veins, pulsing in her head.

As she waited, lying rigid in the corner, almost embracing the floor, the age-rattled house began to make itself heard. Wooden houses breathed. Wooden houses spoke. Wooden houses were friendly. This was the truth according to her mother, and with all of her heart Traudi hoped she was right. But their house wasn't only made of wood because there was also the cellar – a cold, grey tomb made of concrete and stone. It was a place of cobwebs and spiders, crammed with chopped wood, old furniture and jerry cans of oil. The cellar spoke to no one and it cared for nothing. It simply existed. It was there. And though it protected the upper floors from the wet of the snow, it had never been a friendly place. It was cold and damp – nothing more than a box into which everything unwanted, broken or ugly was thrown and forgotten. And because she felt the cellar's resentment, and because there was a trail of blood leading to its back door, Traudi had hidden as far away from the basement as she could possibly get – on the top floor, deep inside her mother's bedroom, under the bed, squeezed into a corner, praying for a miracle.

"Our Father who art in heaven, hallowed be your name, your kingdom come, your will be done, on earth as it is in heaven..."

Traudi opened her eyes and her heart lurched, realising she had fallen asleep. She couldn't say for how long – the only clock in the house stood on the mantelpiece downstairs – but the near-black of the room and the intense cold that made clouds of her breath revealed it to be long into the night. She pressed her ear to the floor, listening for sounds that she may have missed, but there was nothing, nothing but the dry whispers of a wooden house and the beating heart of a frightened girl.

71

From the moment Traudi had looked out of the window – expecting to see her family and finding only fear – she had felt constrained by a torturous need to stay calm. She wanted to scream, to run, to hurl herself through a window and shatter the nightmare around her. But she couldn't do any of that. There was a reason she had to stay calm. So she had retreated from the window, inching away slowly, hoping to quietly disappear. Though every limb, muscle and nerve screamed at her to run she resisted because even though wooden houses were friendly they were also indiscriminate with their affections. A wooden house would talk to anyone should they stop to listen. And knowing this, Traudi had turned from the window and crept to the hallway, step by careful step, pressing her weight slowly, from heel to toe onto the floorboards, desperate not to pressure them into speaking. Once in the hallway, she stared at the door that led down to the cellar. There were two ways in, one from the inside and one from the outside, but she hadn't the courage to reach out and check whether the door was locked. Instead, she lowered herself onto her hands and knees and crawled away.

As Traudi passed the open door to the kitchen she had glanced up at the window, but there was nothing she could see but the pale grey of the sky, and so she had continued, past the toilet, its door still standing open, until she reached the bottom of the stairs. For a second she had paused before the front door, listening for anything that might warn her. She then sat a while longer, four steps up, under the window that cast light onto the staircase – waiting for the day to leave so she could continue upwards knowing the house would be dark from the outside if anyone looked in. As Traudi fought to control each of her steps her legs had ached with the strain of trying to contain them. The blood pounded in her head, but she tried to ignore it, listening instead for the sound of a door opening, or a shout, or a scream. Traudi was terrified, yet even in the grip of the greatest fear she had ever known in the nine years she had been in the world, Traudi had continued to hope – to hang on to the possibility that the movement she had heard under the floorboards had come not from a monster, but from her brother or mother. It seemed impossible, but greater miracles had happened, and perhaps her prayers had been answered and her family had returned, only to find themselves distracted by things she couldn't imagine. And perhaps there was a simple reason for the blood streaking the snow. And perhaps she had mistaken the tracks due to the fright of seeing the blood and there were actually two pairs of footprints walking to the house. In the place where hope still lived, Traudi continued to believe she wasn't alone, and that her family was alive, and coming to get her.

"Our Father who art in heaven, hallowed be your name, your kingdom come, your will be done, on earth as it is in heaven. Deliver us from evil. Deliver Mama and Heini safe. For thine is the kingdom, and the power, and the glory, forever and ever. Amen."

As the night crawled by Traudi's eyes intermittently closed, but there was no sleep she could recall – only the long hours of blindness, the ache in her legs and the fear, that tight grip of fear, squeezing her stomach, urging her to flee, to scramble out from under the bed and run screaming for help. But there was nowhere she could run to without the risk of being caught. The nearest house in the valley belonged to Herr Mayer and a kilometre of track and black wood stood between them. Under normal circumstances it would be a distance that meant nothing, with nothing to dread but the walk itself. But now there was the dark, and in the dark there was something, and that something had dragged another something into the cellar. The snow was red and something was dead or, at the very least, near to dead. Near to dead – oh merciful God, it might be them and they might be alive!

"Our Father, our Father, our Lord in heaven... oh God, no..."

Dead or dying – her own mother and brother, lying in pain, praying for her help as she lay there, under a bed, cowering in fear, whilst those she loved, the two people who would have sacrificed anything to keep her safe, even themselves, lay within the cellar's cold, uncaring, walls bleeding their last.

"What would Heini do?" Traudi asked urgently, her breath short and sharp, her voice rising to an audible whisper. She couldn't think, the beating of her heart was too loud. Her head was buzzing with hope and blame and a new kind of terror, that of believing she had betrayed her own family.

"What would Heini do?" she hissed again, clenching her fists at her own selfish stupidity. She was a worm, a cowardly slug, and the truth was she knew exactly what her brother would do. Heini would fetch his knife, and once he had his knife he would head for the cellar.

Chapter Eight

"I think I was meant to find you."

It was one of the most impressive sentences Leo had ever heard – simple and powerful and exquisitely loaded. Deployed with the force of a heat-seeking missile, it aimed for the heart, seemingly primed to obliterate all that had been built. It was a brave, almost reckless statement of intent, and as a consequence Leo thought of it often. Saying that, he had never known the memory to interrupt his sleep before – surfacing in his dreams like a penance for the sin of neglect.

Of course, context was everything as was the source. Had the sentence been uttered by Günter – say, on the couch in Leo's dingy living room – there may have been a moment of awkwardness followed by a quiet reappraisal of their friendship. But it wasn't. It was Ana who had spoken the words, whispering them in the lisping lilt that inflected her German, and she had been lying in his bed, her dark hair cascading over his pillow, their noses almost touching. *I think I was meant to find you...*

"Isn't it my job to find people?" Leo had asked, immediately wary whilst keeping his voice friendly.

"You're a geography teacher," she replied.

"And local hero," he added.

She had cast him a look that bordered on weary, and to his surprise Leo felt a pang of regret. There was no excuse for the flippancy – no mitigating circumstances to claim or redemption to be had from the Ghost of Heartbreaks Past – he was merely a man, a man from Hallstatt, and the truth was that men from Hallstatt were all too often idiots. Luckily, Ana seemed to recognise this fact and with brutal efficiency she quickly changed tack – employing humour to deftly turn the tables and allow him to take responsibility for his luck.

"So if I'm hearing you right, you're telling me that in your capacity as 'local hero' it was actually you who found me?"

"That would be correct," he replied. "Four months ago in the Post Office, you may recall."

"Then I guess I should count myself lucky," she said. "I've seen the missing list in your study, don't forget."

"Harsh!" Leo protested.

"But true," she insisted. She flipped onto her back, apparently unaware that one of her breasts was exposed. "You know, it's amazing really: according to the museum in town, you Austrians have managed to find Neolithic excrement in the mountains, dating back thousands of years, and yet a few dozen skiers who went wandering up the Dachstein continue to evade you."

"I think you'll find that archaeological digs are somewhat different to rescue missions."

"Well, they certainly find more shit than you do."

Ana threw back her head, letting her laughter fill the room. Leo tried to keep a straight face, but it wasn't easy. Her laughter was as subtle as a foghorn in a church and he found her blatant, ear-shattering ebullience nothing short of breath-taking. Ana was unlike any woman he had ever known – beautiful, confident and competitively droll. She was also extraordinarily lazy. Almost to a rule, Leo's previous girlfriends had been blonde, good-looking, sporty types fond of Nordic walking, skiing and climbing, whereas Ana, dark-haired and curvy, appeared to do nothing. She was almost cat-like in her laziness; a languid, claw-stretching predator, content to spend the day in a pocket of sunshine playing with a mouse. But it was her laugh that truly separated her from the other women he had known; that loud, uninhibited explosion of glee that bore no regard for place or propriety. It was the kind of laugh mere mortals could only envy. Not dirty, just huge. And it was a laugh that Ana deployed with devastating effect, joyously disarming him before she moved in for the kill.

"I know it might sound lame to a rugged mountain man like you," she continued, "but what I'm trying to say is that I came to Austria to find my past and instead I think I may have found my future."

Ana had paused at that point and though Leo had recognised the danger he had been too shocked to react. So instead of trying to lighten the moment he had merely smiled as his brain frantically processed the bombshell that the naked woman in his bed had thrown into his equally naked lap. Apparently a smile was the appropriate response as far as Ana was concerned because she kept on talking.

"I lived my whole life in Valencia, a truly beautiful city, vibrant and passionate, and yet I spent a lot of my time there thinking of Austria, especially after my parents divorced. It was a pretty messy time and it kind of took the shine off everything for a while. So when Dad moved back to Salzburg – before I got to see where he lived – I would walk in the sunshine and imagine what he was doing. In my head, he was always alone, looking sad, in an old wooden house somewhere impossibly snowy, sitting in front of a roaring fire..."

"Toasting marshmallows?"

Ana paused, her eyebrows knitting together in what Leo correctly interpreted as mild irritation. "Do you even do that in Austria?"

"No, not really, no."

"Then he wouldn't be toasting marshmallows, would he? Most probably he would have been gutting a deer whilst practising his yodelling, dressed in Lederhosen and plotting another World War."

"For pity's sake," Leo had groaned. "Do our fellow Europeans think so little of us?"

"I think we both know the answer to that."

Leo tried to look wounded.

"ok, I'm joking," Ana relented. "I apologise. He probably wasn't plotting another World War."

"Apology accepted, although that was probably the most accurate part of your stereotype. Of course next time we won't make the error of relying on the Germans."

"Leopold Hirsch!"

"Ana Valderas-Schmitt!"

"That's a terrible thing to say."

"It was a joke!"

"You shouldn't joke about war!"

"You started it."

And there it was again – that enormous, happy laugh.

At the time of this exchange, Leo had felt pretty pleased with himself. Sex had been instigated and successfully executed, the post-coital obstacles had been skilfully negotiated, and the girl in his bed was still laughing at his jokes. It was the perfect treble – the dream of all fancy-free bachelors sliding towards middle-age. But that was then, when Ana was happy, and now he could no longer muster the same sense of satisfaction as he lay alone in his bed, his head resting on the pillow they once shared, with the room bereft of her things and her fat, carefree laughter. Somewhere along the line he had messed up and, given the chance, he would willingly change things – perhaps say things better, be better, make her time with him better. After all, she hadn't asked for much – only to be with him.

"I thought that coming to live with my father would be the answer to my problems," Ana had told him. "Of course life is never that simple. I was twelve years old when my parents divorced and when my father returned to Salzburg, leaving me behind, I was furious. He had always been an emotionally distant man, but now there were all these kilometres between us as well."

"It couldn't have been easy."

"No, it wasn't." Ana slipped sideways, turning to face him, her head balancing on her hand. "Do you know I never once heard my dad say he loved me? I felt that he did, of course I did, but he never said the words. Can you imagine such a man? A man who never once thinks to tell his wife or kid that he loves them?"

Leo shifted uncomfortably in the bed. His own father had never said the words to him, and Leo had never felt it necessary to say them either. It wasn't a conscious decision. There was no sinister motive behind the omission. It was simply the way it was. This was Austria not Hollywood. But because Leo was weak, and horribly infatuated, he explained none of this to Ana, he simply shook his head in sympathy, allowing her to take the gesture as one of empathy.

"Anyway, by the time I was a teenager, I came to the conclusion that everything that was wrong in my life was due to the absence of my father. So, I studied hard, graduated with honours, got a teaching job, fell in love, fell out of it again and plotted my escape from Spain. And that's how I ended up in Salzburg."

"It's a pretty city to end up in," Leo offered.

"Yes, it is. But it wasn't how I'd imagined it would be. As you might expect, my father has his own life now, he has a new girlfriend. It was kind of difficult."

"You didn't get along with the girlfriend?"

"No, we got on fine. Inge's great, very sweet. But my dad's house was more her house than mine, if you see what I mean? Nothing was really keeping me there. It wasn't quite right. Still I wasn't ready to return to Spain so I started looking for work. After a number of rejections I applied for the post at the technical college here – close to Salzburg and to my dad, but somewhere new, to find my own space."

"And how do you feel now?" Leo had asked.

"Well, seeing as you're asking; a little bit tired and a little bit hungry. You know you've got nothing in your fridge?"

"Yes, I know, it's my fridge. But I was actually wondering how you felt now you're in Hallstatt, whether you feel settled."

"Oh, I'm getting there, I think."

Ana moved towards his lips and as Leo wrapped his arms around her he had done his best not to balk at the responsibility hanging heavy in the air.

On the bedside table, the alarm clock screamed 6am. Before Leo had time to react, the mobile phone rang and he was appalled to discover the call tone had mysteriously tripped into 'Crazy Frog'. Leo cursed Günter's name loudly as he grappled first for the clock and then for the phone, sending them both flying to the floor in the process. Only one of them continued its hellish racket.

After reinserting the battery into his mobile, Leo checked the missed calls. 'Günter Home' showed on the display, which came as something of a surprise because he thought Günter was asleep on the sofa. He hit the 'call' button. Lisa picked up.

"Did I wake you?" she asked.

"I was just getting up."

"Did I wake him?"

"What do you think?"

Lisa sighed, somehow managing to make the effort sound both resigned and annoyed. "OK, Leo you can tell the stupid bastard he can come home."

"So he's forgiven?"

"I didn't say that."

"Then why call me? Why not call your husband's cell phone and tell him yourself."

"I'm not speaking to him."

"But he can go home?"

"Yes."

"Yet you won't speak to him when he gets there?"

"No."

"And you call that a punishment?"

"Very funny," Lisa replied drily. "Oh by the way," she said, just as Leo thought the conversation was over, "I think you need to have a word with Reinhardt."

"The bus driver?"

"Do you know any other Reinhardt?"

"I know one in Gosau."

"It's not him."

"OK. So why do I need to speak to Reinhardt?"

"Because his wife says he's cursing you."

"Cursing me for what?"

"Something about the rescue – he says he saw too much and now his life isn't worth living. This is your fault, apparently. Oh, and he's no longer a bus driver."

"Is that my fault too?"

"Perhaps, but the official reason is that he kept turning up for work completely out of his skull."

"Shit."

"It happens. Now don't forget to tell the useless slob he can come home."

"Should I also tell the 'useless slob' that you missed him?"

"Fuck off, Leo."

By the time the sun had risen, Leo was in his car, heading for Linz. The thermometer on the dashboard revealed an unusually warm temperature for the time of year and during the drive north, Leo watched the sun's assault on the wintery landscape become increasingly marked, with patches of green and puddles of brown blotting the snow the further he travelled from the Dachstein. Linz was only 130km away, but being a few degrees warmer than Hallstatt it could have been another country if the road signs weren't in German.

Leo turned on the radio only to switch it off again as soon as he heard *Lemon Tree* by Fool's Garden introduced – it was too early for pop whimsy, far too early – so he opted to concentrate on the job he was heading for instead, even though Günter's departure coupled with the knowledge that an unemployed bus driver resented having his life saved combined to distract him.

It was in the car that Leo usually worked on his lesson plans, a symptomatic consequence of his general apathy towards teaching. It was a passing nod to obligation that proved increasingly harder to come by as school terms came and went in a seamless tide of indifference. And the older he got the less he could believe he had ended up in such a dreary, soul-sucking profession and in Linz of all places, an industrialised casket an hour and a half from where he lived. Clearly, there was no justice in the world, and the conveyor belt of students that passed through his classes each year did little to dispel that belief. Now and again he forced himself to remember that his pupils were actually individuals, each possessed of their own dreams and fears of what the future might bring, but more often than not he found that they merged into one indolent mass of recalcitrance, their dead eyes staring at him through multi-coloured, emo-heavy fringes. Only on one occasion could he recall anything resembling interest from a class, and it had had nothing to do with the marvels of geography, but rather the AWOLNATION T-shirt he wore. He had never repeated that mistake again. He had no desire to be friends with his students – he simply wanted them to listen, to possibly learn something and then to file out of his classroom as quietly as possible at the first sound of the bell.

Leo shook his head. "Glaciers," he instructed. "Think glaciers."

Having rejected the idea of taking the class to the final frontier, for reasons of commonsense and curriculum, Leo rehearsed his basic introduction to the class. He would most likely start with something informative but visual, a few slides of Dachstein and his trip to Les Bossons. He would then reveal that 10 per cent of the world was covered by ice, locking in enough fresh water to raise global sea levels by 70 metres.

"Should the ice melt it would be catastrophic," he would tell his pupils, possibly illustrating the scale of this potential calamity with the revelation that 70 metres was equal to the height of the Cathay Building in Singapore, once the tallest building in Southeast Asia.

"Oh, who am I kidding?" he muttered. He could almost guarantee that none of his students had even heard of the Cathay Building. In fact, they'd probably have a job locating Singapore, or even which part of the globe constituted Southeast Asia. It was staggering really, their level of ignorance. And he was all too grimly aware that as their teacher he might be partly to blame. Unfortunately, they were caught in a vicious circle, a modern-day Catch-22 – his students barely listened to what he had to say so he told them nothing they didn't need to know, which left a gaping hole in their education that he made no effort to fill because he knew they were barely listening. In fact, Leo was almost certain he'd have gained greater job satisfaction digging trenches for a living, and by the time he had parked the car and grabbed a coffee from the staff room, he had worked himself into such a heinous mood of despondency that he decided to ditch the colour and stick with the facts.

"Once upon a time, ice covered approximately one third of the earth's surface. Are you writing this down?" Leo stopped to stare at the class and sixteen pairs of hands immediately began their frantic shuffle of notebooks. A few of the more able or diligent students had their pens poised above paper.

"Glaciers are sensitive barometers of climate change," Leo continued. "They respond to changes in temperature and snowfall. They also influence local and global climates, altering pressure systems and wind directions, and keeping vast areas in perpetual cold. But why, where and when do glaciers form? Any ideas?"

Leo looked around the classroom at the collection of fringes being stroked with a mixture of disinterest and fear. He turned to the board, a black marker pen at the ready.

"Think of glaciers or ice sheets as SYSTEMS," he said, raising his voice at the clue word before writing 'SYSTEMS' upon the board. "These systems have INPUTS and OUTPUTS, and they interact with other systems such as the ATMOSPHERE, OCEANS, RIVERS and LANDSCAPE. The basic components of a glacier system are MASS and

ENERGY and they enter the system in the form of PRECIPITATION, ROCK DEBRIS, GRAVITY, SOLAR RADIATION and GEOTHERMAL HEAT. They leave in the form of WATER VAPOUR, WATER ICE, ROCK DEBRIS and HEAT. This mass and energy is transferred through the system at a variety of rates with intervening periods of STORAGE within or beneath the glacier. The most important input to glacier systems comes from direct snowfall, blown snow and avalanching from slopes above the glacier surface. These inputs are known collectively as ACCUMULATION. The snow and ice is then transferred down the valley by glacier movement until it reaches areas where it is lost to the system, either by melting and evaporation or by the breakaway of ice blocks or icebergs, known collectively as ABLATION."

Leo stopped talking and put a slide on the overhead projector showing the front cover of Benn & Evans' *Glaciers and Glaciation*. The next slide presented the class with a diagram he had copied from the book, credited to Brodzikowski and van Loon, that showed an idealised cross section of an ice sheet. Leo told the class to draw it. He then positioned himself at his desk in front of the class and pretended to read.

In the silence that followed, with his students distracted and largely unobtrusive, Leo's thoughts took up their customary march backwards, dragging him into the all-too familiar territory of retrospection. Within seconds, Ana's wide, honest face was all that filled his mind and, reacting to his present location, his memory recalled how she had positively glowed whenever she had talked about teaching. On one occasion she had even gone as far as to describe her pupils as 'inspirational'. Of course, Leo's immediate reaction had been one of fascinated wariness, rather like the time he'd answered the door to a good-looking woman holding up a copy of the Watchtower. But in her defence, Ana had spent only five years in the profession, compared to his ten, and she taught sculpture. Maybe that was the key. Maybe her students were in fact different. Maybe they were inspirational. Either way – either right or deluded – Ana's love of teaching was one of the great differences between them. One of many to become apparent the more time they spent together.

By the time Leo began the long drive back home, the way was lit by streetlamps and headlights. He turned on the radio wanting the news, but had to endure Europe's *Final Countdown* first. When the bulletin finally began at the top of the hour it led with the Dutch Prince, Johan Friso. Caught in an avalanche during a skiing holiday in Lech, the royal had been in a coma for more than a week and the reporter gravely reported that doctors feared he may never regain consciousness. Leo grimaced with genuine sympathy. There but for the grace of God, he thought.

Four winters ago Leo had experienced a similar terror. Three hours into a search he felt the rumble before hearing the shouts. Glancing backwards he registered the wall of snow thundering his way, understanding instantly there would be no escape. Dropping his poles, he pulled the activation lever on the strap of his rucksack and hoped for the best as 150 litres of air ballooned at his back, raising him above the avalanche, like a pebble shaken in sand. Within seconds that dragged by like a lifetime, he came to a stop 60 metres down the mountainside, on the edge of a precipice, scratched and bruised, his ski mask torn from his face, his head and neck caught in the grip of a giant red airbag. Dazed, but alive, it was a moment Leo would never forget. He knew more than most just how lucky he had been. Without the right equipment an avalanche could bury a man as surely as a grave, with the snow setting like concrete as it settled, obliterating any trace of where a body might lie. Rescuers had only twenty minutes to locate a victim for a maximum chance of survival without brain damage. After that, the odds decreased sharply. The Dutch Prince may have been an experienced skier, but he had been skiing off-piste, without an airbag, and it had taken 25 minutes to pull his unconscious body from the snow. Ability and social status counted for little in the mountains. Sometimes it was only luck that mattered.

"In other news, the risk of avalanches in Tyrol remains high..."

Avalanches, rolling snow, ice sheets, glaciers... Leo's thoughts resumed their backwards march, leading him not to Ana this time, but to the lack-lustre lesson he'd given that day, belatedly wishing he had done more to engage his students, to make them realise just how fragile the world was as well as their place in it. Unfortunately, he was so utterly done with it all he could see no way to pull back. One day into the half-term and all he could envisage for the next six weeks was the relentless grind of alarm-drive-students-drive-bed. It was not what he had wanted for himself. As a boy he had only ever considered skiing and hunting, like most boys in the region, and when it came to picking a career he had been caught on the hop. He opted for teaching, but it was always meant to be a stop gap – a way to earn money while he thought of something better to do. Regrettably, he never discovered what that was. And exacerbating this misery was the very real fear that there was actually no light to be found at the end of the tunnel. From where Leo was sitting, which was currently at the traffic lights coming into Gmunden, he could see nothing to aim for, nothing to work towards, and no happy ending to be had. His life had gone to crap, the earth was hurtling towards an apocalyptic end and it bothered him more than he let on. In fact there were a lot of things that bothered him more than he let on and most of them involved other people – Ana, for one, and most recently Reinhardt.

Bowing to the inevitable, Leo reached for his mobile.

"*Servus*, Leo."

"*Servus*, Harri."

"And to what do I owe the pleasure?"

With little fanfare, Leo relayed the conversation he had had with Günter's wife earlier that day only to be surprised by Harald's lack of surprise.

"I've heard Reinhardt's been bothering the police and the Church for most of the week, convinced he's on to something," Harri said by way of explanation.

"On to what exactly?"

"Hell, if I know. I don't think they do either."

Leo groaned. "I suppose I better speak to him."

"And say what?"

"No idea."

"Well, that sounds like an excellent plan. When are you going?"

"In 45 minutes, I imagine: when I arrive home."

"Do you want me to join you?"

"Would you mind?"

"I've nothing else to do: the wife's at one of her Tupperware or *Jahrgang* parties. I'll meet you at *Konsum* in an hour."

"Great."

Leo threw his phone onto the passenger seat and turned up the radio, recognising the opening chords to *Strada del Sole* – Rainhard Fendrich's hapless account of being a tourist in Italy. Because he liked the track and he was feeling more affable after speaking to Harri, he sang along.

There were many reasons why Leo had called Harri. For one, he had been there the night they'd rescued Reinhardt; he had helped drag the man home; and he had heard, first hand, the outlandish claims that had bedevilled that journey. But the main reason Leo had phoned Harri was because the older man happened to know a lot more about life, in particular Hallstatt life, than Leo did.

Though Leo was born-and-bred in Hallstatt, there was a bond within the community that he had done his best to avoid. Whilst being content to lead the rescue team and down the beers at Berni's, Leo had never involved himself in the minutiae of town life. He had his job and his interests and he would gladly pass the time of day with anyone who wandered into his path, but he didn't immerse himself in the small world around him, even less so in recent times thanks to a belated realisation that there was more to life and most of it had just walked out of the door. But Harri was different. A former police officer, he knew Hallstatt and those who lived there. He knew their history, he understood their fears and he was fond of them all – even the 'Drunk Dogs' who dragged him away from his wife in the middle of the night. In fact, there wasn't a man – other than his father – that Leo would have so readily turned to in times of crisis and though he wasn't worried about what Reinhardt might have to say, he did want to understand it, which is why he had called Harri.

Emerging from the tunnel leading into the town, Leo stayed on the main road until he arrived at the small supermarket where Harri was waiting, still as a statue despite the cold, a silhouette against the streetlight. Leo opened the passenger door, pocketed his phone, and Harri climbed in.

"Brisk night," the older man said by way of greeting.

"No clouds," Leo replied, and he spun the car around and headed back towards the tunnel, turning left before he reached it to park in a small lay-by. The two men got out, and set off on foot up one of the small lanes leading to Reinhardt's house. The path was icy after the earlier melt and the night air was sharp.

As they neared Reinhardt's home, it was obvious, even in the dark, that the house had seen better days. Only a narrow path leading to the door had been cleared of snow, the rest of the drive lay under a lumpy white blanket covering whatever debris had been dumped there before winter set in. Even so neither man felt it necessary to comment on the lack of order: if a person had no wish to shovel snow that was their business.

Reaching the front door, the cleared steps revealed evidence of a minor concession to conformity although it was unclear whether the snow had been removed for the benefit of visitors or cats as there were a number of plastic bowls cluttering the porch way. Naturally, Leo assumed that the cats must belong to Reinhardt's wife. Men had dogs.

On the wall, to the right of the door, Leo found himself impressed by a cast iron bell pull, having failed to notice it the last time they had visited.

"Must be worth a bit," he said to Harri.

"If it works," Harri replied.

With a quick tug, Leo ascertained that the doorbell did in fact work and inside the house, they heard the distant 'ding' of their arrival announced. Having seen a light on, they waited for someone to come. They then waited some more.

As the two men stood in clouds of their own breath, debating the merits of ringing again or going to Berni's, a harsh shout was heard from inside the house. A minute later, Reinhardt's wife answered the door and rather like the house it was clear she had also seen better days. Though Christine could never have been considered a good-looking woman, she had done little with what had been provided. Her lank shoulder-length hair shone with grease in the dim light of the porch. The clothes she wore were a mismatch of tweed and denim that clung too tightly to the vast expanse of her waist. Before she even spoke the two men smelt whisky on her breath.

"What do you want?" she asked.

Opting to ignore the hostility, Leo greeted her warmly before asking to speak to Reinhardt.

"He's busy," she replied.

"Well, he's not busy driving from what I've heard," Harri replied curtly, cutting through the crap to get down to business.

"For Christ's sake, woman, let them in!" a voice bellowed from inside the house.

Christine responded by opening the door a fraction, wide enough to allow the two men passage. As Leo squeezed by he got the uncomfortable feeling that Reinhardt's wife was one comment away from spitting in his face.

Following the light creeping into the hallway, the two men made their way to the kitchen. It was perfectly clean, if bare, and at a table under a hanging light, to the right of a shuttered window, sat Reinhardt. Without a word, he reached for two glasses on a nearby shelf and poured two generous measures of whisky from the bottle on the table. Both Leo and Harri took their glasses, knocked them against Reinhardt's and slid themselves onto the bench opposite their host, their eyes registering the open Bible in front of them. Reinhardt closed the book, offering no explanation. His fingers shook on the leather-bound cover and his face looked shocking, like a man who'd known no sleep. His beard was unkempt and his eyes were bloodshot. He was barely ten years older than Leo yet he looked like a man of his father's generation.

"So what brings you here?" Reinhardt eventually asked.

"I heard you were upset," Leo replied honestly.

"Show me a married man who isn't." Reinhardt laughed, though there was clearly no joy in the sound. He refilled his glass and tilted the bottle at his guests who both declined the offer, having made little impact on their own drinks. For a moment or two none of them spoke. Had another moment passed by, it might have begun to feel awkward. Fortunately, Harri ended the brief impasse.

"What's going on, Reinhardt?"

Reinhardt stared at him, in a way that hinted to an intrigue the two men had yet to grasp. "Well, that's the million dollar question, isn't it?" he slurred. "What's going on? Nobody knows – nobody that is, but them and me." He paused to scratch his armpit. "You think I'm mad, don't you?"

Leo and Harri both shook their heads, carefully avoiding each other's eyes.

"Yes, you do," Reinhardt insisted wearily. "I see it in the way you won't look at one another. But I'm not mad. In fact I've never felt saner. This is what happens when you finally see the light. And that's exactly what I saw up there – up there on the mountain. And after seeing the light I've now worked it all out. Everything I saw. How it all is, and was. It's written in the Bible, you see, word for word, for anyone to read." Reinhardt paused to bang a fist on the book in front of them and raise his glass. "*And the Lord will send a plague on all the nations that fought against Jerusalem,*" he shouted. "*Their people will become like walking corpses, their flesh rotting away. Their eyes will rot in their sockets, and their tongues will rot in their mouths.* This is the prophecy of Zechariah. And this is what I saw."

"On the Strenhang slope?" Harri asked steadily.

"On the Strenhang slope," Reinhardt confirmed.

"Well, that explains why you might need a few drinks."

Missing the dig, Reinhardt nodded his head before dropping it heavily into his folded arms, slumping on the table before them. Leo and Harri chanced a look, finding only bafflement in each other's eyes.

"Reinhardt, maybe you should talk to someone," Leo ventured softly.

"Talk to someone!" Reinhardt scoffed, his head lurching in his arms, but staying on the table. "And who should I talk to – police or priest? I've tried, oh, believe me I've tried, but none of them listen. Not that I'm surprised. They're not willing to see, that's the problem. It's all too awkward for them. So, there's only me; it's me who's the one chosen to carry the burden."

Leo glanced again at Harri, who raised his hands in a lifting motion, urging him to continue.

"Perhaps you should see a doctor," Leo said gently. "After the rescue, we never had you checked over and I'm sorry for that, it was irresponsible. Also – and I'm in no position to talk, I know that – but it seems you're drinking much more than you used to. Maybe, if you were sober, things might become easier... clearer."

"There's nothing wrong with my eyesight, Leopold!" Reinhardt barked from the valley of his arms. "Why else would you be here now? Believe it or not – and I don't care either way – but I saw too much that night, more than any man has a right to see."

"We were also there, Reinhardt. And the only thing we saw was snow."

"Well maybe there's a reason for that, eh? After all, not everyone deserves to know what's coming. The Establishment – all of you old policemen, politicians and minions of the State – you reap what you sow, friends, you reap what you sow, and I'm telling you now that the truth won't be buried forever. Eventually it gets out."

Not knowing how to respond, and finding it increasingly difficult to communicate with the thinning crown of Reinhardt's head, Leo raised his hands in defeat. The man was too wasted for coherent conversation and no different to the gibbering wreck they had pulled from the mountain more than a week ago, apart from the fact that he was no longer employed and he was reciting the Bible.

"I hear you lost your job," said Harri.

Reinhardt's shoulders shuddered with another burst of humourless laughter. "Yes, that would be correct. Twenty years' service and they show me the door – without so much as a by your leave, not even a few drinks to send me off with. But that's the Company for you. All they care about is profits and margins."

Not to mention their safety record, Leo thought, though he stopped short of saying so. He sipped at his whisky wondering what to make of the man before him. If he hadn't known better, he'd have assumed the snow had addled Reinhardt's brain, but the cold was incapable of causing such damage. If Reinhardt's brain had frozen he would no longer be breathing, let alone discussing conspiracies – ice crystals would have ruptured his brain cells turning them to mush. No, he was simply a drunk, and possibly depressed following the loss of his job, and as a consequence he was itching for a fight with those he felt responsible for the downturn in his fortunes. Coming to this conclusion, Leo recalled the last time he had seen Reinhardt, standing in front of the *Grüner Baum* restaurant, arguing with Bergmann. Leo thought he might as well mention it, but when he did Reinhardt made no effort to respond. In fact he was so still Leo and Harri simply assumed he'd passed out. But as they emptied their glasses, silently agreeing to leave, Reinhardt began talking.

"Bergmann knows," Reinhardt muttered darkly. He lifted his

head and both Leo and Harri were astonished to see tears glistening in the man's eyes. "Bergmann knows better than anyone."

Reinhardt reached for the whisky bottle, shaking off Harri's hand as he tried to dissuade him from having another glass. His tumbler refilled, he held his drink to the light and his eyes took on the glazed appearance of the madman he so strenuously denied being. "*Behold!*" he shouted, "*I am coming soon, bringing my recompense with me, to repay everyone for what he has done. I am the Alpha and the Omega, the first and the last, the beginning and the end.*"

And with that Revelation, Reinhardt dropped his head to the table and began snoring.

Leo and Harri left Reinhardt's house none the wiser than when they went in, and as a result they both agreed they had earned a 'little beer' at Berni's. In the car, neither of them spoke for a while as they each tried to make sense of what they had witnessed.

"I never had Reinhardt down as a religious man," Harri eventually offered. "His Old Man had his moments before the cancer took him, but not Reinhardt, as far as I knew."

"Could be a primeval reaction," Leo offered. "He was pretty scared that night we rescued him. People have turned to the Bible for less."

"Perhaps," Harri conceded, "but they don't often predict a plague of zombies descending."

"Zombies?"

"Walking corpses, rotting flesh, eyes rotting in sockets, tongues rotting in mouths – sounds like zombies to me."

"And what if he's right?"

"About the zombies?"

"Yes."

"Well, it's not easy to kill a zombie," Harri admitted. "So if they are coming I guess I might take the wife to Vienna for a week, just until the plague passes."

Leo laughed, feeling a rare sense of relief rush through his body as he shook off the gloom that had dogged him throughout the day, not to mention the weirdness of the evening. If he was honest, Reinhardt had freaked him out. It wasn't the talk of zombies or conspiracies that had touched a nerve, but the speed in which the man had descended from being an almost respectable bus-driving member of the community to a whisky-soaked doomsayer who looked ten years older than he ought.

"What do you think will become of him?" he asked.

"Who knows," Harri replied honestly. "When a man loses himself to drink it's hard to find the way back. And if by some miracle he does get back, he's got that wife of his to face each morning – sober."

"It's a tough call," Leo admitted. Driving up *Malerweg*, he slipped into second gear as the wheels briefly lost traction on a patch of black ice. As the tyres reconnected with the road he felt a pang of nostalgia for the old car. He had bought it with his very first pay cheque and over the years they had been through a number of scrapes, but the chances of it passing another *Pickerl* looked less likely with each coming year. Of course, nothing lasts forever, not even a vw Golf.

Turning into a small row of orderly houses painted in the pastel colours that were the hallmark of the town, Leo's attention was caught by a light switching on. He saw that it came from Bergmann's place and he was about to suggest to Harri that they should pay him a visit, given Reinhardt's belief the old hunter possessed all the answers, but then he realised Bergmann had company. No more than a silhouette in the porch light, the visitor glanced towards the road, almost furtively, and Leo's mouth fell open. The swift, backward glance revealed the visitor to be a woman. More than that, Leo recognised the dark auburn hair and pale face of his mother.

Chapter Nine

Traudi slowly descended the staircase, easing into each step to keep the house quiet. From the small window she saw the new day approaching; turning the dark mountain grey; making ice glint in the snow; and changing the shadows into trees. On the horizon, the sky shifted from black to purple to pink, and she gripped the knife tighter.

Stopping at the door, she put her ear to the wood. But there was nothing she could hear above the call of the birds or the river's distant rumble. And though a morning frost continued to scuff the window nearby, she recognised the world was getting warmer. This is what the river told her. The snow was melting, the world was waking, and what lay hidden would be found.

Traudi took a deep breath, having to force herself to move: treading carefully past the toilet, past the kitchen, turning left at the sitting room and down the corridor until she faced the cellar door. Beyond the door there would be another door and one more after that – leading to the trail of blood that stained the fields that surrounded the house – and in between that door and where she stood now was the shapeless form of her fear beating a vivid red, like an exposed heart. The sheer strength of it seemed to make the ground pulse beneath Traudi's feet. It sucked at her conviction, wetted her hands and caused her own heart to thump in her chest. When she reached for the key, her lips trembled. Traudi had never felt so scared or so utterly alone.

Beneath her fingers, the lock groaned as the key turned. Holding her breath she waited, afraid of what the smallest sound might bring. With a dull click the lock released and Traudi pushed at the door, keeping the knife held out in front of her. Crossing the threshold between wood and stone, she edged down the stairs, walking blind into the gloom. Immediately the air felt clammy and close: moist with damp and decay and the rusty smell of blood.

"Mother Mary, Mother Mary, Mother Mary, Mama..."

Traudi reached for the angel at her neck as her feet came to a halt on the bottom stair. After allowing time for her eyes to adjust, she saw a number of crates stacked against the wall holding chunks of wood and broken roof tiles. On a shelf stood a collection of jars holding pickles, jams and preserves, underneath them were hessian bags filled with salt and flour. In one corner of the room she noticed an adult's bicycle, one of its wheels bent out of shape. Traudi couldn't recall having seen it before. It was too big for Heini, her father had never ridden one and her mother, well, it was clear she would have no use for such a thing. Traudi couldn't think who the bicycle might belong to or how it could have got in the cellar. But she recognised the long-handled scythe standing behind it, propped against the wall, gathering dust in the gloom, and the sight – familiar though it was – made her heart skip a beat.

With nothing else to see beyond cobwebs and spiders, Traudi looked at the door that led to the second room of the cellar. Clenching her teeth and holding her knife steady, she stepped forwards only to stop as a freezing wind pushed under the door bringing ice to her knees and the smell of raw meat to her nose. Traudi slapped a hand to her mouth, her legs turned weak and her head swam with red-tinged images snatched from a nightmare. This wasn't how it should be and she wanted to run, to flee the tomb of concrete and save herself, but she couldn't. Her mother's pleas crashed in her ears, her brother's eyes implored her to be brave and so she gritted her teeth, turned the handle and pushed.

The dead eyes were the first thing she saw, and she screamed.

On the far wall, caught in a grotesque parody of flight, there hung the lifeless form of a deer. Its front legs were hooked over a line of rope and its hooved feet scraped the floor as though leaping for freedom. Its belly was slit, the organs were gone, and its head lay on a worktop, having been severed from its body. Beneath a huge set of antlers, two eyes stared at her from under long lashes, looking empty and sad. Protruding from the mouth was a piece of pine about the width of a man's hand. 'The last bite' Heini used to call it; an offering from a hunter after taking an animal's life. Traudi leant against the door, her legs close to buckling. However, the sight, gruesome as it was, was not the one that she had expected and it took her a while to slow her heart and clear the tears from her eyes.

Inspecting the corpse from the doorway, Traudi looked for the bullet hole, quickly finding it between the shoulder and chest. Hunting was nothing new to Traudi – every man in the region possessed a gun, even the priest – and so she knew that whoever had killed the deer, offering it a 'last bite', would also have dipped a second twig into the bullet hole. This twig would be worn by the hunter in the brim of his hat. And though Traudi wasn't squeamish she found the ritual disrespectful; like stabbing an animal while it lay dead on the ground because shooting it wasn't quite enough.

Traudi slumped to the floor, exhausted and overwhelmed.

Slowly the tears began to fall, wetting her cheeks. It had taken every ounce of courage to come to the cellar and now she was there she felt like the victim of a cruel and bloody joke. She was relieved yet depleted. Horror images of her mother and brother lying injured or worse had urged her to act, but her bravery had brought her no nearer to knowing their fate. If anything at all she was more confused than ever. She simply couldn't make sense of the scene. Nobody in their right mind would bring a dead deer into somebody else's house and cut off its head. No one would do it, at least no one sane or normal. And to even contemplate such a thing, the hunter must have known that the house was empty – or mostly empty – but how? How could a man walk into another person's cellar and use it as a butcher's storehouse unless he knew that the house was empty, that there was no one inside to challenge him at the door and ask him what the hell he was playing at? Her mother and brother were missing. That was still a fact – a fact that the hunter must have known, and if he had known they were missing then he must surely know why, and if he knew why then he must surely know Traudi remained in the house, and if he knew that...

Traudi squeezed her eyes shut only to open them again when fear reminded her that she was sat alone in the cellar with only a headless deer for company. Still too shocked to move, she looked about her, inspecting the place for clues. Through the uneven slats of the back door, the sun seeped into the room, lighting the floor, and Traudi noticed that the stone tiles were streaked with icy traces of blood and water, making it clear that whoever had killed the deer had attempted to deal with the mess. But why bother? Why wash the floor? And if the floor had been washed this time, did it mean it had been washed before? And if it had been washed before did it mean that there had been more blood spilled, perhaps belonging to something or someone other than a deer?

Traudi jumped to her feet, knowing she had to get out of the house before whoever had been in the cellar decided to return. Running to the back door, she pulled at the handle only to find it was locked. But the outside door was never locked. There was no key. Starting to panic, Traudi ran back through the concrete rooms of the cellar, slipping on blood and ice. She glanced at the bicycle that didn't belong there and gripped her brother's knife tighter.

Climbing the stairs, Traudi thought quickly. She needed to get to the town. She needed to find *Opa*. The day was warm, the snow was melting and it might mean the road had been cleared, not that it mattered now because the chances were it was no longer safe. Anyone could see her on the road, good or bad. Had her mother and brother been seen there? It was more than possible. It would have been the route they would have taken, up or down from the town, cleared or not. Their mother couldn't walk through the forest; it was too dense, there were too many obstacles, even with help. No, it was clear that the road had become a danger, one that Traudi must avoid, which meant she would have to cut through the trees. With Hallstatt lying downhill from the valley, it was a direction she could easily navigate. And even if she did become lost, the river would help her, she would hear its call. Wherever she was, wherever she went, she only had to listen and the river would lead her home.

Back in the hallway, Traudi quickly locked the cellar door behind her and put Heini's knife in her pocket before hurriedly doing up the buttons of her coat, ready for the cold outside. She needed to be fast. The day had started. The sky was no longer pink but blue. All she had to do was clear the white fields and she could lose herself in the trees. Within an hour, possibly two, she would reach the town. She would find *Opa*. He would send for the police and everyone would be saved. There would be no shame in it. Heini couldn't be angry. Something was terribly wrong, and too much time had passed for her family's absence to be a mistake. On top of that, there was a dead deer and a bicycle in the cellar that had no right to be there. Everyone would understand. Heini would see there was no other choice. And Traudi ran to the kitchen to fetch the key for the front door.

Before she reached it, she froze.

Somewhere outside the snow crunched. It was the unmistakable sound of ice compacting under feet. Clamping a hand over her mouth, Traudi dropped to the floor and the noise stopped abruptly. Crawling further into the kitchen, Traudi hid herself under the window, placing her back to the wall, all the time listening, waiting for the footsteps to resume. But there was nothing, and now she couldn't be sure she wasn't going mad. With her heart hammering, she turned to get to her knees. With one hand holding the knife, she raised herself slowly, inching up the wall, reaching for the window above. An icy draught met her face as the chill wind forced its way between glass and wooden frame, but there was nothing to see but the frost on the pane. Then, as her nose touched the window, a hand appeared from nowhere, slamming into the glass. Throwing herself backwards, Traudi caught only a glimpse of a grotesque, distorted image of a man with gnarled flesh and ice-blue eyes fired by winter and death.

"I can see you!" the creature screamed, its mammoth fists banging upon the glass above her, its voice a growl like rolling thunder.

Traudi fell to her knees and crawled in panic to the front door. But she was too slow. As she reached it, the handle rattled. Traudi thought of the key, still hanging in the kitchen. She knew the door was locked yet she pulled on the handle as though her very life depended on it.

"I know you're in there! I *know*!"

Traudi hung onto the door handle. She wanted to scream, but her throat was paralysed. Her arms felt weak with sickness and fear, and when a heavy boot connected with the door the shock of it travelled all the way through her body. Her hands slipped, but it was impossible to get a better hold while the handle flailed wildly on its spring. As she struggled to gain a grip, blow upon blow battered the door, each strike rendered with such anger and intensity Traudi thought the house would collapse. She knew there was nothing more she could do, she was simply too small to battle something so big, and so she fled – running up the stairs because there was nowhere else to go.

Chapter Ten

"The last ice age began about thirty million years ago and ended some fifteen thousand years ago, which I'm sure you will agree is a fair amount of time."

Leo examined his class, finding no visible sign of a willingness to agree or disagree. So far so par for the course, he thought.

"Given that it *was* a considerable amount of time, glaciers were immense and they covered nearly 30 per cent of the earth's surface, stretching from the North Pole all the way south to what is now New York City. Then, for reasons as yet unexplained, the planet began to warm up and the glaciers retreated. Approximately 12,000 years ago the weather cooled again, but only for 1,000 years. The great glaciers of the past had had their day, although they did make a brief comeback between 1500 and 1850, most notably in North America and Europe. This period has subsequently become known as the Little Ice Age."

"Was that the sequel to *Ice Age: The Meltdown*, sir?"

Leo allowed time for the ripple of sniggers to subside. "No, Tobias, the Little Ice Age was actually the sequel to the Pleistocene epoch."

He balanced on the edge of the desk, waiting for the boy to reply. However, glacial periods tended to be unlikely territory for class comedians and his patience was met with silence.

"During the period of the Little Ice Age superstition was rife,"

Leo continued, "and as melting glaciers were held accountable for a number of disasters, such as floods and avalanches, they were believed to be the work of the devil. It was also widely believed that dragons lived in the mountains and that witches gathered around the peaks to cast spells. In fact, so terrifying were glaciers deemed to be that no one even attempted to explore them until the 1700s."

Leo glanced at his students, most of whom were scribbling on notepads. He regarded their diligence with a mixture of satisfaction and despair. Unbeknownst to the class he was conducting an experiment. Generally favouring a more academic approach to education, his conscience had been pricked by recent thoughts of Ana and her passion not only for teaching but also for the pupils she taught. Her enthusiasm made him feel old. It was a debatable truth that he stubbornly refused to accept as fact. Therefore, for one lesson only, Leo had decided to ditch Benn & Evans' glacier bible for James M. Deem and his more child-friendly work *Bodies from the Ice*. Although it felt like serving up J.K. Rowling when the curriculum demanded J.R Tolkien he couldn't fault the book's accuracy – or the change in gear it provoked in his students.

"As we have previously discussed, an alpine glacier forms when more snow accumulates on a mountain than can melt during the summer. This snow becomes a dense, hard ice called FIRN, which is snow that's at least a year old. The French call it *névé*. If this process continues for a number of years, the firn turns into a mass of larger ice crystals and a glacier is created. Once formed the glacier becomes what is essentially a moving river of ice with two main parts, a higher accumulation area and a lower ablation area. Although snow accumulates and melts in both parts, the accumulation area pressures the glacier ice to advance to the ablation area. As the glacier moves downwards it carries rocks and other debris, both on and below the surface."

Leo paused to inspect the class, noticing he'd lost a large section of the audience now that dragons had departed from the scene. But not to worry, he had something better than dragons up the sleeve of his *North Face* fleece.

"As the glacier moves downhill it carries rocks and debris, on and below the surface," Leo repeated. "And in some cases it also carries bodies... human bodies."

Leo watched the interest level rise before his eyes, thinking it was not unlike witnessing a Mexican Wave ripple through a chess match.

"Should someone fall through a crevasse in the ice, and should their body not be retrieved, the ice will eventually transport the body to the glacier's lowest point of ablation. Obviously, the weight and pressure of the ice tends to crush it to smithereens and transportation times may vary – not unlike the Austrian Federal Railway." Leo stopped to give his pupils time to appreciate the joke. Naturally, they didn't need long. "Glaciers all advance at their own speed," he continued. "Their velocity will depend on how much ice has melted, how steep the mountain is, how thick the glacier is and what type of terrain lies beneath the glacier. To give you an example, in 1923 a woman died after falling into a crevasse while crossing the Madatsch Glacier in the Tyrolean Alps. Her body resurfaced 29 years later at the snout of the glacier about 300 metres from where she disappeared. In contrast, in the early 1990s, at the snout of Switzerland's Porchabella Glacier, the skeleton of another woman was found. Subsequent tests revealed that this unfortunate young lady was 22 years old, and most probably a dairymaid, and that she had died about 200 years earlier."

"Ötzi was much older than that," remarked one of the girls sitting at the edge of the second row of desks. Leo nodded at the interruption, having expected it. Ötzi was a national treasure after all. The Italians might have commandeered the body, after scientists discovered its worth, but it was the Austrians who had brought Ötzi down from the shared border. It was the Austrians who had recovered history.

"You're correct, Astrid. Ötzi was roughly 5,100 years older than the Swiss dairymaid and he was in remarkably good shape for his age. But can you guess why his ancient body wasn't pulverised along the way?"

"Because they don't make men like they used to?" inquired Astrid and Leo laughed along with the rest of the class because it was exactly the kind of sharp retort that he so rarely enjoyed in a class of fifteen year olds.

"I'm sure that is also correct," Leo admitted. "Another reason, however, is that the rocky depression in which Ötzi was found protected his body from the gliding ice."

"Shame it didn't protect him from the hatchet that hit him in the head," quipped Tobias. Almost immediately, the boy turned in Astrid's direction and she answered his look with a shy, closed-lipped smile. Though irritated, Leo held his tongue, unwilling to burst the bubble of their brief flirtation. Both blessed and cursed with the clarity of age, he recognised the moment – the first flutter in the chest of a boy, the uncertainty and hope. Sadly, he also saw that Astrid was by far the better catch of the two. Not that the girl would be aware of this, she was too young, but in a year or two when the train-track braces were dismantled and the older, taller boys began to take notice, the chances were high that young Tobias might have to lower his sights. This was the grim reality of love; it was a pleasure that sucked in the innocent, holding them trapped for a while, before spitting them out and leaving their heart crushed, as surely as a dairymaid frozen in a glacier.

****

"Leo?"

"Yes."

"Do you think you might be a sociopath?"

It was Ana's voice Leo heard, coming to haunt him on the long drive home as he vaguely pondered Tobias and Astrid's potentially doomed coupling, and how a man of his record was in no position to judge.

"Do you think I'm a sociopath?" he had asked calmly and Ana had shrugged noncommittally. She placed the magazine she was reading on the table between them.

"It says here that sociopaths have little thought for others, that they are incapable of love, that they don't get nervous easily and they show no remorse or shame when they abuse other people."

"And you think that's me?"

"Do you?"

Leo had frowned, buttered his bread and tried to think of a response. In the end he simply asked, "Is this about us moving in together?"

"But we're not moving in together, are we?"

"So, it's about that then?"

"I didn't say that."

And in fairness, Ana hadn't said that. He had said it. However, in his defence, what Ana *had* said was that it was 'fine' when he told her he saw no reason for them to move their worldly belongings under one roof. Unfortunately, Ana's definition of

109

'fine' and his definition of 'fine' appeared to have been taken from two very different dictionaries and when Ana said things were 'fine' she actually meant that things were 'very far from fine' and that she had come to believe she was dating a sociopath.

Leo was perplexed; there had been no indication of Ana's paradoxical approach to language when they first met. If anything, they had seemed uncommonly well-matched – she liked to talk, he preferred to listen; she could be irrational, he could switch off; and they both enjoyed a late night Leberkäse from the Shell garage. Within a few weeks they were spending more time with each other than without and the passion of summer gently simmered into dating by autumn and into a relationship come winter. Two years later, Leo had slipped comfortably into the role of being one half of a couple, and he had believed things were going well. They had twice visited Ana's mother in Valencia; they had visited her father in Salzburg several times more; she had become a regular guest at the table of his parents; and he had celebrated the two birthdays that had passed with a meal and the champagne she had asked for. Not only that, he had taught her to ski, he'd picked a tick from her scalp, taken her to the hunter's ball, appreciated the *dirndl* she bought and, in the chaos of the last *Fasching* carnival, he'd told her he loved her. Of course, they had been extraordinarily drunk at the time – and she had said the words first – but remembering her father's aversion to the phrase and seeing the question in her eyes, he saw no reason not to reciprocate, and when he told Ana he loved her too, he had meant it – or at least he had meant it as far as his understanding of the words went. To his surprise, Ana's eyes had welled in response, which was touching but no doubt assisted by the enormous quantity of alcohol she had consumed. In turn, Leo had remained calm. Warm, but calm. For him, it was no thunderbolt moment. He had heard the words, he understood the question, and he had answered honestly. And if love was being in the company of a woman he wanted to be with, then he was in love. Ana was remarkable. She was funny, intelligent, honest and beautiful. When he looked into her eyes he felt he understood her. When he imagined her near he could smell her perfume. When she smiled in his presence the world seemed to grow brighter. When she laughed in his arms it carried him away. And when she reached for his hand, he often gave it freely, feeling no sense of irritation. This was the wondrous, almost magical, view of their relationship from Leo's side of the stage, and it was a view that appeared to be slightly askew to Ana's.

"We don't spend any time together," she had said.

"We're together at least three nights a week."

"No, we're not."

"Mostly we are."

"No, we're not."

To prove her point she produced a calendar. A black felt tip pen marked the days they had shared during the past six months. Leo dutifully inspected the evidence – mainly because Ana had gone to the trouble of charting their relationship, but also because his future sex life might depend on it. But no matter which way he looked at it, he thought the black marks and the blank spaces were relatively balanced. Time together, time apart, for the life of him he couldn't see the problem. But there was a problem, apparently. Quite a few of them, in fact: arriving late from work was a problem; his daily run in the valley was a problem; nights with the boys were a problem; exercises with the rescue team were a problem; weekends climbing in South Tyrol were a problem; sleeping on his own because he wanted to go on a pre-dawn ski tour was a problem; and telling her that she kissed like a cow when she was drunk was one of the biggest problems of all.

"You just don't get it," Ana had sighed. "Couples are supposed to share experiences. They make plans. They respect each other's feelings. They try to work out ways in which they can spend more time together, not less. You're supposed to want to be with me, Leo. And you've made me so paranoid I'm frightened to kiss you."

"You're blowing that comment out of proportion, Ana. And, whether you believe it or not, I do want to spend my time with you – and the time I do have I spend with you."

"It doesn't feel like you do – and you don't."

"ok then, tell me what you want me to do. Are you asking me to give up my job? Give up the rescue team? Stop meeting my friends? Stop doing my sports?"

"That's not what I'm saying."

"Then what are you saying?"

"I need to feel like you want to be with me."

"Jesus," Leo had cursed, shaking his head in exasperation, completely at a loss as to how he was supposed to make a woman feel something he thought she already did. What did she want – a notice in the paper? Matching tattoos?

"Look Ana, are you on your period?"

As soon as the question left his lips, Leo recognised he might be in trouble – but he woefully underestimated just how much trouble he might actually be in. Ana's response was nothing short of apocalyptic, and when the door slammed behind her Leo was stunned.

Three days later Ana had calmed down enough to reach for the phone.

"I thought you'd have called me by now," was her opening gambit, and immediately Leo was riled.

However, as her voice had sounded genuinely wounded he

had resisted the urge to vent his disbelief, replying instead that he had been busy, which was partly true. Of course, they both knew that the real reason he hadn't attempted to mend the bridge he had set fire to was because he was kind of mad. Ana had blamed him for something he couldn't comprehend and after smashing his *Österreich Über Alles* mug in the process of trying to connect it with his face she had stormed from the room, making it abundantly clear that she never wanted to see him again.

"Being busy is what got us into this mess. You're always busy," Ana replied wearily, and Leo had sat on the sofa in readiness for round two.

To his surprise, and slight suspicion, Ana had left it at that. There were no recriminations to counter, no holes to dig and Ana's voice remained steady, almost businesslike, throughout the duration of the call. Quite rightly, she apologised for breaking his mug. She also assured him her love was intact before claiming to understand him more than he realised. Leo wasn't sure this was true, but he let it go.

"People are like jelly," Ana stated, seemingly out of nowhere. "They get poured into situations, or places, and even relationships and they mould themselves to fit. People adapt because they want to belong – whether it be to a place, to a time or to a person. But some people are different. They simply cannot adapt. This could be as a result of experience or old age or it could be that it's simply the way they are. So somewhere along the line these people stop being jelly and they turn into something harder, like rock. They cannot bring themselves to fit the occasion. And it doesn't necessarily mean that they're stubborn or that they don't want to belong: sometimes it's simply because it's not within their power to mould themselves. They're no longer jelly, you see? They are rock."

As Ana finished, Leo hadn't answered immediately as he had wanted to give himself time to carefully consider all that had been said. Ultimately, he found himself troubled on two accounts; first, he was of the belief that only children talked of jelly; and second, he was pretty sure his girlfriend had just compared him to a rock. He wasn't sure what was going on in Ana's head, and he was wary of knowing too much, but he also knew beyond doubt that he wanted to make things right.

"Perhaps we should try living together," he finally replied.

****

"Never get married," Günter moaned.

Naturally, Leo didn't answer because the advice, heartfelt as it might be, hardly seemed applicable to him under the circumstances.

"Listen to me," Günter continued, oblivious to the sensitivities of a newly single man, "there are three distinct stages of a relationship and they directly correspond to a woman's attitude to a man's testicles: fun bags, sperm bags and punch bags."

"I take it Lisa's still kicking your balls?"

"Daily."

"And you bring none of it on yourself, of course." Leo raised an eyebrow along with his glass. "*Prost*."

"*Prost*," Günter returned, before emitting a sigh of despair. He looked around the room. There wasn't much to see other than Berni struggling to accommodate two female tourists who appeared to have mistaken the hut for a wine bar. "Have you heard anything from *La Bella Princesa*?"

"You make her sound like a cruise liner," Leo responded flatly.

Before Günter could reply, Berni returned to the bar, a scowl

114

further creasing his deeply lined forehead. Muttering "women," under his breath, he reached for a couple of glasses and two bottles of *Zipfer*.

"Pop a cherry in the glass," Günter suggested. "Inform the ladies it's a Salzkammergut Cocktail."

"And what if it catches on?" Berni replied. "The damn place will be overrun with hairspray and handbags."

"So why not show them the door, like the good old days? Tell them it's a men-only establishment."

"There are laws against that now."

"There are also laws against harassment, but it doesn't stop the *Weiber* from abusing their law-abiding husbands."

"I take it your Old Lady is still making life difficult?" Berni asked, and Leo smirked as Günter admitted she was.

"She'll drag me to the grave eventually."

"They take us all in the end, friend." Clearing his throat, Berni placed two beers on a tray and took them over to the women waiting at the other end of the room. Under fur-trimmed hats their painted lips thanked Berni in the effeminate *Schönbrunn Deutsch* of well-heeled Vienna. Günter grimaced. Leo glanced out of the window.

The light was receding and the heat of the day would quickly drain away. Picturing the sun dipping behind the peaks of the Dachstein, a shiver ran up Leo's spine, yet it had nothing to do with the cold. It was the feeling of something amiss. Not so long ago they had all been trapped – there was no way in, there was no way out – the winter had had the town clamped in its jaws. Now the unseasonal thaw and its uncommon speed was distorting the very fabric of Leo's existence; disturbing the natural order of life in the mountains and luring tourists from the capital when it was far too early in the year to have to tolerate them. But it wasn't just tourists; there was something else he couldn't quite put his finger on, a nagging feeling gnawing at the back of his mind. Something was wrong, badly wrong. And as the Dachstein cast its shadow over the hut, the creeping darkness worked to increase Leo's sense of unease.

"Did you hear about Sepp and Bergmann?"

Berni returned to the bar, pocketing a ten euro note in his wallet.

"Butcher Sepp?" asked Günter.

The landlord nodded. "The police were on his doorstep this morning, Bergmann's place too, not that he was anywhere to be found."

Leo glanced at Berni, the hairs on his neck freezing as he recalled his mother's twilight visit to the old hunter's porch.

"What did the police want?" he asked.

"Meat."

"Well, they went to the right shop, then," Günter muttered.

Berni reached for a bottle opener, offering the men two fresh beers and pouring one for himself, before continuing. "According to the talk – which is of course different to the gossip of women – it seems that perhaps Sepp has been selling something he shouldn't, and Bergmann has been the man supplying him with it."

"Venison?" Leo asked.

"Well, it's not likely to be buffalo meat, is it?"

"As long as it's not dog meat I couldn't really give a crap," Günter interjected.

"That's because you don't hunt," Berni replied.

Leo scratched at his beard, recalling something Harri had once told him. "Hasn't Bergmann got form for illegal hunting?"

"So they say," Berni confirmed. "But Bergmann's a law unto himself. I have to say though, I'm surprised at Sepp."

"So, who tipped off the police?" Leo asked.

"God knows." Berni lit a cigar, and pulled up a seat behind the bar. "The police asked Sepp a few questions, asked to see his cold room, that sort of stuff. Sepp denied any wrongdoing, but refused the police entry, so they've had to apply for a search warrant. The shop's been shut all day so maybe they got one."

"And Bergmann?" asked Leo.

"At home, from what I hear. The police waited for him, probably expecting him to turn up dragging a stag through the snow, but when he arrived he was empty handed, mad as hell, and they found nothing in his house."

"And what do you think?"

"It's not my business to think, Leo. I just pour the beer. However, if the two of them have been up to no good, and I'm not saying they have, it's sure to be bad news for Sepp. For Bergmann, well, I can't see it making much difference to him – only to his pocket."

Leo nodded in agreement. Berni was right; illegal hunting could be a death sentence within a community and at one point in history it literally was – perpetrators were hanged. Of course, these days the offence brought possible prison time, but more commonly a fine. It was the loss of standing that was the real killer though. In the old days, before the revolution, illegal hunters were seen as rebel heroes, men defying the autocratic rule of the day to feed their families with meat stolen from the land of over-privileged barons. But those days were long gone, the romantic shootouts a thing of the past, and illegal hunters were no longer heroes, but criminals. For Sepp it would be a disaster, but for Bergmann Leo could see few repercussions – the man had always shied away from the community. He was a loner with no discernible friends, a shadow living among people, with no desire to be anything more. His face was scarred with a story untold – although there were rumours of a lost love, a bottle of schnapps and a loaded gun – but in truth, no one seemed willing to ask. Bergmann simply wasn't a man who was easily approached, and in a way Leo had always admired that; the chosen isolation and resolute refusal to play to the expectations of others. And yet Leo was also troubled. For a man who had purposely lived his life away from the scrutiny of others, Bergmann had become increasingly visible lately. First there was the tense conversation that had taken place in Berni's and his bizarre interest in Reinhardt's rescue; then there was the argument with Reinhardt in the square; there was this latest episode with the police; and, most troubling of all, the memory of his own mother skulking at the man's door. Something wasn't quite right, and it unnerved him.

"What do you make of Bergmann?" Leo asked Berni.

"Nothing much," the landlord admitted. "He's not much of a conversationalist, but he pays for the beer he drinks and that's good enough for me."

Behind them, a group of teenagers burst into the room.

"Shut the damn door!" Berni barked before they even had time to finish their entrance. Pulling a weary face, he rose from his seat to take the group's orders as they settled themselves at a table nearest the window.

Leo pulled up the zip on his fleece, glancing as he did so at Berni's new customers and noticing a teenage girl amongst the gang of boys. Though her hair was blonde and her skin was pale she reminded him of Ana as he watched her easy laughter light up the room with the flash of perfect white teeth. He turned to Günter.

"I miss *La Bella Princesa*," he quietly admitted.

Instead of berating the lapse in machismo, Günter gently knocked his bottle against Leo's.

Later that evening, after Günter had dutifully gone home to his wife and the Hut had grown lively with men apparently lacking jobs to attend to in the morning, Leo felt the time had come for answers. He looked at his watch. Ten thirty. The hour wasn't ideal, but he took the phone from his trouser pocket and dialled.

"What's wrong?" a sleepy voice demanded on the other end of the line.

"Why should anything be wrong?" he asked.

"If you call your mother in the middle of the night what is she supposed to think?"

"It's only 10.30."

"Exactly, so what's the matter?"

"Nothing's the matter."

"Are you drunk?"

"No."

"You sound drunk."

Leo sighed before confirming that he might have had a 'few little beers' but this did not in any way constitute being pissed. Before his mother could berate him for his language, he asked if she'd heard that the police had questioned Bergmann and Sepp. In the background, he heard the low grumble of his father's voice.

"It's your son," he heard his mother reply. "He wants to talk about Bergmann and the butcher."

"What on earth for?" asked his father, loud enough for Leo to hear.

"Because he's drunk."

"I am not drunk!" Leo shouted down the phone.

"He's shouting now," his mother said.

"I can hear him," his father replied.

Leo blinked, slapped a palm to his forehead and cut to the

chase, opting to discard the gentle preamble he had prepared in his head to ask his mother outright why she had been at Bergmann's house the night before.

"At whose house?" she asked.

"Bergmann's," he repeated.

"Who says I was there?"

"I do – I saw you."

"Then you must have been drunk last night as well. Whoever you think you saw I can assure you it wasn't me. Now go to bed, Leopold. You've got school in the morning."

The line went dead.

Chapter Eleven

Traudi was convinced she was being eaten from the inside out. She imagined her organs turning on one another, feasting like cannibals and stripping her bare of the means to survive. She was so hungry it was painful and the ache that came and went like waves crashing against the wall of her stomach also brought a feeling of rot that pulsed deep within her belly. Her arms and legs felt remote, weighed down by bones too heavy to lift. Her neck ached with the strain of supporting her head. And she guessed she was dying.

"Traudi, you must trust in the Lord."

It was her mother speaking, returning as a whisper at the child's ear and the memory of a cool hand on her shoulder. *I am the bread of life; whoever comes to me shall not hunger, and whoever believes in me shall never thirst.*

"But I believe!" Traudi whimpered. "Can't you see I do?"

Never once had Traudi questioned the Lord. She had always, resolutely, believed in Jesus. But right now, as the hours ticked by like the tap-tap of a cane leading her closer to heaven, she struggled to hang on to her mother's blind faith. She was starving, she was scared, and she felt sick from the onslaught of both.

"Religion is simply a trick dreamed up by the rich to stop the poor from asking too many questions."

That's what *Opa* believed. Of course, he never said it in front of their mother who needed the strength of her convictions to see beyond the prison of her eyes. But he'd said it to Heini who had repeated it to Traudi and the two of them had concluded that their grandfather might have a point. The Bible expected the poor to live on a promise – that all would be well once they entered the Kingdom of Heaven. But there was nothing to stop the rich from receiving the very same reward, and they appeared to have an easier time getting to it.

"If God exists why did he take our father?" Heini had challenged.

"Because God loved him so much that He wanted him near," Traudi replied, repeating the words her mother had once spoken to explain their father's loss.

"And us? Does he not love us?"

"God is love."

"God is a lie," Heini retorted angrily and Traudi had been shocked by the venom in his voice. But now, lying under her mother's bed, with hunger gnawing at her insides, and being too afraid to venture downstairs to the kitchen, Traudi found it difficult to understand how a loving God could be so deaf to her prayers. If the Lord loved her so much why had he abandoned her? What had she done to deserve such a punishment?

"The eye that mocks a father and scorns obedience to a mother will be pecked out by ravens and eaten by vultures."

The Bible's warning was clear. She had known it all along. Yet the words, memorised by her brother for their grotesque imagery and ability to torment, had meant nothing when everything was normal – when Traudi felt safe – but now she remembered her mother's joke, and how she had repeated it with childish glee. *'A family may live without kisses, but not without salt.'* Had she mocked her father by saying such a thing? Of course she had. It was clear she had. Not once did she utter the words after he died, so why did she do it when he was alive? It was like respecting the memory while mocking the man. Not that she had meant to mock her father. She had loved him. She and her mother had only been playing. It was a stupid joke, nothing more. And what of her mother – had she disobeyed her? Traudi was almost certain that she had, but she was a child, what did the Lord expect? No one wanted to wash dishes every day of their lives.

"I'm a child, God. I'm a little girl. How can you be so angry?"

With only the sun to guide her, Traudi had to rely on guesswork to count the number of hours that passed. By her reckoning a full day had come and gone since the thing from outside had tried to kick in the door, and she wondered how many more were left in her.

After fleeing upstairs the hammering had stopped only to start again from another place – underneath the house, inside the cellar, at the top of the stone stairs. But that door was closed, she had locked it herself, and the thing, whatever it was, whatever evil had risen to hunt her down and take her, couldn't get in. It was confined to the cellar, to the cold, unfeeling concrete and its uncaring walls, and to the frozen plains beyond the house leading to the dark, sharp fingers of the forest. As long as she stayed under the bed, hidden from sight, Traudi believed she was safe. The house would work to protect her because her mother had been right. And wanting to show her gratitude, Traudi's fingers stroked the dusty floorboards hoping her home might feel the strength of her appreciation and continue to help her.

During the long hours Traudi stayed under the bed, there were no more shouts through the window. There was no nightmare face or ice-blue eyes. The doors no longer rattled, no boots kicked against the wood, there was nothing, nothing but the beating of her heart. It thumped under the weight of terror that pressed heavy on her chest, like it was ready to explode. In some ways the silence was more stressful than what had gone before, and Traudi's previous concern that she might starve to death was undermined by a new belief that she was on the verge of a heart attack.

She touched the angel at her neck, but it did little to calm her thoughts.

The thing that had come to their house, whatever it was – whether a madman or demon – would not have gone far, not now it had scented her fear. And Traudi was convinced it would be waiting – either skulking in the cellar or lurking in the forest – expecting her to make a move, for her to slip up and show herself. Without doubt, she knew that as soon as she unlocked the door it would pounce. She also understood that her mother had done what she could to keep her daughter safe, and that this thing was the reason for her disappearance. This malevolent thing – this creature alive or dead, man or beast – was the cause of her family's absence, if not their deaths.

The thing waiting outside was the reason she was alone.

Chapter Twelve

Leo hit the accelerator, moving dangerously close to the silver Audi in front. Almost bumper-to-bumper he swerved left, overtaking the car before returning to the middle lane and switching on his fog lights. The point made, Leo dipped sharply into the slow lane and looked in the rear view mirror, hardly believing his eyes as the Audi continued its fascination with the middle lane, seemingly undaunted by the lesson Leo had administered. It was irrational, perhaps even childish, but the indignation that swelled in his stomach made Leo's nostrils flare. He glanced again at the Audi behind him, focussing on the German number plates, finding his irritation somehow justified.

Glancing at the dashboard, Leo clocked the temperature – a balmy 5 degrees Celsius – and the time, 4.05pm. In another hour, maybe less, the light would be gone. Yet another day wasted in the torturous pursuit of wages. Subconsciously, Leo's left hand drifted to his belly. He felt his waistline escaping over the belt of his jeans and the softness of it repulsed him. He ought to be more disciplined. He should do more sport. He needed to forego the beer and start eating more healthily. Unfortunately, the days were short, his spirit was weak, and once he got home he knew that darkness and fatigue would work to rob him of the will to rectify the damage. He needed more time.

Looking at the roadside Leo saw the snow was melting fast, its icy existence largely relegated to pockets of white clinging to the darkest corners of passing fields. Though the warm weather was unusual it was not unheard of at this time of year, but seeing the winter in such a full and hasty retreat added to Leo's panic. Time was slipping away, as surely as the season's grip on the landscape.

With a hand still cradling his stomach, Leo thought of the journal in his 'study'. It was a thought that compounded his sense of failure. Started as a boy, the pages documented every ski tour he had ever undertaken; the places; the routes; the elevations; and the completion times. Every year the number of tours had increased until they reached a peak of 43 in 1998. Smug as it sounds, it was a phenomenal achievement and it was one that had left him pretty much isolated from the world. Even so, with every coming winter he promised he would beat that personal best. And every year work, alcohol, women and life conspired to defeat him. This year had been exceptionally poor – only twelve, barely challenging tours – and now the snow was already receding. The winter had arrived early, but after a fierce and promising start it was sprinting towards the finish line whilst Leo found his foot wedged in the starting blocks. Imprisoned in his car, Leo watched the world rotate with a mixture of envy and despair, feeling robbed and thwarted and something close to self-loathing.

He relaxed his foot on the pedal as the steering wheel shuddered in response to the high speed. Not for the first time, he felt a pang of nostalgia for the old car. It was a twinge of affection almost immediately followed by a pulsing sensation deep within his trouser pocket. Leo dug frantically, but time, as ever, remained his most consistent enemy and having failed to undo Günter's mischief the hellish tone of Crazy Frog's be-ding-ding-ding rattled his nerves. Fittingly, Günter's name appeared on the display.

"You bastard," Leo swore.

"Well, that's a nice way to greet someone," Günter replied. "Where are you?"

"I'm on the highway."

"How was school?"

"Are you really interested?"

"No, not really."

To his left, Leo saw the Audi driver drawing parallel. A round, doughy face stared in his direction and a fat fist appeared at the man's ear in a clumsy imitation of Leo on the phone. The driver shook his jowls in admonishment.

"Fucking Germans," Leo grumbled. He met the man's look with his middle finger and the Audi cruised ahead, at a speed Leo's Golf couldn't hope to match, all the while glued to the middle lane.

"What's with the Germans?" Günter's voice asked.

"Bah, ignore me. It's nothing, just another arsehole on the road."

"I've got a good joke about Germans."

"I'm sure you do."

"No, really, it's a good one."

"Go on then..."

"There was an Austrian couple staying at a hotel..."

"I thought this was a joke about Germans," Leo interrupted.

"Don't interrupt," Günter snapped. He coughed theatrically and started again. "There was an Austrian couple staying at a hotel. One morning they went for breakfast to find two other couples sitting in the dining room – they were GERMANS. As the Austrians took their seats, they overheard one of the Germans say to his wife, 'Could you pass me the sugar, Sugar?' A little while later, the other German turned to his wife and said, 'Could you pass me the honey, Honey?' The Austrian guy noticed the expectant look on his wife's face and after gazing around the room he turned to her and said, 'Pass me the bacon, you pig.'"

Leo snorted down the phone, laughing in spite of himself. Günter was right; it was a fine joke, one his mother might even appreciate after four decades of marriage. "So what do you want Günter? You can't be ringing just to tell me jokes on the drive home."

"No, I guess not," Günter admitted. For a moment the line went quiet and Leo felt a prickle of suspicion rise up his neck. Eventually, and with no preamble, Günter revealed, "Lisa's left me."

"She's left you?"

"Yes."

"As in packed her bags?"

"Yes."

"As in taken the kids?"

"Yes."

"Jesus."

Leo didn't know what to say. Günter and Lisa had been married seven years and they had two children, a boy and a girl. The girl had come first and Lisa had named her Delilah. Two years later, Günter had punished his wife by insisting on naming their son Samson. Although the children became affectionately known as Deli and Sam, they were the living proof of the unconventional nature of Günter and Lisa's relationship, which had always been rocky if not always Biblical in its complexity. Even so, Leo had thought the two of them were solid, and it was a belief that dulled his ability to react to the news that they weren't with anything other than confusion. He relaxed his foot on the accelerator, willing his mind to catch up with the slower speed.

"So where's Lisa gone?" he finally asked.

Günter sighed heavily down the phone. "She's gone back to

her mother's."

"To her mother's?"

"Yes."

"But her mother lives downstairs."

"I know. It's kind of awkward."

Leo blinked in bewilderment. It wasn't that unusual for families to share homes in Hallstatt. The houses were large and many were divided into separate dwellings as the older generation clung onto life denying the younger generation their rightful inheritance. Even so, a trip downstairs hardly smacked of abandonment: rather, it was a change of scene, a kneejerk Feng Shui. It wasn't like moving to another country. It wasn't like running off to Spain.

"Fancy a little beer?" Leo asked.

"I thought you'd never ask," replied Günter.

****

When Ana moved her belongings into Leo's house he had been astonished to discover she owned more knickers than knickknacks. Of greater surprise, however, was the realisation that there wasn't a part of him that even remotely resented the intrusion – possibly because he was so utterly overwhelmed by the assault on his senses. His fridge, so long a hub of humming dejection, became a place of wonder filled with crisp salads, colourful vegetables, litres of milk, fish fillets and meat. The kitchen was transformed into the heart of the house pumping the aroma of freshly ground coffee into the hallway, or spices and herbs flavouring the dish of the day. His bed sheets smelt of Ana's perfume, and his bathroom carried the scent of feminine secrets with shelves parading pots of face creams, body lotions, and fruit infused bath salts. As a result, Leo found himself in an almost constant state of arousal.

And though he might now be remembering the time through rose-tinted glasses, it seemed to him that his home woke with Ana's arrival, becoming somehow bigger, more generous, warmer and lighter. The two-bedroom house that had been little more than a place to sleep and store skis, became a shared oasis, an escape from the world, inside of which they laughed often, fought occasionally, and made love, albeit a little less frequently than they used to. Leo was happy with the arrangement. More than that, he was content. And for a while, he thought Ana was too. But somewhere along the line the earth began to shift, slipping beneath their feet like debris under a sliding glacier, moving so slowly as to be almost imperceptible until it belched the crap of the world out of its snout.

In May Ana was told that her services would no longer be required at the technical college. The dismissal had nothing to do with incompetence, but rather a cut in funding, and it had only ever been temporary. Leo tried to be sympathetic and he acted swiftly to comfort Ana, assuring her that she needn't pay her half of the rent until she found other employment. Ana thanked him, in a way that struck him as possibly sarcastic, but this may have been due to the pronounced arch of one eyebrow. Either way, he didn't have to foot the bill for long. Within weeks of losing her teaching post, Ana acquired a new job in town; serving in one of the shops that mainly catered to tourists with a penchant for salt.

"We sell salt candles, salt scrubs, salt licks, salt crystal lamps, salt shakers and salt blends for the culinary adventurous," Ana had sighed. "In fact the only item not salt-related is the pepper spray behind the counter."

Leo had laughed at that because he thought it was a joke. Unfortunately, Ana hadn't been joking and she found the unexpected change in her fortunes far from funny. She was annoyed. And Leo failed to understand why. He recognised the pay was minimal and the hours were few, starting at 9am and finishing at noon, but it sounded like paradise to him. At least five days a week he hauled himself out of bed before dawn, knowing it would be dark by the time he returned home. Each sunset signalled another day lost. That was misery – that was the glorious gift his own life had bestowed him – whereas Ana had the world at her feet with the freedom to enjoy it. In all honesty, he would have loved to stand in her shoes and quite often, during the relentless slog back and forth from Linz, he imagined what he would do with the hours, picturing himself running through the Echerntal Valley, biking to Gosau, climbing the Kasberg and skiing on Feuerkogel. A few times he even spent the drive fantasising about ski tours, returning home to triumphantly notch up another success in his neglected and age-battered journal. For Leo, time was the Holy Grail of his existence, but of course Ana was a very different creature to him. She had a sloth's interest in sport and instead of embracing her freedom she simply felt trapped by it.

"You'll never understand," she had said.

"Try me," he had challenged.

Ana looked up from the sandwich she was eating, having lost her appetite for cooking along with her job. "Well," she said, pausing in search of the words that might adequately express how she felt. "When your day is filled with so many hours, it's the things that are missing that become more apparent."

"And what's missing?" Leo had asked.

"You."

****

131

Five shrill beeps interrupted Leo's memories. He reached for the phone, now lying on the passenger seat, and felt a familiar rush of adrenalin as he read the message on the display: 'ACCIDENT. HALLSTATT. CLIMBING GARDEN.' Nothing too unusual, he thought. Could be something, could be nothing. He dialled the control centre.

"What have you got?"

"Missing male, 43 years, possibly injured."

Leo pulled into a lay by, stopping to search for the pen and paper he kept in the glove compartment. He hurriedly took down the information at the control centre's disposal. They both agreed it didn't amount to much.

"I'm forty minutes away," he confirmed.

Putting his foot to the pedal, Leo drew a mental picture of the area – a rock face left of the Echerntal Valley, no more than 50 metres high and fitted with permanent anchors. Given the location, it was probable that there had been a fall leading to an injury of some kind – perhaps a sprain or a broken bone, or even a split head. What was harder to work out was why the climber had been reported missing. Leo shook his head. It was useless to speculate, the possibilities were endless, and the mountain had a habit of throwing up surprises. He reached for the phone intending to call Günter, but deciding to wait until he cleared the highway. Once he reached the ring road passing Gmunden he dialled.

"You there?" he asked.

"Just arrived," Günter confirmed.

"Any details?"

"It's Reinhardt who's missing."

Leo's heart sank. The fool was fast becoming the rescue team's

132

sole source of business. "For crying out loud..."

"I know, I know...Apparently he was out with his old woman, blind drunk, there was some kind of fight and she left him to it."

"What the hell were they doing in the climbing garden?"

"They weren't in the climbing garden. Reinhardt's deeper in the valley."

"Where exactly?"

"As you know, it's hard to be exact, Leo, but I'm sure we can follow the noise."

Günter removed the phone from his ear and held it at arm's length, facing the expanse of rock growing black with the fading light. Leo listened on the other end of the line, unable to decipher what his ears were receiving. It wasn't a scream he heard – the sound was barely human – it was more like the bellowing rage of a wounded animal. Günter returned to the phone.

"Did you hear him?"

"I heard something," Leo replied.

"If I'm honest, it's creeping me out," Günter admitted. "Have you got everything with you?"

"That bad?"

"It might be."

Leo mentally catalogued the contents of his boot. "If I'm coming straight to you I'm going to need a radio."

"Sorted, there will be plenty by the time you get here – the rescue bus is on the way."

"Well, that's one piece of good news, I'm starving. What's on the menu?"

"I'm told to expect *Wurstsemmel* and coffee."

"Save me some. I'll be with you in thirty minutes."

"I'll be waiting," Günter replied. "Oh, and Leo..."

"Yes?"

"Drive carefully, friend, we don't want you taking any unnecessary risks."

As both men knew the unnecessary risk would start at the setting of the sun, Leo laughed as he killed the call.

A rescue was rarely easy – and the dark increased the difficulty tenfold – and if Günter was advising the use of full kit, the mission promised to be tricky. Experience had taught Leo to keep the basics in the car – a full harness, a set of carabiners, a first aid box, a helmet and headlamp, waterproofs and boots. Should it all be needed it could mean that Reinhardt had tested his luck one time too many. Leo looked at the dashboard – 4.45pm and already -2 degrees Celsius. He glanced upwards, towards the greying sky, wide open and cloudless. In twenty minutes the light would be gone and the temperature would plummet further.

With a growing sense of trepidation, Leo motored past Bad Ischl, slowing only for the speed traps. He then sped through Bad Goisern, rattled over the railway line that split the village of Au, pushed along the pass that sloped down to Hallstatt and flew through the tunnel like a bullet. After running the red at the traffic lights, he turned right towards Echerntal following the avenue of houses until the road forked on the brow of a hill. The right lane degenerated into a gravel track leading deeper into the valley, weaving past a couple of farms until it came to an end roughly a kilometre from the House of the Blind Woman. The left turning would take him to a small bridge and another gravel track which would wind its way towards the climbing garden and the edge of the forest. Leo turned left.

Once over the bridge, the chassis of the car took a hammering as the wheels kicked up stones and Leo slowed his speed, shifting into second gear. He reached for his phone, but before he had chance to dial he saw the blue lights of a police car through the trees. Leo pushed the phone into his pocket and let the lights guide him in; past the climbing garden, into woodland, until he came to a halt at a dirt clearing at the base of the mountain.

By the time Leo parked up, two police cars and an ambulance were already in attendance, as was the rescue team's minibus, spilling men and equipment from a side door. On the ground he saw a number of harnesses, all receiving a last minute check whilst the ropes were counted and coiled. He noted the dark silhouette of a waiting stretcher and somewhere, amongst all the paraphernalia, he knew there would also be a body bag.

Leo got out of the car to join the gathering rescue team, most of whom were working in near silence while a police siren wailed intermittently; a signal to Reinhardt that the emergency crews had arrived. Only when the siren ceased, did Leo hear again the strange, amplified moan of distress that he was told belonged to Reinhardt. The sound was as eerie as Günter had suggested and Leo was surprised to find the blood chilling in his veins. Opening the boot of the car, he hurriedly pulled on his waterproofs as Günter approached, bearing sausages. Leo thanked him and ate as he dressed. Once his harness was on, both men checked each other's equipment; tugging at belts, clips and knots.

"I've spoken to the police," Günter said. "They know no more than us. But Reinhardt has to be in some kind of pain because that's a God awful racket he's making out there. I'm guessing he's fallen."

"But where?" Leo asked.

"Hard to say for certain but it looks like the waterfall."

Günter pointed upwards and to his left. Leo needed no light to see a seemingly impassable wall of rock, the face of which was broken only by the deep groove of one of the area's waterfalls and a smattering of trees that had somehow defied the laws of gravity.

135

"Where's Harri?" he asked.

"On his way," Günter replied. "His wife had to drag him from the sauna."

"He'll be happy then."

"Tell me about it. My ears are still ringing after I told him it was Reinhardt missing."

Right on cue, the bizarre howls of their rescue pierced the quiet of the valley and one of the police officers hit the siren again in an effort to keep the man calm. Günter shivered.

"Damn cold tonight," he muttered, his eyes holding Leo's for a fraction of a second. He then turned to join the rest of the team.

In all, twelve men answered the emergency call. When Harri finally arrived he brought the number to thirteen. Though Leo had never been a superstitious man, it made him uneasy.

"If that Drunk Dog comes down in one piece I swear to God I'll break his neck myself," Harri threatened, his face still flushed from the effects of the sauna and a justifiable rage. Leo was about to placate him, but Reinhardt beat him to it.

"What the hell?" Harri shouted in response. His eyes scanned the rock face, searching for the source of the noise. As his eyes hovered around the waterfall he added more quietly, "How in God's name?"

The men paused in their preparations to consider his face. No one knew the area better than Harri. He had spent a lifetime charting the peaks, hollows, trails and ridges of the Dachstein. There wasn't a hut he hadn't visited or a path he hadn't trod. And when a man like Harri takes one look at the area they are about to go into and asks 'How?' grown men grow nervous.

Once everyone was ready, the team gathered around a map placed upon the bonnet of a police car. The men quickly went through their options, debating the merits of setting out as a single unit or dividing into two before agonising over the necessity of taking a stretcher. In the end they agreed to leave the stretcher behind, deciding it would be better to locate Reinhardt before worrying about how they might bring him down. They further agreed to start the search with a six-man team heading directly for Reinhardt's wails whilst the rest of the men attempted to find a passable track to take them to the waterfall.

Swallowing a last bite of sausage, Leo assumed the lead of the first team, taking with him Günter, Harri and three of the less-experienced members of the group; Andy, Joe and Christian. Their headlamps on, they walked into the dark with strong, purposeful steps, crashing through the brittle branches of the surrounding pine trees, the tread of their boots quickly picking up mud.

For fifteen minutes the six men trudged through the under-growth, their calves tightening with the added weight clinging to the soles of their boots and the steadily increasing incline of the terrain. No one spoke because the night was young and they had no idea how much breath they might need. Besides, the soundtrack of Reinhardt's screams was hardly conducive to easy conversation, and because it was dark to the point of black they all felt the need to concentrate.

Twenty minutes further into the rescue, their headlamps picked up the stony floor of a dry riverbed and they followed its path upwards. As they climbed higher every step seemed to grow steeper than the last. The ground was soft, treacherous with wet twigs and sodden earth, and it easily gave way beneath their feet. Occasionally, one of them would lose balance, slipping to their knees, grabbing hold of whatever passing rock or branch they could find to stay upright.

Behind him, Leo heard the labouring breaths of his men

accompanied by the dry rattle of Harri's chest. It was nothing to worry about, the older man was as fit as any of them on the mountain, yet the noise still scratched at his nerves, reminding him of his own age and mortality. Above Leo, the light from his headlamp bounced off slabs of grey rock – mammoth shards as old as the world itself, standing like magnificent monuments to the power of nature. When he looked down he saw only black mulch. This was him, he thought. This was man. This was their worth here on Earth. They were the crap under the feet of giants, the decaying remains of a plan gone wrong, and instead of nourishing the soil they were poisoning it. Leo shook his head and blinked rapidly, silently counting his steps to keep his mind focussed. To his side the darkness was all encompassing, broken only by the faint beams of headlamps and the occasional glare from the team's reflective jackets. And through it all, through every slip and grunt, through the ranting of his mind, through the wet and the harsh, biting cold, Reinhardt's distress rang in his ears, increasing the pressure, compounding a growing sense of unease.

After thirty-five minutes spent following the riverbed, the men arrived at a small plateau. Above it stood an almost vertical granite wall and the team had no choice but to stop. They were getting close. They could hear it. Reinhardt's screams were almost deafening. Without a word said, Günter stepped forward, easily the strongest climber among them, and Leo worked quickly to secure his friend as he hauled himself upwards, searching half-blind along the rock feeling for slots in which he could anchor a chock. As Günter climbed higher, his boots slipped and scraped upon the wet surface, raining grit and mud onto the men below. Leo spat the dirt from his mouth, holding the rope fast – all-too conscious of the danger and all-too aware that it was his best friend risking his life in the dark. He kept his headlight steady, working with the others to position a guiding beam on the wall. But the higher Günter climbed the weaker the light became.

"Fuck it!" Günter eventually roared in frustration.

No one moved. Everyone kept their lights trained in Günter's direction, but it was clear that having scaled four metres of rock he was now at a standstill. Leo braced himself.

"What's up?" he shouted.

"Not me, anymore," Günter said as he grudgingly admitted defeat. "There's nothing here but flat rock. It's impossible. I've nothing to hang onto, nothing to use. The damn wall is vertical."

"OK, leave it!" Leo ordered. "Come down. You've done what you can."

Leo felt Günter leaning into his harness and he balanced himself to counter the weight, slowly feeding the rope to facilitate descent. Once Günter's feet hit the ground they unclipped themselves. Leo pressed the push-to-talk button on his radio.

"Rescue Bus, this is Leo. We're at a dead end. Over."

A static crackle met their failure before a response came.

"This is Rescue Bus, Leo. Rescue Team Two is somewhere to your right having found a path to follow. Over."

"In that case Rescue Team One will head back to the coordination point. Over."

"Roger that."

Leo clicked the radio back into its holster, feeling deflated by the dead end they had come to and slightly envious of the other team's chances. Appearing at his side, Harri gave him a soft nudge.

"I'm not so sure about this path the other team have found," he said after waiting for a pause in the almost constant cacophony of Reinhardt's terror.

"No?"

"No."

Leo was about to ask why when Reinhardt resumed his screeching, and something to the right caught his eye. Following Leo's gaze, the other men peered into the dense black of the forest, blinking rapidly and finding nothing. Around their feet an icy breeze began to gain in strength, rising to freeze the sweat on the men's faces. Somewhere above them Reinhardt released another animal roar. A second later there was a flash of light.

"Did you see that?" Leo asked of no one in particular, the words almost catching in his throat.

Reinhardt again bellowed his presence; another thunderous, bestial lament that ricocheted on the rock around them. The men tensed. The light flashed again. Not once, but twice, three times and then...

"Oh Jesus," Leo sighed wearily.

"Fuck it!" a voice erupted angrily from the trees.

Two minutes later Gerhard approached, closely followed by the rest of Rescue Team Two.

Once the men had regrouped, and with nowhere else to go, all thirteen members of the rescue team carefully retraced their steps to the coordination point, all the way chased by Reinhardt's distress. By the time they reached the clearing, exertion and tension had made lead of their legs. All of them were frustrated. All of them were cold. All of them were worried. Reinhardt was a fool, but he was a fool that was known to them, and he was lost in the dark in the kind of terrain that didn't suffer fools gladly.

From the rescue bus two volunteers rushed to meet the team, carrying trays of refreshments. Leo grabbed a sausage before clasping an icy hand around a polystyrene cup steaming with hot, sweet coffee. He broke off from the group to speak to one of the police officers, relaying the difficulties that had so far thwarted the rescue. He then returned to his men who had gathered around a map, their breath visible in the light of their headlamps.

Though Reinhardt's deranged calls had pumped up the pressure, they had managed to confirm that the team was heading in the right direction. Even so, it was clear they needed to find another route. To the left of the waterfall there was nothing but smooth, vertical rock – almost impossible to negotiate. Everyone turned to Harri, currently leant over the map, scratching at the grey stubble on his chin.

"We might have a chance if we start a lot further to the right, if we make a bigger arc towards Reinhardt. Higher up, beyond the waterfall, I seem to recall a small plateau. Of course, there has to be a way in before that, after all the Drunk Dog got there somehow."

Leo nodded. "Let's start as one group and divide up if and when necessary," he said. "I also think we should take the medical kit, I've got a feeling Reinhardt might need sedating."

Christian stepped forward. "I'll carry the bag," he volunteered, and though no one said a word, the relief was palpable.

At twenty-one, Christian was the youngest on the team. Mop-haired, blue-eyed and built like an ox, he was the son of a church organist and displayed an extraordinary sense of civic duty for a man of his tender years. Also a member of the dog rescue team, Christian was a lively and visible component of Hallstatt's charitable conscience and every Christmas he blacked his face and donned the robes of one of the Three Kings to go house-to-house collecting money for the Third World. Günter wasn't a fan of the boy, but Günter harboured a dislike of anyone holding an interest in the contents of his wallet.

Leo lifted the medical kit onto Christian's back, offering a gentle pat of gratitude as the younger man took the weight and tightened the straps at his waist.

"Are we set?" Leo inquired, watching the team recheck their equipment before pulling their gloves back on. Hearing a low, muted chorus of confirmation, he stepped forward, leading the men back into the black, some way further to the right than the last time they set off.

Once again, dense woodland barred the way and the men had to push back branches as they lugged themselves and their equipment over great blocks of fallen rock, half-climbing, half-crawling, their feet slipping on the mulch of rotten needles, their hands all but paralysed by the cold as the temperature continued to drop and the sharp wind whipped their heels. But the higher they climbed, the firmer the ground became until eventually they reached snow. An hour later, Reinhardt's insane bellowing was almost upon them.

"I think we're level," Leo grunted to the men behind him.

Each of them stopped to catch their breath before pulling at the zips of their rucksacks, unearthing chocolate bars and water canisters. Winded by the climb, none of the men spoke, and the freezing air stabbed like daggers of ice in their lungs. Their muscles trembled with exhaustion and Reinhardt's insanity was stretching their nerves to the point of snapping. It was Günter who lost it first.

"Shut it, Reinhardt!" he yelled. "Just shut the fuck up for five minutes – we're trying to get to you!"

As the last of the order echoed around them, the guttural screams and bellowing lament that had guided and dogged the team abruptly ceased. It was so unexpected the ensuing silence didn't feel like peace, but a vacuum.

"Thank Christ for that," Harri muttered, but his relief was

unconvincing and the men next to him laughed awkwardly.

Leo stamped his feet, rubbed his hands together and began to suggest they divide into two teams again when a huge gust of wind stole the words from his mouth. It was followed by a furious incantation, amplified by the hard rock around them, giving its delivery an unnatural power.

"We cast you out! Every unclean spirit, every satanic power, every onslaught of the infernal adversary..."

"What the hell? Is that Reinhardt again?" Günter looked to the men for confirmation. In the crossed beams of their headlamps, every face looked baffled. Christian stepped forward and raised a gloved hand to his lips.

"...No longer dare, cunning serpent, to deceive the human race, to persecute God's Church, to strike God's elect and to sift them as wheat..."

The younger man nodded, as if to affirm his own knowledge, and his eyebrows arched. "I'm no expert," he admitted, "but I'd say Reinhardt is performing an exorcism."

"A what?" Günter demanded.

"An exorcism," Christian repeated, "a ceremony to expel spirits of the dead."

"Brilliant..." Leo sighed, "just brilliant." He rubbed his nose, attempting to bring the blood back to the tip. "Come on," he urged, "let's get this old fool down from here before we all freeze to death."

Though a couple of the men nodded, none of them spoke – a dark mountain was fertile ground for the superstitious, and none of them looked happy.

"...God the Father commands you. The Son of God commands you. God the Holy Ghost commands you..."

Leo quickly divided the team into two groups. He would

take six men in the direction of Reinhardt's unholy screeching. Gerhard would lead the others further up the mountain, in the hope they might stumble across an established path that would allow them to take over the rescue should the lower team find their way blocked.

"As good a plan as any," Gerhard admitted and after wishing the others good luck, he led the second team away, into the dense dark of the trees.

Leo turned to where Reinhardt's shouts were loudest, noting the breath falter in his chest as he did so. Beneath his clothes, he could feel the sweat building on his skin. Knowing he couldn't afford to cool down he wiped roughly at his face with the sleeve of his jacket and he forced himself to move. Bizarrely, his feet seemed unwilling and it took a monumental effort to get them to comply. Leo shook his head. He was frozen to the core and the wind that battered his ears was messing with his head; torturing his senses with howls and whistles and occasionally the sound of a young child crying. He looked at Günter to see if he was dealing with the same torment, but his friend's scowl suggested he was simply annoyed.

Perhaps it was fatigue, or the men's increasingly frayed nerves, but the closer the team got to Reinhardt the more effort it took to keep on walking even though they were no longer climbing, but going straight. Movement had somehow become a discipline requiring concentration and the hard ground, though it should have made the going easier, seemed to drag at their boots as though they were wading through treacle. The cold numbed their faces. The wind bit their fingers. And the night cast shadows around them that took on shapes they all tried to ignore.

"...to save our race from the perdition wrought by your envy..."

144

Finally clearing the trees, they arrived at the icy vein of a small stream cutting deep into the vertical rock, one of many feeding the frozen waterfall in front of them. Somewhere, in the thick of the darkness, beyond the waterfall, shouted Reinhardt – almost close enough to smell if not to yet see. But though the waterfall was silent and the stream barely trickled, the craggy terrain shone in the moonlight like polished stone making it treacherous underfoot. Furthermore, Leo could see no way across, it was simply too steep and panic started to grip him as Reinhardt's voice pounded against his chest.

"...upon a firm rock, declaring the gates of hell..."

Leo closed his eyes, needing to count, to calm himself down. One, two...

"...should never prevail against her..."

He felt the rush of darkness closing in, as though he might faint. Four, five...

"...He would remain with her all days..."

Eight, nine...

"...even to the end of the world..."

And he opened his eyes to see Ana.

An arm's length in front of him, Leo watched her brown eyes filling with tears as her full lips trembled with words unsaid. He reached out to comfort her, wanting to touch her hair, to feel his fingers gliding through silk, but as he raised his hand she turned abruptly, staring straight at him. He registered the confusion in her face before clarity arrived, and as quickly as they had started Ana's tears dried and the softness of her gaze hardened. 'You did this to us,' she sneered through angry thin lips. 'You broke me on this rock and then you crushed my heart. Well, I hope you're happy now, Leo.'

"Leo?"

145

He blinked in surprise, shocked to find Harri looking straight at him.

"Where...?" Leo looked around him, searching in the dark until he felt Harri's grip on his arm. The older man handed him a chocolate bar, the concern evident in his eyes, and Leo ate quickly. Almost immediately the sugar hit his system and as he began to understand his own foolishness he offered a shy smile, feeling boyish under the care of his friend.

"Is everything fine?" Harri asked softly.

"Everything's fine," Leo assured him.

He pulled his water canister out of his rucksack. After drinking deeply, he gave his cheeks a quick slap before stamping his feet and retaking the lead, guiding the men away from the stream to a place someway higher.

As Leo walked, he radioed Gerhard who informed him that his part of the team were covering good ground, and that they had recently spotted the small plateau Harri had mentioned, above the waterfall, some 10 metres from where they guessed Reinhardt lay preaching.

"We'll look for anchor points to secure the ropes and then we'll go down. Over."

"This is Rescue Team One. We'll continue searching below you. Out."

Leo clicked the radio back in its holster and with a slight shrug of his shoulders, he led the men higher.

"...the holy apostles Peter and Paul and the other apostles command you. The blood of martyrs and the devout prayers of all holy men and women command you..."

Leo and his men battled through the undergrowth, slipping frequently, their exhaustion evident in the slowing pace, their backs aching under the weight of equipment. As they walked, Leo found it increasingly hard to think straight, unable to comprehend how Reinhardt could have lodged himself in such a remote place without the use of a parachute or a crane. The man was a drunk lunatic so how could it be that he could traverse the mountain whilst they, the professionals, failed at every turn? It didn't make sense. And he was fast losing the will to work it out.

"Hey! I think I've found something!"

Leo scrambled down the incline to reach Andy, losing his footing in the process to arrive at the man's feet on his backside. Günter helped him up with a grin. After catching his breath, Leo moved next to Andy and followed the beam of the other man's headlamp now shining on a small trail barely half a metre wide leading out of the trees. Relief instantly coursed through Leo's veins. He walked to the front of the group, inching along the path until it brought him to the edge of the waterfall and a small ridge, a hand's span in width.

"I guess it could be done," Leo said as he bent to the ground to measure the space. He glanced at Günter who responded with a sharp nod before directing his own headlamp to a place above the ridge.

"I'd say it's possible to anchor some points over there," he said. "We could then use the ropes to pull ourselves across."

Leo looked at the wall and then looked at the fall. It was a long way down and he was fully aware of his limitations. "Günter, how do you feel about going first?"

"I'm good with that."

"Then, I'll follow." Leo turned to the other men. "Andy you secure me. The rest of you stay put, in case we get into trouble."

At Leo's shoulder the radio crackled into life.

"Rescue Team One, this is Rescue Team Two. Over."

"This is Rescue Team One," Leo replied. "What have you got, Gerhard? Over."

"We have sight of the Missing, but no way to reach him. Over."

"Is the Missing injured? Over."

"Hard to tell from this angle, but I'd say his throat must be sore," Gerhard paused. "The Missing appears to be standing. Over."

The men around Leo chuckled. It was good news. If Reinhardt was on his feet, it would be easier to bring him down.

"This is Rescue Team One. We are preparing to cross the waterfall now. Over."

"Roger that. Out."

Günter stepped onto the ledge, shaking the tension from his shoulders before removing his gloves. Gingerly, he tested further along the ridge with the weight of one foot. Satisfied, he took one of the chocks from his belt and searched for a crack in which to wedge it. Moving carefully, he clipped a quickdraw to the chock wire and fed through the rope. Glancing backwards, Leo gave him a thumbs up and Günter repeated the process.

"...every diabolical legion, we adjure you by the living God, by the true God, by the holy God..."

Leo kept his headlamp pointed in Günter's direction, praying the light would be enough, willing the chocks to hold, damning the strong wind snapping at his friend's heels.

"...that whoever believes in Him might not perish but have everlasting life..."

Günter continued to slide left and Leo stepped closer to the ridge, feeding the rope, feeling it tighten.

"...Be gone, Satan, father and master of lies, enemy of man's welfare..."

A fourth chock squeezed into the rock and Leo watched Günter leaning precariously to the left, searching for another opening.

One more should do it, one more anchor and he would be across.

"...*Give place to Christ, in whom you found none of your works. Give way to the one, holy, catholic, and apostolic Church...*"

Günter landed on the other side of the waterfall, the thud of his feet sounding triumphant in their emphatic arrival. Leo immediately pulled himself into the wall, feeling for the rope above him. Gripping it tightly, he nodded to Andy and began inching his way across the ridge, his heart thundering in his chest.

"...*Bow down before God's mighty hand, tremble and flee as we call on the holy and awesome name of Jesus, before whom the denizens of hell cower...*"

Leo reached Günter in six steps, coming to rest on a small shelf in the rock. The two men exchanged the briefest of handshakes, the adrenalin evident in the shine of their eyes. Leo looked about him, searching the ground with the beam from his headlamp. To the left he spotted a narrow trail and after unclipping his ropes, Leo slipped past his friend, retaking the lead.

"...*to whom the heavenly Virtues and Powers and Dominations are subject...*"

The trail took them to the sharp edge of a corner. As Leo negotiated the bend a larger ledge became apparent, roughly eight metres ahead. Standing on it, with his back to the mountain, was Reinhardt.

In the moonlight the older man's face was a contortion of shadows. Spittle hung from his lips. His hair was wild, as though electrified. And he looked like a creature insane. Shouting into the wind, he brandished a bottle of whisky in one hand and a shed antler in the other, wielding it as though it were a wand. His eyes were covered by a ski mask and around his neck he wore a white handkerchief, tucked into the collar of his coat, giving him the look of a deranged priest.

"...*God of heaven and earth, God of the angels and archangels, God of the patriarchs and prophets, God of the apostles and martyrs, God of the confessors and virgins...*"

"Reinhardt!" Leo shouted.

"...*God who has power to bestow life after death and rest after toil; for there is no other God than you...*"

"Reinhardt!"

"...*the Creator of all things visible and invisible, whose kingdom is without end...*"

"Reinhardt, it's me, Leo!"

For a second Reinhardt faltered and the ski mask span towards Leo. But it was only a second and before Leo had chance to speak the mask whipped back to face the black void, rubble falling into the darkness below as Reinhardt's feet balanced precariously close to the edge of the ledge.

"...*deliver us by your might from every influence of the accursed spirits...*"

Reinhardt staggered forward, screaming louder and throwing his hands into the air. The whisky bottle shot from his grasp to crash on the rock below and a knot hardened in Leo's stomach.

"...*from their every evil snare and deception...*"

Leo clipped a rope to his belt.

"Hold me!" he shouted at Günter, and with no time to think he lunged forwards, forgetting the drop below, seeing only a man in need of saving.

"...*and to keep us from all harm...*"

Leo landed closer to the ledge on his hands and knees. He immediately crawled towards Reinhardt, feeling the rope tug at his harness as Günter shouted a warning he didn't catch.

"...*through Christ our Lord!*"

As a mighty roar split the sky, Leo hurled himself forwards, arriving within an arm's reach of Reinhardt whose head turned sharply in his direction. Though Leo couldn't make out the man's eyes, he thought he saw a flicker of recognition pass over his face, an understanding, some form of clarity in the fog of insanity. The air around them seemed to turn still and Leo carefully raised himself to his knees. But the movement was enough to break the spell. The wind picked up and Reinhardt wavered, shuffling away from Leo towards the edge of the plateau.

"Careful!" Leo shouted, but the warning was snatched by the wind. "It's me, Reinhardt. It's Leo."

Again Reinhardt stopped. He tilted his head to one side, as though listening to something or considering his options. Leo took the opportunity to try and placate him, raising an arm as he rose to his feet, trying to keep his movements smooth, though every muscle trembled. To his relief, Reinhardt began to smile, a familiar softness returning to the man's face, and Leo's shoulders relaxed. But it was too quick, too soon, and a harsh gust of wind surprised him as it swept down the black mountain. Reinhardt's head reacted immediately, shooting backwards as though seized by an invisible force. His mouth twisted in anguish as his arms flailed in front him. The priestly frock of his coat whipped about his legs and under the ski mask he wore his face contorted beyond all recognition. He shrieked in agony – releasing a high-pitched, furious pain that ripped from his throat.

"Give me back my girl! " he screamed. "Give me back my girl! "

Then clasping his arms over his chest, like a corpse in a coffin, he tipped himself forwards. The noise stopped, the ledge stood empty and Leo dropped to his knees.

Chapter Thirteen

The house shook. Ice particles spat at the windows. The snow was snatched from the mountain and hurled into the valley. The night came alive with a terrible fury, and Traudi could only cower under her mother's bed, her hands covering her ears, as the wind lashed her home. It was a storm like none she had ever known. There was nothing about it she recognised. The rumble she heard was not the sound of thunder, but the charges of hunger, and the darkness of the room belied the cloudless sky. Something was wrong.

Outside, the wind continued to crash into wood, slamming against glass, ripping at shutters, and battering the doors. It was no longer a storm, but a search. Traudi didn't know how, but she knew it was seeking a way in. At her back, the walls shuddered, as though trembling under the onslaught. The floorboards groaned in despair. The house, for all of its care, was helpless in the face of the entity swirling around it. The power was monstrous, the intention coldly clear, there could be no defeat, there would be no escape, and it forced its way inside, bursting through the slats, bending the roof, digging up the cellar, searching every room and climbing the stairs until it scented her fear.

With a thundering crack, the door flew open, hitting the wall and splintering on impact. A victorious howl rode on the wind as it rushed through the room, invading the wardrobes, twisting the curtains, grabbing at drawers, throwing up clothes and stealing the sheets before it swooped to the floor, surging under the bed to grab her by the feet.

"God, no!" Traudi screamed, but it was a strangled, pitiful cry instantly swallowed by the wind.

The noise was tremendous and Traudi's hands flailed in the dark, desperate, blind, reaching for anything that might keep her grounded. With a sharp pain, her knuckles connected with a bed leg. She immediately grabbed hold of it, pulling herself forwards, clinging to the stump as invisible hands tightened their grip. Skeletal fingers, colder than ice, penetrated her boots, pressing against her ankles, trying to pull her clear. There was no time to ask why. There was no feeling but fear. It was a nightmare turned real, and it descended like a sack over her head, throttling all thought.

"No!" Traudi screamed. "No!"

With a violent jerk her body lifted upwards. She was airborne, a rag flapping between wood and coiled springs. The wind whistled past her ears, tearing at her hair, whipping her clothes, showing no mercy. Its icy tongue lashed her bare legs, its cry sounding shrill and demonic. Its purpose was clear; to suck her into another world through the gaping hole of its soul.

Like a leaf blown from a tree, Traudi lost her grip and her nails scratched along the floorboards as she tried to hold on, but it had her by the legs and it was dragging her clear, into the room, into the chaos of something hateful. With a desperate panic, Traudi kicked out; fighting to free herself from fingers she couldn't see. As the room loomed behind her, she flung out her arms, grappling for an anchor, looking for something, anything, to keep her safe. In the dark, her hands slid over the frame of the bed, finding the cold ball of a post. She held on and the furious wind responded by throwing her into the air before slapping her to the floor. Every bone in her body was ready to break. But Traudi refused to let go. Flying blind in the tempest, with tears streaming from her eyes, she struggled to breathe. Her neck strained under the pressure, but she forced her head straight and tried to ride the gale before it snapped her like a twig. Traudi screamed, God how she screamed, but the force was too strong and it wrenched her hands from the bedpost. It hurled her through the air and she slammed into the wall, stunned and suffocating under a weight that landed on her chest. She was pinned, hanging like a picture, high above her mother's dressing table.

"You cannot do this!" Traudi yelled.

The wind replied by throwing her across the room. The back of her head smashed into the beams on the ceiling, her right arm crashed into glass. She plunged to the floor, dropped for a second, before the force turned direction to slip under her back. It launched her again – flinging her body against the wall with such violence she heard the crack of her head hitting the wood before she fell onto the dresser. Somewhere in the distance, like a memory from the past, a voice shouted. It was the call of a name and the squall shrieked in reply. It span around the room like a hurricane in a jar until it found the door and slammed it shut.

The wind died. The house fell quiet. And Traudi slipped from the wooden dresser onto the floor, unconscious.

When Traudi woke she heard birdsong. The sun poured through the window and though the rays were muted by dust, it was still bright enough to make her squint. She rubbed her eyes, and for a second there was nothing, only the knowledge of a new day, until she saw the destruction.

"Oh God!"

Traudi scrambled for the only sanctuary she knew, the dark corner where she hid, seeking the place she felt most safe. But even as she dived under the bed she jolted away, as though bitten. Nowhere was safe. There was nowhere to hide. The outside had come in.

Panic seized Traudi's chest and she instinctively reached for the bone angel at her neck, but she touched only skin. Her protection had fled. Her eyes darted desperately around the room; the wardrobe doors were flung open, the drawers had been pulled to the floor, her mother's clothes lay scattered, crumpled and torn, and a glass lampshade lay smashed in one corner. Within the shards she glimpsed silver and she scrambled on her knees to recover the necklace, relieved to find Heini's angel still attached. However, the chain was broken and there was no way she could fix it. With a sense of urgency, she wound it about her wrist, looping the links twice around her fingers until the angel sat in her palm. Sitting on the floor, surrounded by her mother's clothes, finding further proof of the night's terror in her bruised and battered body, Traudi wanted to cry. But there was nothing left. All hope had been wrung from her body. Exhaustion and fear had stolen her tears. There was no way for her to understand what had happened – and the bright sun only worked to support this disbelief. But something had happened. The nightmare was gone, but the room was in chaos where before there was order, and she knew beyond doubt that those she loved were also gone. Whatever thing had intruded on their lives it had taken away her mother and brother. It had waited outside in the form of a man until its patience ran dry and it had entered her home as some kind of malevolent storm. And now this thing, this terrible thing, with no shape and no voice, had set its sights on Traudi and she knew it wouldn't stop until it got what it wanted.

With a rising sense of grief, Traudi got to her feet. In the midst of all of the confusion one thing had never been clearer. She had to leave the house, and she needed to be quick.

Around her fingers Traudi felt the chain digging into her skin, and the angel pressing against her palm, gently reminding her she was not completely alone. She reached into the pocket of her coat, feeling the cold blade of Heini's knife. Then, her mind made up, she headed straight for her brother's room where she was momentarily shocked by the order she found after the chaos of the night. Carefully, she placed the knife on Heini's table, even now, after everything that had occurred, mindful of its correct position; fourth from the right, in merit of size. She then reached for another blade, stronger than the last, bigger and sharper. She put the knife in her pocket.

"I wish you were here, Heini," she whispered. With a last look around, she left his room and closed the door behind her.

On the landing Traudi waited, suddenly caught in suspense, not knowing whether the thing that had broken into her home might be waiting downstairs. However, the house was quiet. Nothing moved. The air was still. There was no wind, no breeze, not even a draught. Traudi looked through the window, casting light on the bottom of the stairwell. To her relief she saw only sunshine and patches of green, wet grass. So now is the time, she thought. Now she should go. Traudi held on to the knife, far too scared to deal with the pain racking her body. She pulled up her socks, buttoned up her coat and stepped off the landing. Her feet had barely touched the third step when she felt it approaching.

There was no sound to warn her, only the certainty of her senses. Traudi's eyes grew wide and her heart fluttered in her chest like a trapped bird. She knew she should hide, but her legs were heavy as stone. "Not again..." she whimpered, "please, not again."

Traudi stared at the door below, the bone angel digging into the palm of her hand. She saw the handle jolt and a key rattle in the lock. Traudi watched, unable to move, rooted to the floor even as the door flew open and the shape of a giant filled the doorway, his face grey against the light, his mouth tight with rage, his eyes burning like ice. By his side, standing vertical, like a crutch, was the silhouette of a gun.

"Ready?" he screamed, throwing the challenge into the hallway as he kicked the door shut with the back of his foot.

Traudi looked wildly around, her eyes coming to rest on the stairs leading to her mother's room. But it wasn't safe anymore, she knew that now, and she no longer trusted the space that once hid her. With no time to think, she backed quietly into her bedroom.

Downstairs, she heard boots stomp upon the floorboards, their thunderous beat accompanied by the scrapes and groans of furniture being pulled and pushed, followed by doors being slammed. Among the heavy thuds, the sound of fists hitting walls reverberated around the house. As quietly as she could manage, Traudi slipped under her bed, pulling the blanket down as she went, using it as a screen, praying it would shield her from whatever it was that was coming to get her. She slid herself backwards until she hit the far wall. This was the end. This was as far as she could go and so holding Heini's knife in front of her she waited.

"I know you're here!" the voice shouted and Traudi winced as the strength of it invaded her room.

Below, the sound of the search became ever more frantic, ever more frustrated, until finally the heavy tread of boots thumped on the stairs. With unnatural speed, the door to Traudi's room seemed to burst open, causing her to flinch and hold her breath.

She heard the wardrobe open, the curtains pulled roughly. And she could only watch helplessly as a pair of cracked leather boots, filthy with soil and the dead of the forest, dirtied her floor, stamping their presence with such fury that the ground seemed to shake.

As the boots stormed out of view, Traudi gasped for breath. Every inch of her trembled as she heard the door to her brother's room open. A minute later the boots thudded upstairs, heading for the only place left. Traudi listened as the intruder entered her mother's room. To her confusion, the house fell silent. The thing stood still. And Traudi shivered under her bed, unnerved by the pause. Within minutes the bangs, scrapes and slams resumed and Traudi recognised her chance had come. It was possibly her only chance. She had to get out. She had to run while the stairs were clear. And she had to leave now.

Traudi pushed herself from under the bed, determined to leave, only to feel one of her feet clatter against a musical ball – a long forgotten gift gathering dust in the corner. With heart-sinking alarm, she watched the metal sphere travel across the floor, filling the room with the tired strains of Beethoven's *Für Elise*, the tune rendered discordant by the passage of time and the uneven roll of the ball. Almost immediately, the thing upstairs stopped its search and thundered downstairs. Traudi barely had time to throw herself back under the bed before the door pushed open.

It re-entered the room quietly, almost carefully. She watched it walk to the ball, silencing the music beneath the toe of a huge, dirty boot. From under the bed, Traudi saw a gnarled hand reach down to take the ball. As the boots turned slowly she sensed their indecision, but finally they came towards her. Traudi pressed her back to the wall, wishing it could swallow her. The knife trembled in her hands, but she was ready to stab the beast in the eyes as soon as it bent down. But no face came. Instead, the thing turned, presenting Traudi with the back heels of its boots. She had no time to think as the bedsprings suddenly wheezed and dipped, scraping against her head as they responded to the pressure of weight. Traudi held her breath, trying to keep herself small, seeing no hope of escape. And then the monster above her – that irate and furious thing – suddenly gasped.

As its sobs shook the bed Traudi could only lie there and listen.

"Will you never forgive me, Lord?"

Chapter Fourteen

They drank steadily, with no real sense of thirst, thirteen men sat in a pub because it was easier than facing the solitude of home or the attention of others. The first round of beers had been on the house, the subsequent beers had come from other drinkers, offering their support with few words spoken. This was Hallstatt – a place where news travelled on the wind and where respect was given in fermented hops. Leo lit one cigarette after another. Though his fingers had thawed, the cold had penetrated deeper than skin tissue and nerves, and he smoked like a man trying to get warm from the inside out. He glanced around the table, finding his confusion reflected in the eyes of them all. It was the same question that teetered on the edge of everyone's lips – what the hell had just happened?

After two hours descending the mountain the team had spent a further two recovering the body. From his injuries, it was clear that Reinhardt had died on impact; his neck was broken, his head was fixed at an impossible angle, and the ski mask he wore had fractured, leaving plastic shards embedded in his eye sockets. If the man had found peace they saw no evidence of it. It was a hell of a way to go.

Berni approached the group, bringing with him fresh beers and a wet cloth, which he handed to Leo.

"For your face," he instructed. He pointed to a cut under Leo's eye, just above the cheekbone. "We don't want your blood scaring off the ladies, now do we?"

Leo wiped at his cheek, surprised because he hadn't felt anything. He inspected the cloth; nothing serious; simply a scratch caused by a tree branch or the hard edge of the mountain.

"Better?" Leo asked.

Berni shrugged. "You can only work with what you've got."

The men around the table smiled at Berni's teasing. They lifted their bottles to salute the men who had bought them their drinks, and when the landlord returned to the bar they each drifted back to their own personal space – their aching bodies recalling the climb, their ears humming with Reinhardt's wails, their eyes still traumatised by what they had witnessed.

Every one of the team had known Reinhardt, and though none went so far as to call him a friend they felt bereaved nonetheless. It was a grief aggravated by a sense of failure. Hours earlier Reinhardt had been alive – physically unscathed if mentally unstable – and having succeeded in reaching him it felt like they had dropped the ball at the last, crucial, second. None of them were strangers to death, whether by accident or design, but being a spectator to such an end was a harsh reality to accept, even for those familiar with the brevity of life. Leo looked at Harri and the older man met his stare. Not so long ago they had rescued Reinhardt from the Strenhang Slope. More recently they had sat in his home. They had both listened to his craziness and they had both walked away. Leo recognised the look in Harri's eyes because he felt it in his own. They had rescued Reinhardt once, and they had tried to rescue him again, but they still wondered whether they could have done more.

"What I don't understand is how he even got on that ledge."

It was Christian who finally spoke up, and being the first to voice a common bewilderment he broke the spell hanging over the men.

"He must have flown there," Gerhard declared.

Gerhard was a heavy-set man, weathered by life and a bitter divorce. He was one of the few in the town still working at the mine. Even so he hadn't been afraid to shed a tear when Reinhardt fell.

"Fly there?" Andy scoffed. "I saw no wings."

"We saw no path either," Gerhard reminded him.

"That's true enough."

Leo listened but added nothing to the discussion: his brain was numb from what his eyes had seen and his mind struggled to understand what his ears had heard. The body resting in the morgue might suggest the nightmare was over, but he couldn't shake a nagging disquiet that he had missed something, something important. He couldn't explain it, but it felt like unfinished business.

As shock gradually receded in the warmth of the Hut, and the flow of free beer, each of the men offered up their own differing opinions of the night's events, placing possibilities on the table to be carved up, scrutinised and eventually discarded as they all came fumbling to the conclusion that what had happened was nothing any of them could explain. There was no obvious route to the ledge Reinhardt had found. Even in daylight reaching the plateau on the far side of the waterfall would have required a certain level of expertise. And at the very best, Reinhardt had been a rambler.

"It's beyond me," Harri said to no one in particular. And they all nodded in agreement.

As the night grew old, the rescue team departed one-by-one, either walking or stumbling from the hut, returning to wives and girlfriends who would discover their failure within a fog of confusion and alcohol. Only Leo and Günter remained – both of them suffering from the shared affliction of having no one to go home to.

Covered in dirt and dry sweat, feeling dog-tired and increasingly drunk, it seemed a lifetime ago since Leo answered Günter's call in the car, and in some sense it was. But now the Hut was quiet, they were alone, and Berni was distracted by the debris of another night's business, it seemed as appropriate a time as any for Leo to inquire about the state of his friend's marriage. He didn't expect a reply – at least, nothing enlightening – but Günter surprised him.

"Lisa's done nothing I don't deserve," he admitted glumly.

Leo raised an eyebrow and Günter rubbed his face, feeling shame warm his cheeks.

"There was a girl," he revealed. "It was nothing serious, but there were a few texts and well, you can guess the rest."

"What kind of texts?"

"The kind of texts that send a wife running to her mother."

"Shit."

Günter reached for Leo's cigarettes, an act which deftly indicated the severity of the crime. Günter hadn't smoked for more than a year.

"Who was the girl?" Leo asked.

"No one you know," Günter assured him. "I found her on the road to Gosau, flat tyre, I helped her change it, we got talking, swapped numbers and then, well it was just a bit of harmless fun, nothing more."

"You didn't meet up?"

"Only once; a quick drink about a week ago; I was passing through Gosau, seemed churlish not to."

"So you had a quick drink and nothing more?"

"Well, maybe there was a kiss, but no more than that, I swear." Günter held up his hands and Leo held his stare until his friend eventually confessed, "She lives with her boyfriend."

Leo shook his head and lit a cigarette of his own. Günter's infidelity, or attempted infidelity, was none of his business. What a man chose to do with his life and his wife was his own affair. Even so, he liked Lisa – enough to have dated her once.

"You're an idiot," he said simply.

"I know," Günter replied, and by the slump of his shoulders Leo saw that he meant it. Leo waved to Berni and two more beers arrived at their table. Günter scratched at his head; his scalp itching with the combination of salt and remorse.

"Was there ever a greater fool than man?" he asked. A sheepish grin brightened his face, but it had the decency to fade quickly. "Have you heard from Ana?"

Unwilling to contribute to the confessional air of their discussion, Leo replied that he hadn't and he gave no indication of wishing to elaborate. However, Günter was a man unused to suffering alone.

"You've heard nothing at all?"

"Nothing," Leo confirmed, feeling the walls close in as his friend scrutinised his face, clearly expecting more. "She won't be coming back," Leo finally offered.

"Not ever?"

"I very much doubt it."

"So that makes two idiots sitting at the one table."

Leo agreed, happy to end the conversation there, but then he recalled Ana's face coming to him on the mountain – the tears and the venomous accusation that he was to blame for their failed relationship – and the world began to tilt as his mind contemplated unfamiliar territory. With a sigh of disbelief, he reached for his wallet. Inside was a sheet of paper, folded many times over to fit behind his driver's licence. He handed it to Günter.

"Read it," he said.

Not attempting to hide his surprise, Günter took the letter, opened it up and scanned the page for a signature before reading more carefully. Once he was finished, he gave a low whistle.

"Some pretty words there."

"Yes."

"And pretty sad too."

"Yes."

"Did you know?"

"No."

Günter scanned the page again. "So you weren't around much, then."

"I was there all the time."

Günter raised an eyebrow and Leo met the challenge by returning to his beer. Unfortunately, Günter felt he had a point to make and he gave a succinct, if damning appraisal of the previous three months of Leo's life, cataloguing the days he spent working in Linz; the hours devoted to skiing, climbing, hunting and running; the three-day exercise they had enjoyed in Upper Austria; the overnight in Tyrol attending the federal AGM; and the week vacationing on the Stubai Glacier, south of Innsbruck.

"Wasn't it Christmas week when you went to Stubai?" he asked.

Leo winced, yet he heard himself defending the decision using the same justification he had previously given to Ana. Even as he spoke he felt the words turn to ashes in his mouth.

"Andy and I had been talking about it for a while – long before Ana moved in – and as she wanted to visit her mother in Valencia I couldn't see a problem. Besides I joined her for four days."

Günter reacted with a snort. "You're living behind the moon," he said bluntly. "Andy is a single man and even if you did agree to the trip before you shacked up with Ana, you were still dating her at the time. Knowing women as well as I do, I'm pretty sure that Ana would have assumed you'd be spending the whole of Christmas with her." Günter folded the letter in his hands and handed it back to Leo. He then added, more gently, "Ana was a keeper, Leo, but when she walked away you practically opened the door for her."

Resisting the urge to remind his friend that he was in no position to talk, Leo bit his tongue and simply said, "I know."

And he did. He really did know.

During the past three weeks hardly a moment had gone by in which he hadn't thought about Ana, and of the role he had played in her departure. With the benefit of hindsight, he recognised he had been blind, worse than blind – but it was easier to spot the obvious once someone had written down the answers.

During the summer Leo had vaguely wondered whether Ana might be depressed – given her mood swings, the loss of her teaching job and her subsequent immersion in salt – but he had accepted her explanation that there was nothing psychologically wrong and she was merely suffering from a case of being 'extremely fed up'. Though she added 'and mainly with you' she had laughed, and he had therefore assumed she was joking. But now, as his mind travelled back through the past year, he wasn't so certain. He was seeing things differently and understanding how these things might have fallen into place – each inconsequential episode stacking up, one on top of the other, higher and higher, until the wall between them became too great to scale. The moments were nothing and yet everything and they had brought such a gradual change in their lives that the danger had crept up on him unnoticed. He now recognised that one of the first things to change was Ana's laugh. It wasn't as ripe or infectious as it used to be. It was weaker somehow, less convincing, and he remembered feeling strangely excluded by it. Then there was the time Ana had suggested they buy a house together. He had told her it was a crazy idea, a disaster-in-the-making in the current economic climate. That it made no sense whatsoever. But of course, he now realised that Ana wasn't looking for an investment opportunity – she was seeking a place to nest.

"What about Mauritius?"

"I'm sorry? Have you won the *Lotto*?"

"OK, well how about somewhere closer, like Montenegro? It looks kind of pretty."

Ana had passed him the brochure, and it did look kind of pretty – blue waters, white buildings, and secluded bays. It also looked pretty boring, and the hotel she had marked, pretty expensive.

"Here's a thing," he had said, "just what is the point of four and five star hotels? Why pay all that money just to sleep in a bed? I mean, when you think about it, it's insane. But of course, Montenegro is full of criminals."

Ana's considered response to this was to snatch the brochure from his hands and dump it in the bin. "Is there actually anywhere on God's earth that you do want to go on holiday?"

Leo bit his lip. He wasn't a complete fool. And he wisely gave no mention of a quickly receding glacier in China's Yunnan province. Instead he moved to the sofa, forced Ana's face to meet his own, kissed her full on the lips and said: "We live in Paradise, my love. We have mountains on our doorstep, lakes in abundance and as much salt as a man could wish for. Why would you even want to go anywhere else?"

Though Ana had screamed in reply her exasperation had come

with a smile and so life continued, bumbling on in the same haphazard fashion, until one day – not long after he returned home from a boys' weekend in Croatia – he was informed that the time had come to talk. As it was Ana's idea she mainly did the talking, but over an occasionally awkward meal of pizza and salad they both offered up their own differing perceptions of the relationship they were in, in what they hoped was a calm and adult fashion. Ana felt lonely, she said, as though she had been cut adrift having anchored her hopes on Leo. In turn Leo tried to ignore the nautical theme of her discontent to reveal instead that he had been unaware of how she felt. Though he didn't say it, he felt sorry for the upset he had caused.

"Maybe it's me," he admitted. "Maybe I'm simply not meant to be someone's boyfriend."

"Perhaps if you were with the right woman..."

"No, that's not it," he had said, and Ana had fallen quiet.

Eventually, once the silence grew uncomfortable and enough time had passed to indicate they had absorbed each other's points, they both arrived at the same adult conclusion: that ultimately it was up to the individual to take control of his or her own happiness.

Despite there being no immediate feeling of having fully cleared the air of the poison that threatened their relationship, once the summer cooled into autumn the perpetual raincloud that hovered above Ana's head suddenly lifted. It was laughable now, given all that he knew, but when he witnessed her new positivity he had thought he was responsible for it because, at least for a while, Ana became more active; taking walks in the valley; even cycling on occasion. With quiet relief, Leo watched the spring return to Ana's step and the light come back to her eyes. She had plans, she one day informed him, and though she didn't go into any great detail it apparently involved taking over his shed at the bottom of the garden. Naturally, Leo had done his best to hide his irritation when Ana demanded he relocate the work tools he rarely used and the deer heads he had yet to mount in order to make room for her equipment.

"I'll be sculpting again," she informed him. "It's what I do, it's who I am."

"What about the salt shop?"

"I'll stay on. After all, I need the money to pay my half of the rent."

"Maybe they will let you sell your sculptures there," he suggested, and Ana had laughed.

"Maybe," she had said, and she threw him a look he wasn't able to interpret.

Glad that Ana had found a plan to occupy her time, Leo willingly accompanied her to the lumber yard where she picked out the biggest stump of tree trunk she could find and which he and his poor aging Golf subsequently carried back home. Once that was done Ana went to the local hardware store and bought a hasp and a padlock, which Leo was then instructed to attach to the shed door. Afterwards, and with a glint in her eye, she pocketed the key.

"So I can't even go into my own shed?" he had asked.

"It's not a shed, it's a studio. And no, you can't."

And despite being curious, he never did try. If Ana needed her space she was entitled to have it and as a consequence of getting that space she awarded him his own. No longer did she check her watch whenever he walked through the door. She never asked what time he would be back when he went for a run. She practically encouraged him to go out with 'the boys' if they called. And she started to venture into the kitchen

169

again. Of course, this newfound domesticity rarely stretched to cleaning, much to his mother's irritation, but the house once again breathed with the aroma of fresh coffee, meat paella, chilli con carne and herb crusted vegetables. Her inimitable laughter bounced again from the walls. And their bedroom shrugged off the cold, battleground atmosphere of the previous few months, to become a place of familiar, longed-for refuge. Somehow, somewhere, their relationship had rediscovered its balance, and Leo was both relieved and thankful. The hostilities ceased, the fun returned and Ana became someone easier to come home to. And only once during those gentle autumn months did he glance at the shed from the front room window and wonder aloud what lunacy his girlfriend was carving inside.

"I really wouldn't advise you to go in there," Ana had warned him. "It would only make your hair curl."

And of course Leo had laughed, trusting she was right. Earlier that year he had attended an open day at the technical college only to be dumbfounded by the sight of horned monsters carved out of wood and daring frescos of the female form sculpted in astonishing detail.

"And that's art?" he had asked, staring incredulously at a somewhat abstract interpretation of a woman's pubic region as they sipped coffee in the canteen.

"As Oscar Wilde once said, a work of art is a unique result of a unique temperament," Ana had assured him.

"It's the unique result of too many hormones," Leo had retorted, only to later understand that it would have been wiser to keep his mouth shut because when he reached his 35th birthday Ana presented him with that very same fresco. His mother had been appalled at the gift and whenever she visited, Leo felt obliged to turn the offending 'art' to the wall.

For much of the autumn Ana had appeared content, almost buoyant. She took care of herself. She was livelier. And she kissed him like she meant it. There was a return of the warmth they once shared, and he had sorely welcomed it after feeling the heat of their passion inexplicably collapse into smouldering resentment. It seemed amazing to him now, but at the time he never suspected a thing. He simply believed that women were difficult and beyond the comprehension of men. They looked for meaning where there was none to be found. They insisted on happiness but remembered only faults. And they struggled to live within their own skins. Men, however, were different. At least he knew he was. And he was pretty certain Günter was the same. They tended to react to life rather than think about it. Ana once asked him why he had joined the rescue service and he had replied that it was cooler than joining the fire brigade. To his surprise, she had thought he was joking, that underneath his Vortex jacket he was concealing a more noble reason, chiefly the need to save people. But he wasn't. He simply liked being in the mountains, staying fit, going on missions and returning home tired. He wasn't a hero. He was a man. And perhaps the greatest divide between the sexes was their differing perceptions of life – women saw the world through alien eyes and the rose-tinted spectacles that covered their expectations could only lead to bitter disappointment. Worse than that, when it came to the really big issues, the problems that properly needed discussing, breaking down and solving, the deal breakers of a relationship, women had a habit of going quiet – which is how it was after he returned from a three-day exercise in Upper Austria in which the team had been put through their paces learning the latest Dyneema rope techniques. Entering the house shortly before midnight he had found Ana sat in the front room, a blanket wrapped around her shoulders and the old gloom of the summer seemingly back with a vengeance. He threw his rucksack to the floor, bent to kiss her and she offered him her cheek.

"What's wrong?" he had asked, genuinely perplexed.

"Why didn't you phone?"

"We were busy and there was no signal in the hut."

"That's convenient."

"It's not convenient, it's the truth. What's the big deal? What's happened?"

"Nothing has happened," she snapped, "and even if it had, would you care? Just keep on living your life, Leo. It's perfectly obvious to anyone with half a brain that you know no other way."

And that's as much as he had been told. From that day on, Ana stopped working in her studio, she went to bed early and she paced the periphery of his life with a resentment that grew in ferocity as the winter moved in. As she suffered in silence, Leo kept his distance and did nothing to salvage the situation, partly because he was annoyed, but mainly because he was blind.

****

Having left Berni's at 3am, giving him barely two hours of sleep, Leo drove to Linz where he downed copious amounts of coffee before congratulating himself on having had the foresight to tell his class to prepare a three-minute talk on anything they wished, as long as it involved glaciers. Considering the running theme that permeated his lessons he should have known that most of his pupils would choose some aspect of global warming, and star-pupil Astrid gave a particularly impassioned plea about polar bears 'literally walking on thin ice'. However, it was Tobias – the class clown and lowly fool for Astrid's love – who surprised Leo the most by presenting a brief biography of Louis Agassiz, affectionately known by those with a fascination for the subject as the Father of Glaciology. Born in 1807, Agassiz had studied glaciers the hard way, by calling them home for five years. And it was by driving a line of stakes into the ice that he subsequently discovered that glaciers moved forwards. It was a major discovery in its day, but perhaps more remarkable to Leo at that present moment in time was Tobias' demonstration of Agassiz's experiment using two poles, a plastic sheet, a handful of pipe cleaners and a glutinous mass consisting of washing powder, water and glue.

"Bravo!" Leo congratulated the boy, genuinely impressed despite the mess that ensued. The boy's cheeks flushed red, his fellow pupils gave generous applause and feeling a little better about the world, Leo dismissed the class, returned to his car and slept through the lunch break.

The brief nap offered some respite from the interminable fatigue that weighted Leo's shoulders and reddened his eyes, but the day failed to pass any quicker, and when the final bell of the day tolled Leo knew he was game over. He then drove home with the vague melancholy that always proved to be his most faithful companion during times of hangover. Afraid he might fall asleep at the wheel, Leo negotiated the traffic with the window down, barely feeling the cold. Even so, when he reached Hallstatt he ignored the pull of his bed because his body craved soup.

Turning into an orderly row of pastel-painted houses, the welcome light switched on before he had even finished reversing into the driveway.

"Good to see you, Son."

His mother gave him a tight hug on the doorstep before following him into the house, closing the door on the cold outside.

In the kitchen he found his father, sat at the oak table that dominated the room. Large enough for a family of eight, it was a constant reminder of his parents' unsatisfactory attempts at propagation – and their optimistic belief that they might one day entertain grandchildren. Leo took a seat opposite his father, who acknowledged his presence by putting aside his newspaper.

"Tough night, by all accounts," he commented, informing him in the simplest terms possible that he had heard of the failed rescue and of Reinhardt's bizarre passing.

"It wasn't one of the easiest I've experienced," Leo admitted. He carved the bread waiting on the table and dipped a slice in the bowl that his mother placed in front of him. Ana used to say his mother's soup possessed all the aesthetic quality of a glistening puddle of fat, but he had yet to find anything that nursed a hangover better and it hit his stomach like a salve.

"I went to see Reinhardt's wife today," his mother informed him, coming to the table and smoothing her apron as she sat.

"How was she?" Leo asked.

"Drunk."

Leo nodded. He was little surprised. "Strange couple," he muttered, "or at least they were."

"Yes, it's a terrible shame," his mother said. "Christine never used to drink so much, but Reinhardt, well he's always had his problems. Do you know your father once found him naked in the cemetery?"

Leo looked up from his soup.

"Ten years ago," Leo's father confirmed. "I took him home, had a word with his old man, and said no more about it."

"Why was he naked?"

"I don't know. He never said."

"What did his father say?"

"He wasn't best pleased."

"Did he get professional help?"

"I very much doubt it. And why would he? In my experience, young men are predisposed to public nudity. I seem to recall you were also found wearing little more than a pink ribbon tied to your soldier on one occasion. No one suggested we have you committed."

"It was *Fasching*, Dad, and I had been tied to a lamppost."

"Even so, it wasn't your finest hour," his father teased, "although it may have been Günter's."

Leo shook his head. Yes, it was all very hilarious now, but at the time his mother had chased him through the house with a frying pan for the shame he had brought to her door.

"Anyway the point is, Leopold, that you needn't think there's any blame to be had here," his father continued. "Reinhardt was a sick man – sadly, far more ill than any of us realised."

"I don't blame myself," Leo replied, honestly. "But I do feel, oh I don't know. I'm not sure how I feel. It's not only Reinhardt, it's everything. This strange winter, the heavy snow, the quick thaw, Ana leaving, Reinhardt dying and then, well there was something else, something else that happened on the mountain, and I can't seem to shake it."

Leo stopped talking, pausing to allow his mind to form his thoughts into a more coherent fashion. Under the yellow light of the lamp hanging over the table, his parents watched him quietly, giving him time, their eyes showing a concern that had been there for as long as his memory.

"What happened on the mountain?" his mother gently pressed.

"I'm not sure," Leo confessed. "We had split into two search parties and our group had come to a dead end. I wasn't feeling overly tired – at least nothing more than you'd expect from the climb – and I'd eaten before we set out, but I still had what I can only describe as an hallucination. I was looking around, finding my bearings, and I suddenly saw Ana, as clearly as I see both of you sat here, and I froze. I mean, I completely zoned out. Then, later on, a matter of seconds before Reinhardt jumped, I thought I heard a child screaming – a little girl. I can't explain it, and I assume it was a trick of the wind, but it sounded so real, I mean, really real, and ever since I've been left with this nagging feeling that I've missed something, or that I've forgotten to do something, something really important."

Leo leant back in his chair, overwhelmed by an emotion he couldn't place. He blinked back the tears that threatened to fall and his parents swapped a look of concern. Leo noticed his father nod and after finishing the sausage on his plate, he took his newspaper into the other room, placing a gentle hand on Leo's shoulder as he went.

"You've a good heart, Son," was all he said.

As he left the room, Leo's mother rose from her seat, heading for the stove where she placed three white sausages and a mound of steaming cabbage onto a plate. She presented the meal with an order to eat and Leo did as he was told, fully aware that his mother was watching his every move. Although Ana once accused him of possessing all the sensitivity of a brick, even he couldn't have missed the tag-team approach to parental care that had just taken place. He waited for his mother to speak, but she remained quiet, allowing him to eat.

"Okay," he said eventually, wiping his beard clean after finishing the meal. "I'm now ready for whatever it is you feel you need to say."

Leo's mother smiled, deepening the crow's feet at her eyes. "Am I that obvious?"

"Do you really want me to answer that?"

As she took a moment to smooth her auburn hair, Leo shifted uncomfortably in his seat, sensing the turn the conversation was about to take. His mother's dark eyes looked at him, the pupils huge with concern.

"Perhaps you should go and see Ana," she gently suggested.

Leo leaned back in his seat, not a little surprised. "But you said she was a leftwing lesbian."

"I said no such thing," his mother spluttered, "I simply thought she might be a feminist."

"As if that were a bad thing," Leo teased and his mother shook her head and released a small exasperated laugh.

Shifting her chair closer, she placed a hand on his forearm. Her fingers were small, still soft for her age, but they were different from the hands that used to protect him and he was suddenly conscious of time and the irreversible marks that it left on those that he loved.

"Honestly, I'm worried about you, Leo. It may sound silly, but sometimes I feel like we're losing you."

Leo frowned, slightly stunned by the confession. "I don't get you."

His mother sighed, massaged his arm, and tried to find the words. "It seems to me, not so much to your father, but it seems to me that you're becoming remote. You seem so alone all the time, so stuck in this world of yours that I worry you've forgotten about the real one, and the real one is passing you by. Please, let me finish," she raised a hand to stop him from interrupting. "Look, I know you love everything you do – your sports, the rescue team, your glacier climbing and all that – but when the day is over, what is left? You're 35 years old, Leopold. Most of your friends are married. They have children. They have built their own lives. You can't run like a boy forever."

177

"I'm not running from anything," Leo corrected, no longer able to sit by as his mother rushed to the conclusion that he was turning into some kind of hermitic freak. "And it was Ana who left me, remember?"

"I'm not talking about Ana specifically," his mother replied, releasing another sigh, half-tired, half-defeated. "I'm talking about the kind of man you are. That's what I worry about most because if you carry on the way you are I really do think you will end up alone. Or God forbid, living with us."

"Well, if God wills it," Leo joked, and he saw his mother relax as she understood he had taken no offence. She smoothed her apron again, a subconscious affectation Leo had come to recognise and be wary of.

"You know, Leo, your father wasn't the first man I ever loved."

His mother glanced at him, almost shyly and Leo fought to keep his face straight, to save her further embarrassment.

"No?"

"No," she confirmed. "There was someone else, someone a little like you actually – sporty, good-looking, a little hard on the outside. Of course, we were only young, still teenagers, but this boy, well he seemed hell-bent on living a life of solitude. He never gave himself the chance to be anything different. And now, well, time has passed, we have both grown old and this man, this man who had a lifetime to change his ways, is still alone. He has no family, no friends to speak of, only memories. And the fact is you can't live a life by clinging to memories. They will send you mad in the end. So please, trust me, Leo. Don't be your own worst enemy. Take the blinkers from your eyes, seize life, love it to the best of your ability and find someone to share it with."

As his mother stopped talking, Leo saw the plea on her face, willing him to acknowledge that her words had sunk in and that he was ready to embrace life in a way she found more comfortable to deal with. But the truth was, Leo didn't spend his days clinging to memories, if anything he was doing his damndest to ignore them, and though his mother's concern was sweet, almost touching, he found himself distracted by the riddle of the madman who had once owned her heart.

"Oh God, it wasn't Reinhardt, was it?"

Somewhat abruptly, Leo's mother pushed back her chair, rose from the table and swiped her son about the head before taking his dinner plate to the sink.

****

On the drive home, Leo stopped at *Konsum* to buy a packet of cigarettes and three bottles of beer. As he was leaving he met Günter's wife at the door, which was awkward.

"Leo," she acknowledged.

"Lisa," he replied.

Sam stood by her side, holding onto her hand, looking as tiny and lost as only a five-year-old boy can. Leo noticed Lisa's grip tighten. He looked around.

"No Deli?" he asked.

Lisa jerked her head backwards. "She's outside having a tantrum. Apparently I'm the worst mother in the world today."

"Kids, eh?"

"Well, at least the girls grow up eventually," she sharply replied.

For a moment Leo held Lisa's gaze. The hurt in her eyes was evident and he nodded, conceding that she had good reason to feel angry. Instinctively, he reached out and pulled her into his shoulder, gently placing a kiss on the dark crown of her hair.

"Your husband's an asshole," he whispered. "But he's an asshole who loves you, Ana."

Günter's wife sniffed as she pulled away, briskly wiping at her pale cheeks. "The name's Lisa in case you've forgotten, Leo."

"Shit." Leo shook his head, appalled and confused by the mistake. He knew he was tired, but come on. "Lisa, look, I'm sorry..."

A sudden screech of tyres followed by a young girl's screams interrupted his apology and Lisa let go of her son's hand as she ran from the shop shouting her daughter's name in panic as Leo followed. Outside, standing in the middle of the road, they saw Deli – her face white and her eyes wide, but otherwise unharmed. Facing the girl was an Audi 100, steam rising from its bonnet as the engine ticked over in the fast-cooling night. Lisa ran to her daughter's side whilst within the car, sitting motionless behind the wheel, the driver stared at the child caught in his headlights, his mangled face of scars still and unreadable.

Chapter Fifteen

It was a glorious day: the birds were singing, the sky was blue, crocuses bloomed and Traudi's legs skipped with happiness as she followed the path that traced the river. She was a princess, the forest was her palace, and when she raised her head she looked into the eyes of the most beautiful man. Though the stranger walked by her side she didn't know his name. But she felt that she knew him, and she saw no need to question his presence or ask who he might be because she understood she was dreaming. Traudi knew this because the world was softer than real life could ever be. Its edges were blurred; the leaves were greener; and the river played solely for her, tumbling over giant white stones, splashing its music into the air as sweetly as fingers caressing the keys of a piano. For so long everything had been dark, a place of tears and fear, devoid of comfort and hope, and Traudi was tired of the terror that fed on her bones. So even though she knew she was dreaming she surrendered to the lie. She counted the birds in the trees, displaying feathers more colourful than nature had painted, she skimmed stones across the river, and she enjoyed the warmth of the sun on her skin. All the while, the beautiful man with his messy black hair and coal-coloured eyes, walked beside her, casting his shadow upon the path like a holy shield of God. Shyly, Traudi reached for his hand and the beautiful man smiled. His palm was huge.

His fingers were warm, and she could scarcely recall having felt more protected. Though his eyes were sad and a small cut scarred his cheek, Traudi knew that as long as he was near everything would be fine – she would never need worry because the beautiful man with the messy black hair and the shining black eyes would pick her up and carry her home.

****

Leo woke with a start. He grabbed the clock, squinted at the display and promptly threw it across the room. He couldn't be sure whether he had forgotten to set the alarm or whether he'd simply slept through it, but either way he was furious. It was pathetic. He was pathetic. It was Saturday, there was no school, no long commute, and he had no one to please but himself. Yet time had got the better of him, once again, and his only plan for the day already lay in ruins. There would be no ski tour. There would be no new details to record in his journal. And he swung his legs out of bed, feeling frustrated, incensed and irrationally hard done by.

Walking to the window, he lifted the curtain to find a scene more ghastly than he could ever have anticipated; plenty of sunshine and unseasonably warm – the perfect combination for an untimely end. Leo gazed at the snow, beginning its slow retreat up the mountain. Still only March and yet it felt and looked like mid-spring. Below his window, weather and industry had combined to clear much of the streets and the jagged skyline of the town's metal roofs practically sparkled in the sunlight. Experience told him it would take only a thirty-minute walk to feel the crunch of winter under his boots, but it would take a further three hours to reach the nearest summit by which time the overnight freeze would have thawed, leaving the snow wet enough and heavy enough to trigger an avalanche. As a member of the rescue team making a ski tour under such conditions might appear reckless at best, suicidal at worst. And given Reinhardt's recent passing and his mother's conviction that she had spawned some kind of wayward recluse, Leo was in no hurry to add to the woes of the community or indeed his mother's maternal concerns. He took a last look at the clock now lying at his feet, and kicked it.

After briefly considering a return to bed, Leo headed for the kitchen which was, predictably, cold and bare. If he'd had the foresight to put on socks the tiles might have been more forgiving, but the emptiness was an issue that couldn't be solved on his own. He opened the fridge door, more for the welcome light than the contents inside, and after pouring a glass of water he moved to the sitting room where he found his cigarettes. As the smoke curled in the stagnant air he glanced around the room, itemising his worldly goods; one sofa, a table, four chairs, a few books and a shelf supporting nothing but dust. Thirty-five years on the earth and this was all he had to show for the effort it had taken. He didn't even own a television, and the only work of art was an overly large vagina currently facing the wall. Leo stubbed the cigarette into a saucer – having never got round to buying an ashtray – and went for a shower. Twenty minutes later, he was dressed and heading out of the door.

In the corner store that clung to the tip of *Seestraße*, Leo bought a bottle of sour yoghurt milk and a packet of Marlboro Red. He was no nutritionist, but he recognised it was a pitiful excuse for a breakfast.

"Terrible news about Reinhardt," the woman behind the counter remarked. Her name was Elsa and she and Leo had once attended the same school. Leo knew this not because he remembered Elsa, but rather because whenever they met she felt it necessary to remind him. "I can still hardly believe it. But I guess, crazy is as crazy does. Is it true that you found him with a pair of knickers on his head?"

Leo blinked, not sure whether Elsa was attempting some kind of joke. If she was it seemed highly inappropriate.

"No, we didn't find Reinhardt wearing underwear on his head," he responded flatly. "Who told you that?"

"Oh, who knows, everyone's talking about it. Poor Reinhardt. He clearly wasn't himself though, was he?"

"Well, no. I think that's fair to say." Leo handed over a ten euro note and waited for his change. Elsa delved into the till, taking her time.

"Did you know it was Reinhardt who shopped the butcher to the police?"

Leo raised his eyebrows, admitting that he didn't.

"Well, they say nothing will come of it, not now their star witness is discredited..."

"Not to mention dead."

Elsa crossed her chest and flashed an apologetic smile. Somewhat reluctantly, she handed Leo his money. "It seems a long time since school, doesn't it?"

"Yes," he answered. "Yes, it does."

Pocketing his change, Leo left the shop more perplexed than when he went in, unable to fathom where the line about underwear had entered the story of Reinhardt's last hours. He drank the yoghurt milk in four hungry gulps, discarding the empty bottle in a bin at the side of the road. He then lit a cigarette and considered his options, of which there were few – a coffee at his parents' house, Günter's place or a cafe in town.

"*Servus*, Leo!"

He looked up to see Christian approaching, his Labrador dog padding obediently at his side, its ears standing forward, its tail up, seemingly happy to be alive because he was going for a walk.

"*Servus*, Christian."

"Waiting for something?" the younger man asked.

"Only a slow death," Leo replied dryly.

Christian grinned and pointed to the cigarette in Leo's fingers. "Well, that should quicken the process."

Leo shrugged and tried to smile. Christian was right, of course. But the problem with being right was that it tended to be irritating.

"Don't suppose you want to join us?" Christian asked.

"Where are you going?"

Christian pointed towards the valley. "It's a lovely day. It would be a shame not to use it before nature returns to her senses."

Leo stared at the younger man, the hairs on his neck rising, his mind faltering with the shudder of déjà vu. He couldn't explain what or why but he found his feet turning towards the valley before he had even accepted Christian's invitation.

****

Something pushed on Traudi's face. It wasn't hard, but it was insistent and she found it increasingly difficult to breathe. She opened her eyes and gasped. The underside of the mattress was on top of her, there was nothing below her back but air, and she was floating thirty centimetres from the floor. Panic gripped her body, and the second it did she fell to the ground, hitting it with a dull thud whilst her heart continued to thump in her chest.

"Not again," she whimpered. "Dear God, not again..."

Traudi curled herself into a ball, waiting for the door to crash open and invisible fingers to snatch at her feet. Clutching her knees to her chest, she felt herself trembling. But nothing came. The room remained quiet. There was no wind. No supernatural assault. There was nothing at all. Nothing at all... with a start she stared at the mattress, now sitting above her, noticing the springs no longer dipped and the weight that had lain there had gone. The man, the thing or demon that had entered her room had left. Traudi glanced across the floor finding the mud from its boots still marking the wooden boards. A large spider weaved its way through the trail on dark, spindly legs. At the far end of the room, a woodlouse scurried along the skirting board. Traudi saw the spider turn and she hid her face, unable to watch.

"When a person stops caring they risk everything," her mama once said. But Traudi had never stopped caring, not about anyone or anything, and no words of wisdom, no quotes from the Bible, no haunting demands to be strong, could convince her that she was ever going to be safe again. She was as vulnerable as a woodlouse in a nest full of spiders.

Traudi glanced at the mattress above her, suddenly recalling the indistinct but beautiful face of a man. She had fallen asleep and she could scarcely believe it. After everything that had happened, she couldn't understand how she could have been so reckless. She racked her brains, but there was no moment she could recall when her eyes had grown heavy and she had battled to keep them open. She didn't even hear the intruder leave her room. All she knew for certain was that she had fallen asleep and woken up to find herself floating under the bed. And that wasn't normal. Nobody could think that was normal. In fact nothing had been even remotely normal about her life since she woke up to find her fever had broken and she was alone. If it wasn't for the pain that ravaged her body Traudi would have sworn she was still delirious. She looked at her knees, close to her chin, protruding through the gap in her coat. Where the skin wasn't blue it was purple with bruises.

Traudi turned from her side to rest on her back, biting her lip as the movement brought a new shock of agony. There wasn't a part of her that didn't hurt; not a muscle, not a nerve, not a bone that didn't rattle in protest. And beneath her head, she heard the house groan, as though the two of them were connected, both creaking in misery, one with old age, the other with pain. A single tear rolled down Traudi's cheek. She missed her mother. She missed her brother. She missed their once happy life. But it was clear that whatever had broken into their home was not going away. It had found its way in, it had slept on her bed and Traudi was sure that nothing would change until she gave up the fight and lay down to die, breathing her last among the dirt and the dust that coated the floor. Reaching over the skirting board, her fingers stroked the wooden wall.

Though she was no stranger to death – having grieved for her father and cried for the dog – it was the first time Traudi had ever considered dying. Perhaps it was the fear, coupled with exhaustion and hunger, but as she lay on the floor she dared believe there were worse ways to go. As long as the intruder let her be, as long as she could remain in her room, as long as the doors stopped the vicious wind, and the demons forgot where she was, as long as she could be left alone she would welcome death. She truly believed it. She was prepared to die in her talking house, under her own bed, praying for the Lord to deliver her quickly into the arms of her family. She was ready for an end to it all.

Traudi closed her eyes and, for the briefest moment, she pictured her family waiting for her; her mother, standing tall, holding onto her cane; Heini by her side, his face fixed in the stern look she knew best; and her father, no longer a shadow, but a kind-looking man with dirty blonde hair, his arms circling his wife and his son, with room for one more. Traudi's tears fell faster, streaming down her cheeks, wetting the hair above her ears. Not too long now, she promised. Not so very long to wait.

Below her back the floor shuddered as the house revealed someone was there. To her surprise, Traudi found she no longer cared. She had lost contact with the terror of dying, and having done so she barely reacted when doors slammed in the rooms below and heavy boots stamped across the floor. She was untouchable now. Every drop of fear had wrung dry; she yearned only for heaven. As far as Traudi was concerned, there was nothing more that evil could do.

Her fingers drifted from the wall to stroke the floor. Although her ears continued to listen, her brain instructed them to simply accept the intrusion. After all, there was nothing she hadn't heard before, and she had lived through much worse, and for a while she even felt calm. But then the banging stopped and there was a new sound to decipher, like water being thrown from a bucket. Traudi raised her head, paying a little more attention as the splashes travelled from room to room. Eventually, she was forced to raise her hands to her face as the smell became increasingly overpowering.

It wasn't water being thrown throughout the house, it was gasoline.

****

"Dad tells me Reinhardt's funeral is scheduled for Wednesday."

Leo glanced at Christian, searching for something suitably

sombre to say – something that might befit his leadership status whilst acknowledging his failure to bring the man down alive – but in the end he simply replied, "Oh, right." It was a miserable response, almost belligerent under the circumstances, but at that precise moment in time he had neither the strength, nor the will, to discuss Reinhardt or Reinhardt's funeral or anything else for that matter. He simply wanted to walk, to feel the sun on his head and the breeze in his hair. Quite simply, he wanted to forget about the world, at least for a while.

A little ahead of them, Christian's dog dived into the mounds of snow lining the sides of the road, digging for God only knows what. From where Leo stood it looked like a lot of fun, and he vaguely wondered whether his life might benefit from having a dog in it; after all they were faithful, fond of the outdoors and indisposed towards mindless chitchat. It could work, and it was a nice idea, but even as he considered it, he knew it was impossible. He simply didn't have the time for a dog. And it was a realisation that triggered an ambush of guilt – he didn't have time for a dog and yet he'd believed it to be enough for the woman he loved.

"Albert, heel!"

At the command, the dog bounded towards them and Christian took hold of Albert's collar as a car approached. Once the vehicle passed, the dog was released, free to play once more in the frozen snow.

"Good dog you've got there," Leo remarked.

"Yes, I've been lucky."

"And how's he doing with the rescue team?"

"Good as gold. Of course he gets into a few scraps with the other males, but as a working dog he's superb. Good at all the disciplines or at least he is now, now we've stopped him pawing his rescues."

Leo looked at him quizzically, and Christian explained how the dogs were taught to bark once they found a missing person.

"If the team is called to an avalanche or a search there's a high probability that the victim is injured. The last thing they need is an excited dog jumping on their broken bones."

"I guess not," Leo replied.

"You know, you should come and join us some time, come on an exercise, you might enjoy it."

"If I ever find the time," Leo replied.

"That's true. You always appear to be pretty busy – or drunk."

The younger man laughed, but Leo felt strangely stung by the words. He had always cast himself in a more gentle if not romantic light so it was sobering to hear that the common perception was that of a crapulent bore.

"No. I'll definitely make time," Leo insisted, cringing at the anxiety he heard straining his voice.

"Right you are," Christian replied, but he didn't sound convinced. He picked up a stick and threw it for Albert. Leo lit another cigarette.

As they walked further into Echerntal, the houses began to thin and trees gradually filled the void with the snow lining the road becoming deeper, and the climb a little steeper. Reaching the fork at the brow of the hill, Leo asked which way.

"Let's follow the river," Christian replied. "Albert likes it along there."

"Well, if that's what Albert likes." Leo smiled and the three of them turned right, climbing higher into the valley, away from the town.

****

There was no time to think and even less to feel afraid, she simply knew that she had to get out. She had been willing to die alone, she had even begun to welcome it, but Traudi refused to end her days trapped in her room with flames licking at her feet, smelling the wood burn and hearing the house scream. She would run, and if she was caught, she would do what she had to do. Traudi reached into the pocket of her coat and pulled out the knife. The curved blade was designed for hunting, but now the hunted would fight back. If she had to, she would use it. She was sure of it. Taking grip of the bone angel hanging by her palm, secured by the silver chain tied in loops around her fingers, she lifted the protection to her lips.

"I pray the Lord my soul to keep; if I die before I wake I pray the Lord my soul to take."

Making the sign of the cross upon her heart, Traudi opened the door to her room.

Pausing on the landing she heard muffled steps, too far away to be close. Whatever was down there had retreated to the cellar. She remembered the deer, its carcass hung on the wall as though leaping for freedom, and she crossed herself again. Whatever happened, the intruder would not take her head, not while she still had breath in her body. Without waiting a moment more, she ran down the stairs. Though the blood crashed through her ears Traudi heard her steps thundering through the house. Wooden houses speak, that's what her mother said, but they weren't built to be discerning. Reaching the door, she pulled frantically at the handle, relieved to find it unlocked. She pushed it open and the cold air rushed in. Ahead of her she saw the field, a patchwork blanket of snow and green grass. Jumping from the stone steps, her boots landed in wet mud, almost tipping her over. She looked right towards the path that led to the track that led to the road knowing that was the way she should go. But before she could run, it appeared.

From the direction of the cellar door, it burst around the corner of the house, assuming the form of an old man. However, this demon wasn't wizened by age; it was huge with a chest broad as a barrel, its skin raw with cold and knotted by scars; its eyes hard and blue as the freezing sky. It stared at her, white spittle on its lips, a scythe in its enormous devil hands. More out of shock than fear, Traudi screamed.

"I hate you!" she shouted, no longer able to contain her fury at this thing, this abomination of man, this slave of the witches, who had stolen everything she had ever known, everything she had ever loved. "I hate you!"

Traudi ran, her heart racing as fast as her legs. There was no chance of making the road, so she headed for the forest, running towards the river, hoping to lose herself in the trees. Clearing the field, she quickly looked back. The demon was coming after her.

****

The deeper Leo walked into the valley the more he relaxed. He couldn't remember the last time he had taken a stroll simply for the hell of it, at least not since Ana packed her bags, and it was nice. Of course, his competitive spirit would never allow him to make a habit of such a leisurely pursuit and he recognised he suffered from a form of sporting schizophrenia as the only competition he ever encountered was with himself, or more precisely his old self, the Leo who used to finish a winter season with 43 ski tours under his belt. But today, with the air fresh and crisp, and clean snow crunching under the heels of his boots, he couldn't think of a better way to spend the morning. Hallstatt and the area surrounding the town was beautiful. It was always good to be reminded of that.

Despite his initial reservations, partly provoked by Günter's peculiar brand of anti-philanthropic prejudice, he found Christian to be surprisingly good company. He didn't talk much and he seemed largely content to throw sticks for his dog. But occasionally they pondered some aspect of the rescue team and its members, and they even had a brief discussion on the possibility of Hans Grugger returning to the piste following his horrific accident at Kitzbühel. But by and large they walked through the valley in easy silence.

Following the gravel road that wound its way past a few small-holdings hugging the edge of the forest, they broke off from the main route as the mountain closed in. Hearing the river, they tramped through a small copse of trees to find a well-worn trail. The snow was compact, smooth as tarmac, and the soles of their boots squeaked on the surface. In the deeper snow, within the trees, stick-like holes revealed the tracks of deer. And with the sun shining, the landscape glittered like a carpet of diamonds. In fact it was so warm Christian had taken off his jumper.

Because they heard the river well before they saw it, Leo was little surprised when he got to the bank to find the water level uncommonly high. At this time of year, he'd have expected only a slow running stream with its bed of white stone still clearly visible. But it was a torrent that met them and the water rushed through the channel with the power of late-spring. It was unnatural and because it was unnatural Leo mentioned it to Christian, who laughed.

"Dad says the religious community is preparing for Armageddon. Meanwhile the hippies have consulted the Mayan calendar and are now convinced the end of the world will come sometime in

December. It seems the combination of extremely heavy snowfall and a very quick thaw has made a lot of people nervous. But yes, it's also unusual."

"And what do you think?" Leo asked.

"Me? I think it's got more to do with something called weather." Christian winked at him. "Anyway, I've seen the forecast and if the experts are to be believed we'll be back in our hats and gloves by this time next week. The spring is still a long way off."

"Well, thank goodness for that," Leo muttered. "I also get nervous when the snow leaves too early."

"And so speaks a Hallstatt man, born and bred," Christian joked. He picked up another stick and threw it for Albert.

****

The faster Traudi ran, the more violently the forest attacked her. The trees were so densely packed that the branches snagged on her hair and slapped at her face as she forced her way through. She knew the path would be easier, but anyone could follow her on the path whereas the dark forest, with its sharp spikes and infernal scratches, was the safest place she could think of. No matter how tough the terrain was, or how deep the snow or how close the trees grew, she knew she could negotiate them quicker than any old man. But of course, this wasn't any old man, and whenever she looked back she always saw him near, never clearly, sometimes there was only a glimpse of green jacket or the pale flash of hands grappling with branches, tearing them out of his way, but he was always there, only a fraction behind her. Traudi knew it shouldn't be possible, that there was no earthly way an old man could follow so swiftly, but she had grown used to facing the impossible. After waking up alone she had been trapped in a world where the wind brought invisible hands, where a force with no shape could throw her against walls, where a headless deer could find its way into the cellar and a demon could search for her holding a gun. And now that demon, that old man, that intruder, the thing, the abominable beast, was chasing her.

From the trees, Traudi heard the river. It called to her with the roar of a lion as it crashed against the rocky slopes that contained it.

"The river has sustained this valley and the people in it for centuries..."

Traudi ran for the river, crying out for it to help her.

****

Leo shook himself, feeling a cold breeze settle on his shoulders, causing the hairs of his neck to stand on end. He followed the river with his eyes, his stare running against the current, looking for something, he didn't know what.

"Are you OK?"

Leo glanced at his side to find Christian watching him, wearing the same expression he had seen in Harri's eyes when he came out of his episode on the mountain. Leo ran his fingers across his forehead, convinced he must be coming down with something.

"I'm OK," he confirmed. "I've not been feeling myself lately."

"Perhaps you're coming down with something," Christian replied. And Leo smiled. He reached for a stick and threw it for the ever-grateful Albert who responded with astonishing speed, his tail in permanent motion, wagging with all the glee of a dog that thinks running after a stick is the meaning of life. If only everyone he came into contact with was so easy to please, Leo thought.

****

Traudi didn't know for how much longer she could run. Every step seemed to send her plunging to the ground, her body ached with pain and exhaustion, her skin was frozen to the bone and every time she looked behind her, she saw him coming, his mouth gaping in fury, the words lost in the noise of the river. There were times when he had gained so much ground she could almost count the scars on his face. Traudi fell to the earth, her chest heaving as it struggled for breath and battled her sobs. The river screamed at her – Get up! Get up! – and Traudi hauled herself to her feet with tears streaming down her dirty face, her body protesting every step of the way. I can't do it, she yelled, but the words echoed only in her head. Even her voice had abandoned her; the effort of survival proving too much to bear. Slowly, her legs began to buckle, refusing to move, weighing her down, and dragging her to the ground.

"No!" she shouted.

With a gigantic effort Traudi forced herself to her feet, but the trees were becoming impassable, as though working against her, and she knew she had to escape them. Seeing a break of light further ahead, Traudi ran for it, feeling an overwhelming sense of relief as the branches thinned, making way for a trail. For a moment she stopped to catch her breath. On the flat ground her legs struggled to find balance, as though sprung abruptly from glue and unable to adjust to the lack of resistance. She looked at the path, rolling ahead of her as inviting as a carpet, but even as she took a step forward she knew she should leave. The track was too exposed. Her legs were too slow. She had no choice but to delve back into the dark of the forest, away from the bank of the river.

Her heart sinking, Traudi had to force herself to run. She

crashed through the wall of trees, no longer thinking with any sense of direction. She had lost her bearings. All she knew was that she had to keep the madman behind her. As she ploughed through the forest, the snow grew increasingly deep. With its top layer wet from the heat of the sun, it slowed her body and sucked at her will. Fallen trees, blown by winter storms, lay like traps, waiting under a blanket of white to trip her up and send her sprawling. Traudi stumbled across them all as she pushed her way further up the mountain, half crawling half running. At times she became so dizzy she thought she would faint and the further she ran the more frequently she fell, crashing into the debris of rock slides and the immovable trunks of the trees until her arms became so numb she didn't even notice when the knife slipped from her hand. The only thing she was conscious of was the sound of heavy boots crunching on snow as the noise of the river slipped away and the laboured, wheezing breaths of her pursuer took its place.

"Wait!"

The order thundered through the valley, but Traudi ran on.

"Wait!"

Traudi looked at her hands, suddenly aware she wasn't holding the knife. She moaned in dismay and held tightly to the only protection that remained. Squeezing the bone angel nestling in her palm, she begged it to help her.

"He will give His angels charge of you, to guard you in all your ways."

Ahead of her – she didn't know how, and she no longer asked why – a glow of light appeared, beckoning her through the thick of the trees. Traudi ran for it, her arms flailing wildly at the mesh of branches working to stop her until she burst out of the dark, into sunshine.

In front of her was a small clearing, a perfect white circle hidden within the evergreen forest. Traudi glanced behind her – quickly locating a green jacket and blue eyes – she then looked to the other side of the clearing, somehow knowing that's where she should be. In twenty strides she could make it, in twenty strides she would be free, and with a final gargantuan effort she plunged into the unblemished snow, her hands working like paddles as her feet sank into the cold.

"Wait!"

Traudi dragged herself forwards, refusing to look back as she waded through the clearing, finding her rhythm. Clearing the halfway point the going started to get easier as the snow gradually freed her knees until it came only to her calves. One more leap and she would be in the trees.

"For the love of God, Traudi, wait! It's me!"

She stopped abruptly, the words stunning her into stillness. He knew her name. The thing knew her name. Traudi turned around, facing the clearing. In front of her, close enough to see though not yet close enough to touch was the old man. Standing like opposite points on a compass, the two of them faced each other on the edges of the circle. The old man leaned forward to rest his hands on his knees, his breath coming quick and shallow. Even so, he never took his eyes off Traudi and those eyes, those ice-blue eyes, were streaming with tears.

Wiping roughly at his face, the old man stood straight. "Don't you recognise me, Traudi?"

Traudi felt her head spinning as the world rushed by in a squall of sounds, memories and fear, all of them chased by the wind. It couldn't be...

"Heini?"

The old man's lips trembled and his head nodded in confirmation.

He moved towards her. His arms outstretched, his legs wading through the snow to reach her.

"Yes, it's me, Traudi... Heini."

Another five steps were all that remained between them and Traudi shook her head fiercely. How could this ancient, gnarled creature be her brother? It was impossible. It had to be a trick. The devil was trying to trap her. As he moved nearer, Traudi started to retreat. She inched backwards, not daring to take her eyes off the old man and behind her back she felt the trees looming large, darkening the sky. She shuffled towards them slowly, her legs ready to turn and run. As though reading her mind, the old man's face fell and Traudi faltered at the despair she saw written there. His eyes welled with fresh tears and she stared in disbelief because she had seen those eyes before, and she had witnessed that same unmistakable grief – on the day that Herr Bittner had come from the mine to tell them their father was dead.

"Heini!" Traudi shouted.

She didn't know how, she simply knew it was true – the old man in front of her was the brother she loved. Traudi felt her legs grow weak. Fighting to keep her balance, she stepped backwards into the ankle-deep snow, feeling the heel of her boot stick as though caught in wet mud. She stamped hard, trying to free herself, smiling at Heini as he moved closer to help, but the earth shuddered under the weight of her struggle and the snow shifted. With no warning, the ground opened. It happened so fast she had no chance to scream and the blackness below dragged her into the mountain, bringing soil and rock raining upon her head, burying her deep, cutting off the world.

Even as she fell Traudi knew she had been there before, a long time ago, when her mother was alive and Heini was still a boy. It felt like a dream, but she remembered the drop clearly and the sharp, crack of pain as she landed on rock. Yet this time, there was no ledge jumping out of the dark, nothing to break her neck and her fall. There was only the gentle, angel hand of the river rising up to catch her. Traudi closed her eyes, allowing the water to embrace her, finally understanding that at last she could sleep because the river had come to carry her home.

****

Albert barked – three short very exact calls for attention – and Christian cocked his head to one side, his eyes looking puzzled.

"I think he's found something," he said.

Christian ran further up the river to investigate and Leo followed him, a little more slowly. When he reached the bank, which was as close as the river could get to the spine of the mountain, he saw Albert wagging his tail. The dog barked again and Christian came to his side. He delved into his jacket pocket, offering the dog a slice of ham that had been wrapped in cling film.

"Good boy, Albert. Good boy."

Leo inspected the drop below them finding a shallow pool, elevated from the main body of the river, in which he quickly discovered the cause of Albert's excitement. "There are bones," he said.

"Probably a deer," Christian replied. "We find a few of them around here."

"Perhaps," agreed Leo, but he wasn't convinced, and the nagging sensation that had been dogging him for days told him to make sure. He clambered down the rocky embankment, noticing two larger bones first, brown with age and decay. They could belong to a deer, but as he was no expert in the matter he couldn't say for certain. He jumped into the water, which was freezing but no higher than his knees. He bent down to pick up the largest of the bones. The elongated shape, the bulbous end, it could be a femur. However, it was small, far too small for an adult. To the right of him, a gentle trickle of water caught his attention and when Leo moved closer he saw it came from a small opening at the base of the mountain. The outlet provided the proof he barely realised he was looking for. Leo stepped away. Grabbing a number of larger rocks from the embankment he hurriedly built a makeshift dam, effectively closing the shallow pool from the passing river.

"Call the police," he shouted up to Christian.

"Why, what is it?"

"I think the bones are human. I'm not sure, but you better call them," he said.

Leo continued to build the dam as he listened to Christian on the phone, explaining what they thought they had found and relaying their coordinates. When Leo was satisfied the dam would hold he took another look at the scattered remains; as well as the femur there was possibly a tibia and a few other fragments of bone that could have been fingers or toes. Some of the pieces were tiny, and he felt a pang of regret for the small life that had been lost. Leo made the sign of the cross on his chest, surprised at himself given his atheist leanings, and with his legs growing numb he moved to climb back to the path. As he turned, sunlight fell on the pool through the swaying branches of the trees and its rays picked out a chain that had snagged on one of the smaller pieces of bone. Leo bent to inspect it and when he rescued it from the water he saw it was attached to an amulet of some description. The figure was nothing he could make out, but he recognised the material – it had been carved from the bone of an antler.

Chapter Sixteen

The clouds skulked over Dachstein's jagged peaks, retaking possession of the skies, forcing the grey hue of winter back on the town. The cold lake gleamed, still as polished steel, and a gentle snowfall began to dust the rooftops and walkways. Two streets back from the lake, amidst a tidy row of pastel-painted houses, Heinrich Bergmann sat in his home – a shadow in front of the fire – as the oppressive cloak of the mountain wrapped the valley in a premature gloom. High above the mantelpiece, a stag's empty eye sockets, dark in the bleached skull of a once handsome animal, followed his thoughts with a ghostly dispassion; the only witness to the tears that rolled down the old man's cheeks as he caressed the bone angel in his hands, hanging from a blackened chain that used to be silver.

Only when the flames began to die did Bergmann rise from his leather seat. His body creaked in protest, loud as the boards of an old wooden house. Taking a handful of twigs from the wicker basket, he coaxed the fire into prolonging its life before placing two halved logs on the grate. After wiping roughly at his nose with the back of his hand, he took the poker from its stand and prodded. Despite the growing heat, he stayed where he was, transfixed by the flames which danced along the wood, watching through a gauze of grief that transported him to another time – a time when he was little more than a boy, sat alone, in front of another fire, in a place he used to call home.

With a clarity borne of repeated nightmares he felt again the fierce breath of winter on his face, remembering how those in the valley had been trapped in their homes, cut off from the town and battling a cold that ate into their bones. Under the gaze of the Dachstein, the snow had fallen without respite that year, cementing itself onto the landscape. No ploughs were mobilised to aid the community – the state was still struggling from a war that had left it bankrupt and humiliated fourteen years earlier – and it was up to the men to dig themselves out of the white tomb that engulfed them each night. But of course, some homes didn't have men – they only had boys – and deep in the valley, Heini had struggled from dawn to dusk to clear a pathway from the door to the road whilst hauling logs to the hearth to keep the house warm. However, there was only so much an eleven-year-old child could take, and blisters quickly ballooned and burst on his palms as chilblains burned his fingertips in protest at the extremes in temperature his chores subjected him to. Even so, he never complained. Not once. And his mother, blind and otherwise engaged, never saw the discomfort her son wordlessly bore because that was the winter that Traudi fell ill.

Taken by a common cold, his sister had been grouchy and intolerable for more than a week until one day she failed to rise from her bed. When their mother went to investigate, she discovered Traudi wrestling a fever. Though ice clung to the inside of the window, Traudi writhed in sheets wringing with sweat. Her skin burned to the touch and her hair had tangled in the fight, leaving wet strands clinging to her face. As their frantic mother slapped wet cloths and curd poultices onto Traudi's forehead, Heini watched from the doorway, trying to ignore the chilblains stinging his fingers. At meal times, he dutifully followed his mother upstairs carrying a bowl of soup which he observed her spoon down his sister's throat, as though she were a baby. And when night fell, he listened to his mother praying at Traudi's bedside before settling herself on the floor to sleep, still clutching her daughter's hand. Heini watched all of this, and when he wasn't playing witness to his mother's vigil he dug the snow from the path, cut the wood into logs, stoked the ever-hungry fire, and went for provisions.

Although Heini accepted his mother's worry, he thought it unnecessary and foolish – illness was a part of life and death only happened to the old. Not for a minute did he think the fever was anything his sister wouldn't come through, and in the end he was partly proved right. After a hellish week of thrashing in her bed, Traudi began to recover; the fever broke, she began to sleep more soundly, she started to eat and their mother moved back to her room. Whatever had afflicted her had come and gone, and life should have continued its natural course. But then their grandfather fell ill.

Visiting after the weekly shop – alone because his mother continued to agitate over his sister – Heini arrived at *Opa's* home anticipating venison stew and a few notes for his mother's purse. Unusually, there was no welcome when he stepped through the backdoor and after checking the sitting room, the parlour, and even the cellar, Heini ventured upstairs. He found his grandfather struggling to breathe on the floor of his bedroom, wearing his night clothes, abandoned by speech, and wet from his body's betrayal at the shock of a stroke. Heini was stunned. After that, he was efficient. Hauling *Opa* upright, he leant him against the nearest wall, taking a knitted blanket to cover him, and quickly worked to wipe the old man's shame from the floorboards. Only then did Heini run for help.

Next door, Franz Weber was clearing a path to the road. It was a task he quickly abandoned and once he was at his neighbour's side, Heini ran for the doctor who summoned an ambulance. As *Opa* was driven away, Heini then sprinted for home – and it was at that point, at that precise moment in time, that his world began to unravel.

Though Traudi's fever had broken, she was still confined to bed, and in far too weak a state to be dragged into Hallstatt. It was a terrible decision their mother had to make, but in the end there could be only one choice. Agreeing that Heini would have to accompany her, she went to speak to Traudi – to explain that she would be gone for a while, but that she'd return as soon as was humanly possible and in the meantime Heini would be there, once he'd helped her get to the town. Traudi should be brave, their mother had instructed, and she shouldn't be afraid because her brother would look after her.

As ever, Heini watched from the doorway and though Traudi seemed to hear their mother's promises, he was pretty certain none of them had sunk in. His sister was drowsy and irritable and instead of answering their mother she simply turned her face to the wall because all she wanted to do was sleep.

Three hours later, Heini returned home, anxious and exhausted. His legs trembled with fatigue and his heart thumped with worry. He had no way of knowing whether *Opa* was alive or dead, and his head had become plagued with images of his mother crying alone over the corpse of her father, and by fears for how they would survive without him. Heini was scared, and as the man of the house it made him feel ashamed. So when he returned to discover Traudi had risen from her bed to venture into the pantry, he struggled to hold on to his reason. On the cold shelf, he immediately saw tooth marks defacing the leg of ham that was to be their dinner for the night and chunks torn, not cut, from the bread. Though he knew Traudi had hardly eaten all week, he was incensed. They weren't animals or monkeys in a zoo. And it was a fury further exacerbated when he stomped to the sitting room to find Traudi messing with the fire. Heini went spare. Fires were hazardous; ever since they could talk their father had drummed this into their skulls. Did she not remember how he had fallen into his own parents' fireplace as a child, leaving his right arm a mangle of scars? Was there no respect for the memory of their father? Was she a spoiled brat with no brains?

Heini rushed at his sister, but she evaded his grasp and ran for the door.

"I hate you!" Traudi screamed as he spat his fears into her face. "I hate you!"

And those were the last words she ever spoke to him.

Heini watched his sister run from the house, too angry to give chase, too preoccupied to care. In truth, he thought she should be punished. And for a while he simply wanted to forget – to be left alone, to be released from a responsibility that had left him isolated and unable to ask for help. He wanted his dad back, so he might place a hand on the crown of Heini's head and banish the fear sheltering there. In short, Heini wanted to be a boy again. So no, he didn't give chase. He simply stood in the doorway watching his sister tramp across the field, falling into snow drifts, scrambling on her knees, expecting her to give up quickly, to come home and apologise. But as Traudi neared the edge of the forest, she turned in his direction and pulled something from her pocket. As she waved the object in the air Heini felt the rage building inside him, like steam powering a train, and he bolted for his room. On the table by his bed, he instantly saw that one of the knives was missing – but it wasn't any old knife, it was the most important one, the one his father had given him. The insult felt monumental; Traudi possessed their mother, this was a fact beyond dispute, whereas the knife was his. It was his connection to their father and it was all he had left bar a head full of memories.

Heini thundered downstairs.

By the time he emerged from the house, Traudi was gone, but she'd left a trail in the snow even their mother could follow and it led Heini through the trees, deep into the forest, closer to the mountain, towards the silent river. It was there, a little in the distance, that he spotted Traudi, and as she turned to see the anger in her brother's eyes she panicked, scrambling faster through the snow, falling over a storm-felled tree until she careered into a boulder. Heini watched the knife fly from his sister's grasp and he ran to reclaim it. Finding it almost immediately he wiped the snow from the blade and he was about to tuck it into the waistband of his trousers, out of habit, until he remembered the sheath discarded on the bed in his room. The very thought of such disorder set Heini's nerves on edge and with the knife now safely in his possession his only thought was to get home and put it back where it belonged. As far as Heini was concerned, his sister could go to hell, and so he turned his back on Traudi – he turned his back on the little girl and walked away.

Once at the house, Heini headed straight for his room where he returned his father's knife to its rightful place. He then went to the kitchen where he took another knife to the ham, slicing it clean, eradicating the teeth marks left by his sister. Finally, he moved to the fire and once the flames burned brightly in the grate he sat in his father's old chair and waited. By sundown, when he was still alone, he began to get anxious. When night arrived he started to panic. Scared or not, Traudi should have returned. And knowing this, Heini also knew something had to be wrong. So he put on his boots, lit a paraffin lamp and went to discover what it might be.

By the time Heini reached the forest, the snow had been whipped into a blizzard and in the dark of the night he had to rely solely on memory to retrace his earlier steps. However, once he reached the bank of the river he was at a loss as to where to go next and his search was reduced to shouting into the wind. Heini screamed Traudi's name until his lungs burned and his voice grew hoarse, but there was no reply that he heard, not a sound above the hellish squall of the storm; only the faint, faraway echo of his fear rebounding off the walls of the Dachstein.

As Heini searched for his sister, all concerns for *Opa* became dwarfed by a nightmare image of Traudi lying injured in the dark being buried alive by the winter. In the struggling glow of the lamplight the black trees loomed large around him, menacing his mind, clawing at his face with needle-sharp fingers, throwing shadows in his path that made him start with fright. And by the time the paraffin lamp sputtered to an end, Heini was frozen to the bone with a leaden heart, heavy as a tombstone. He had no choice but to head for home, and as he walked away from the river he prayed with every footfall that he would step inside the front door to find Traudi upstairs, sleeping in her bed. But even as he crossed the threshold he knew the house was empty. Heini was alone.

Once his mother returned home, his isolation was complete.

Arriving with Franz Weber, she found Heini in the front room. But it was Herr Weber who saw the haunted look in the child's eyes, though his gaze barely lifted from the grate of ashes. And it was Herr Weber who approached the boy, telling him not to worry, that his grandfather would be fine. Then, when Heini revealed through chattering teeth that Traudi was missing, it was Herr Weber who shielded the boy as his mother flew at him. It was a beating Heini took without protest.

For three long and terrible days, twenty men or more from the rescue team scoured the area above and around the Echerntal valley, but they found no trace of Traudi or any leads that might give them reason to continue the search. The head of the rescue team was visibly upset when he stated that his men had done all they could possibly do.

"It's as though the Lord has simply plucked the child from the mountain," he said.

However, Heini didn't believe in God, and he stared at the dark rock that stabbed through the carpet of snow knowing that somewhere, amidst the boulders and trees, the mountain had hold of his sister.

Once the rescue team had left for their own homes, the house fell quiet. His mother seemed unable to bring herself to speak and in the growing darkness of their home Heini watched her from his place by the fire understanding that she blamed him entirely for her loss. Her blind eyes never reached for him. There was no attempt to acknowledge his existence. It was only the next morning, once all hope had gone that she finally relented and spoke.

Seated by the window, her sightless eyes unable to stop their search, she told him: "Well, we're even, Heinrich – you lost everything you loved and now you've taken everything I loved."

His mother then rose from her seat. Without uttering another word, she tapped her way through the sitting room, heading for the staircase, and Heini tried not to cry as she passed by because he knew she was right. Their mother had worshipped Traudi – just as he had once reserved his adoration for their father. Now

Heini had robbed his mother of a daughter, like the mountain had long ago robbed him. And that's why he didn't blame his mother for holding him responsible because he thought she had every right to feel aggrieved. And that's why he refused to cry as he added more logs to the fire because he needed to take his punishment like a man – and if that meant listening to his mother unleashing her anguish upstairs, away from him and the cause of her grief, then so be it.

As the screams grew in velocity, coming to fill every corner of the house, Heini knew that from that moment on his mother was lost to him. She would never forgive him. And she never did. Not to her dying day.

As their mother cried for Traudi, Heini had stayed where he was; downstairs, tending the fire, not knowing what else to do. The following morning, after her pain had grown silent he summoned the courage to check on her. At the door of her room he found chaos. Clothes were strewn about the floor, drawers had been pulled from their hinges, a glass lamp lay smashed in a corner, and amidst it all he found his mother, sat on the floor, staring at the wall. Heini moved to her side, hoping to offer some kind of comfort, but when he touched her arm she flinched as though scalded.

"Get your things, we're leaving," she instructed, her voice sharp as ice.

She then walked from the bedroom, taking nothing with her but the clothes on her back and the stick in her hand. As Heini followed he paused by his own bedroom door, thinking of what he might need, but in the end he left the house with nothing because it was all he deserved. But as he watched his mother lock the front door behind them, he suddenly remembered the fire burning in the sitting room.

"Leave it as it is," his mother snapped. "I don't care if the whole house burns down."

She then walked away and Heini could only follow. Glancing back at the house he knew it would never be their home again.

****

Heinrich Bergmann jolted with a start; firstly from the shock of the telephone ringing and secondly at the unexpected sight of an aged hand holding a poker that glowed red in the fire. Shaking his head, he reached for the edge of the mantle place and hauled himself upwards; freeing the man from the ghost of the boy he once was.

On top of a dresser a clock ticked loudly and he looked at it with some degree of wariness as he passed; no longer trusting its concept of time. In the hallway, the telephone rattled on a glass table.

"Bergmann," he answered.

On the other end of the line, a woman's voice caused him some surprise before he scratched at his forehead, frowning.

"OK," he eventually said. "I'll meet you there."

Walking to the front room, he carefully positioned the fireguard in front of the hearth. As he returned to the hallway he noticed a pile of hunting magazines sitting slightly askew on top of the telephone directory. He corrected the mistake before reaching for his coat.

The snow was falling steadily by the time Bergmann reached the graveyard and he found her waiting on a bench, wearing a navy woollen coat, her cheeks pinched pink in the cold. She had loved him once, many years ago. He had loved her too.

"Gretl," he greeted, and the woman smiled.

"No one's called me that since I was a child," she told him. "How are you, Heinrich?"

"Oh, you know..."

He came to sit beside her on the bench. Subconsciously, his hands reached inside his coat and he pulled out the bone angel as his eyes drifted over the tidy row of crosses in front of them. Perched on a cliff, high above the rooftops, facing the lake, the cemetery gave the dead the best view in Hallstatt. There were no family graves, there simply wasn't the space and the mountain's spine offered no room for expansion. So, old bones were exhumed to make way for the new, like a conveyor belt of death. Margarethe reached out to rest a hand on his arm – a peace offering given by another ghost from his past. Swallowing hard, Bergmann kept his eyes on the lake. He moved his hand to cover her fingers and left it there.

"So really," she said, "how are you?"

"Better now," he admitted, "but for a time I really thought I was going mad."

"You were grieving, Heinrich. You've spent a lifetime grieving. This is different to madness."

Bergmann looked at her, understanding she was referring to Reinhardt, but Margarethe shook her head. "I wasn't talking about him specifically, although it's clear the man was extremely unwell."

"Perhaps," Bergmann admitted, his voice breaking with sadness and uncertainty, "but mad or not, and I'm not so sure he was, it seems to me that Reinhardt triggered something the night he went missing."

"The night he died?"

"No, before that – the night he saw ghosts on the Strenhang slope."

Bergmann shifted uneasily on the wooden bench and Margarethe's eyes followed his fingers as they moved along the chain he held, working their way along the links until they reached the angel, like a penitent Catholic contemplating the mysteries.

"The day after Reinhardt said he saw the dead I started to notice something odd at the old house," continued Bergmann. His voice was wary and he watched her closely, but Margarethe kept her eyes steady. "Of course, there was nothing to see. The house was the same as it had always been. But there was this feeling – something I couldn't shake – and a few times I thought I saw condensation on the windows. Of course, nobody had set foot in the house for more than fifty years, and it would have been as cold inside as out. But then one morning after I dragged a deer to the cellar..." Bergmann paused, looking embarrassed and a little sorry, "don't be telling the police now," he joked, and Margarethe smiled and promised that she wouldn't. "Well, I brought a deer back to the cellar to hang it – the only use I've made of the house since the day we left – and it was then that I thought I heard something upstairs, some kind of movement. I told myself it was rats, I mean what other explanation could there be? But the next time I went back to the house, I heard something again. You know, our mother was fond of saying that wooden houses talk. Well, this one was talking alright. I just couldn't work out what it was saying. So, I left the cellar and took a walk around. There were no footprints, no nothing. The place was empty. But then, as I was turning to leave, I noticed a shadow in the kitchen. Well, my heart almost burst from my chest and after it stopped thumping I grabbed a bucket from the cellar, turned it on its head and peered through the window. And that's when I heard a gasp, like a half-scream. Well, as you can imagine, I pretty much exploded – thinking kids were in the house using it as a playground. I ran to the front door, which was locked, and I was so angry I tried to kick it in. But the door was solid, too solid for an old man like me. So I ran back to the cellar. Of course, I only had the key for the outside door, and the door into the house was locked from the inside. It was the way we had left it, you see, the way it had always been, ever since, ever since Traudi…"

Bergmann stumbled, blinking rapidly and Margarethe squeezed his arm. He tried to smile at the contact, to tell her he was fine, but he found himself unable to release the words, there were simply too many emotions in the way, and for a while there was nothing he could do but let them come.

After a while, Bergmann blew his nose into a white cotton hanky. Pushing it into his trouser pocket, he gave an apologetic look. "Not quite the man you used to know, eh Gretl?"

Margarethe smiled. "No, you're not the man I used to know," she confirmed. "You're far more likeable now."

Bergmann managed a smile. Gretl had always been forthright, it was a trait he admired, and he suddenly found himself regretting the years that had passed. Soft lines had come to crease his old friend's face, most prominent at her nose and her eyes, and her once chestnut hair had become an unnaturally rich auburn. He wasn't sure about the colour, but neither of them looked quite like they used to. Self-consciously he brushed his fingers along the scars he had acquired and turned away to gaze upon the still lake.

"What happened after you found the house locked?" Margarethe asked gently.

Bergmann shook his head. "I didn't find it locked," he corrected. "It *was* locked. It had always been locked. That's why I couldn't understand how someone could have got in. There were no broken windows. No sign of forced entry. Anyone in there would have had to climb down the chimney, and I couldn't imagine kids going to that much effort. But I had to find out because it was driving me crazy.

"As the keys were back at the house – the Hallstatt house," he added by way of clarification, "I returned home. When I got there the damned police were outside wanting to know something about deer meat. It was farcical, really. Anyway, I let them search the place, I had nothing to hide – my most recent kill was at the old house..."

"My son calls it the House of the Blind Woman," Margarethe interrupted. "I think he got the name from his grandfather."

"I wouldn't be surprised. That's what everyone called our home at one point – not so easy to hear when your mother is the blind woman though."

"No, of course not... Kids aren't very thoughtful, are they?"

"No more thoughtless than adults." Bergmann tugged at the collar of his coat, feeling the snow slipping down his neck. "So yes, the police were at the house, they had a good look about, asked a few questions and left. To be fair, they didn't seem that concerned, in fact they looked embarrassed if anything, but I've never trusted a policeman, so thinking they might have me under surveillance – I know, the very idea – but thinking they might I didn't want to risk leading them to the old house where they might actually find what they were looking for. So, I left it a day, during which time I managed to convince myself that I was simply an old fool losing his mind. I've heard loneliness can do that to a man – and yes, you needn't say anything, I know I only have myself to blame for that."

Margarethe shrugged, doing nothing to dispel him of that notion.

"Anyway, a day or so later – the day after Reinhardt died, actually – I took my hunting rifle and all the old keys and I returned to the valley. You know, my hands were shaking when I put the key in the lock. It could have been nerves, I suppose. After all, it had been a long time since I'd set foot in the house. Anyway I went in and I was that fired up I charged through the place like a bull in a marquee; I marched through the rooms, banging doors, opening wardrobes, even cupboards, looking for the little sods that had entered my home. But there was nothing downstairs, nothing to see but dust and bad memories. So, I went upstairs and – Christ, it had been so long – the place was like a mausoleum with everything in its place, the same as the day we had left it. I entered Traudi's room; the covers were still on her bed, her clothes still hung in a wardrobe. My room, exactly the same too, but then I went to the attic, to the place where our mother had her bed and, having forgotten some of what had gone on before, I wasn't prepared for the sight that met me. Her room was a mess. It was as if all hell had broken loose in there, which I suppose it had in a way, many years before. I was stunned and yes, I was shocked and I felt all the years of guilt come crawling out of the grave that I'd long ago buried them in. And then as I stood there, looking at the mess, thinking of my mother and the chaos she had created, I swear on my life, I heard music, Beethoven's *Für Elise* of all things. I ran downstairs, straight into Traudi's bedroom and that's when I saw this small, mechanical ball rolling along the floor. Well, I'm telling you, it practically finished me. It had been a present from our father and the year he gave it to Traudi she had driven me mad with it. Like most toys, she gradually lost interest in it and I assumed the ball had been lost, but there it was again... back from the past with the intention of driving me mad all over again. Well,

I'm not ashamed to say it, Gretl. I sat down on my sister's bed and I cried my God-damned heart out.

"For most of the night, I stayed where I was – on Traudi's bed, wondering what the hell was going on with my mind. I was tormented, there's no other word for it. I had all these feelings of guilt, of shame. It was more than I could bear. And the next morning, as soon as the sun was up, I decided to put an end to the craziness once and for all. I walked home and collected a can of gasoline, determined to burn the whole blasted place down..."

"Oh Heinrich, you didn't?" Margarethe's hand shot to her mouth and Bergmann reached to calm her.

"No, I didn't," he said, "but I would have done. I wanted to. I couldn't see any other way out of the nightmare; all those years of wondering, of blaming myself, of being tied to a house that had brought us nothing but pain. I guess I wasn't thinking too straight, but to my mind setting fire to the house seemed the most obvious thing to do, like building a pyre for the past. So, I doused the downstairs with gasoline and then I went to the cellar to find some kind of rag I could light, to throw into the place, and that's when I heard her... Yes, Gretl, as mad as it might seem I heard *her*... I heard my sister, Traudi. Of course, I didn't know it was her straight away, I simply heard someone running from the house so I ran from the cellar to catch them. I was holding a scythe in my hands, can you believe it? It had been in the cellar for as long as I could remember, along with an old bicycle I used to ride before the arthritis set in, and it was the only thing I wanted to salvage from the house before I set fire to it. So, there I was, carrying a scythe in my hand, like the grim reaper, when I turned the corner of the house to see Traudi. I swear on my life, I saw her – she was as real and as clear to me as you sitting here now. And nothing had changed. She was still this skinny slip of a girl, with messy blonde hair, the biggest blue eyes, dressed in her favourite blue coat, wearing a pair of winter boots – just like the day she went missing. I was speechless, but then she shouted at me – no, she screamed at me – using the last words she ever spoke to me. "I hate you!" she screamed. "I hate you!" And then she ran. For a moment or two, I was too stunned to move. I mean, I'd just seen my sister. Still nine years old, still the same as she ever was, but alive. And she was, Gretl. Traudi was no transparent apparition, no floating white sheet, she was flesh and blood. She was real.

"Well, when I came to my senses, I immediately ran after her. I wouldn't lose her again, not a second time, and she eventually led me through the trees to a clearing. Jesus, the place was beautiful and it was there that she stopped to look at me. I tell you, her blue eyes were enormous – wide with panic and fear – and it near broke my heart all over again. But Traudi had stopped and I was finally able to tell her who I was, that I was her brother, Heini. Of course, I saw the confusion in her face, and what could I say to convince her otherwise; this tiny child who used to have a brother just two years older, and who was now looking at a decrepit old man saying he was that boy. I could hardly believe it myself and I saw her backing away from me – this monster that I had become to her. Well, I didn't know what to do, or what to say to make her believe me and I felt tears stinging my eyes as I racked my brains to try and think of something, of anything to convince her that what I said was the truth and what she saw was a different kind of truth, and then, I don't know why, but something changed in her eyes. She called my name, Gretl. She called me Heini. She knew I was her brother. And suddenly all that weight, the sheer burden of carrying a lifetime of hate, just drifted away. Then, that very same second, Traudi disappeared, just like that." Bergmann stopped to click his fingers. "At first I thought she'd fallen through some kind of hole, but I was practically two metres from where she was stood and I followed her footprints right up to that place, but there was nothing; no hole, no more footprints, nothing. I couldn't believe it. I dropped to the snow, digging frantically with my hands, determined to find her. And that's when I felt the shallow indentation beneath my fingers. I got up and stamped my boot on the ground until it started to give way, and then I knew – I finally knew for certain – that this was where Traudi had disappeared; the place where she had fallen into the mountain, never to be seen or heard of again."

Bergmann stopped talking and Margarethe gave him the time he needed. Watching his tears, she could hardly believe he was the same man who had broken her heart all those years before; the young hunter who had romanced her to the verge of marriage only to walk away claiming he couldn't deal with the responsibility. Only now, some forty years later, did she begin to understand that it wasn't the idea of love that had frightened him, but of losing it. Naturally, she found his tale of ghosts uncomfortable and outlandish, but he seemed to believe what he said and right now, sat on the bench with the snow falling around them, she could think of no more plausible explanation for the events of the past few days. At odds with the unseasonal weather, a cold wind had blown through Hallstatt; it had taken away Reinhardt and it had brought peace to a man she had once loved. Margarethe didn't believe in ghosts, but she believed Heinrich was speaking the truth, and perhaps some things in life couldn't be easily explained, and there was no point in trying to find reasons. Perhaps life or God simply stepped forward to tidy up the ends.

"Damn, this snow is starting to come down, look at you,"

Bergmann said after blowing his nose into his handkerchief.

Margarethe looked at her arms; her navy coat was almost white. Subconsciously, a hand reached to her hair.

"You look like you're wearing a wedding veil," he remarked and Margarethe laughed at the image.

"I'd pity the man who'd marry an old woman like me."

"I'd pity the man who didn't," Bergmann replied. He coughed to mask his embarrassment, but he knew there was more he needed to get off his chest. "You were wrong, you know, when you told me all those years ago that I loved the mountain more than I loved you. I didn't. If anything I hated the place. But I couldn't let go. You see, I never stopped searching for my sister. In the early years I used to wonder whether a day might come when I would stumble across her body, half-praying I would, half-hoping I wouldn't. But I never did find any sign of her and in the end it took Traudi to take pity on me. She came to show me the way, Gretl. Whether you believe it or not, and I can see by your eyes that you're sceptical, it was my sister who led me to the spot where she fell. It was Traudi who revealed how she had died. And for that, I will be eternally grateful whether people choose to believe me or not. And I'll tell you something more, there was one more thing that little girl did for me. Before she disappeared, before she vanished again, she called my name and she smiled. She actually smiled at me, Gretl. Traudi had returned not only to show me, but to forgive me."

No longer able to resist the five decades of grief battering his insides, Bergmann leant forward and sobbed. As his body heaved, Margarethe moved closer, taking her old friend into her arms, soothing his cheeks, whispering into his hair as though he were a child; a sweet, blameless eleven-year-old boy who had just lost his sister.

By the time Bergmann had exhausted his tears, the light was fading and another day was drawing to an end, breathing its last in the shadow of the Dachstein. By now the snow was showing the makings of a blizzard and the lake was no longer visible. Winter had returned. Margarethe looked at the bone angel in Bergmann's grip and he followed her eyes.

"You know," he said, "it seems kind of fitting that it was your son who found Traudi's necklace."

"I think so too," Margarethe agreed. She got to her feet, stamping them briskly to free them of the cold that had set in.

"He's a fine man, your boy," Bergmann told her. "You should feel proud."

"Of Leopold?" she asked with a smile. "Well yes, I do feel proud. He has a good heart."

Chapter Seventeen

Leo was attaching the skins to his skis by the time Günter arrived.

"Nice day for it," Leo greeted, taking the chance to wipe the snow from his lashes.

"It's the kind of day Austrians were made for," Günter replied with a grin. He unloaded the car before surveying the landscape ahead – or at least as far as the snow would allow.

Leo checked his watch, almost 6.45am. It didn't happen often but the timing was perfect and it added to the deep satisfaction he felt at simply being outside – right in the heart of the valley, in crisp virgin snow, contemplating the ski tour ahead and feeling privileged to have been born into the midst of magnificence. There were few activities in life that allowed a man to experience something immense, but ski touring was one of them. The resorts were fun, but venturing off-piste was where the challenge lay. No carefully groomed runs, no machines or ploughs to hammer out bumps, the terrain was as difficult or as easy as nature chose to make it, and the relationship between man and mountain felt all the more honest for the respect that had to be shown. Ski touring was hard work. There was nothing glamorous about the sport. There was no fashion to follow. A man paid for his pass in burning muscle and sweat. He earned the right to be there.

Leo poured himself a cup of sweet tea before packing the flask in his rucksack, alongside the first aid kit, a light jacket and a fresh t-shirt. He checked the pressure on the airbag canister and switched the tracking device to receive.

"You ready for the *Pieps* check?" he asked.

Günter nodded and walked further up the track before turning to face him.

"Five metres, position south west," Leo confirmed. The two of them then repeated the process with Günter switching his own tracker to receive.

According to the avalanche situation report today was a Hazard Level Three in the area, which indicated a considerable risk, somewhere between moderate and high. However, the weather report was a little more forgiving, predicting clearer skies by mid-morning. All being well, by the time they reached their goal, namely a hut 1,872 metres up on the Dachstein plateau, the sun would be shining and the view would be nothing short of spectacular. Leo tightened the straps that kept the tracker on his chest before zipping his jacket, stepping into his skis, opening the binding and switching his boots to walk mode. Under his breath, he whispered a welcome to the mountain.

"Show me what you've got, my friend."

Unhindered by any need to hurry, Leo and Günter ambled up the snow-covered track discussing nothing more serious than their chances of survival. As they walked, a slight breeze played around them, still sharp from the cold of the night, and the snow fell in large, gentle flakes, settling on their beards whilst melting on their skin as their bodies responded to the warmth of movement.

"God, I love this weather," Günter remarked, and Leo nodded in agreement.

Ten minutes into the tour they passed the House of the Blind Woman, a little to their left. After everything that had happened,

Leo couldn't help but look and he was surprised to see all the windows open and Bergmann stood outside, clearing the path. Instead of the lederhosen he habitually wore he was dressed in jeans and a jumper, with no hat covering his shock of grey hair. Armed with a shovel instead of a rifle, it was altogether a softer image than the old hunter had previously projected.

"*Servus!*" shouted Leo.

Bergmann glanced up from his work and Leo noted the effort it took to wipe the scowl from his face. Even so, he laid down his shovel and approached.

"*Servus*, Leopold, Günter. Good day for it."

"Yes, perfect," Leo agreed, "care to join us?"

"Only if you're packing a stretcher in your backpack; I've no longer the lungs for such things. But the next time you pass by, join me for a beer. I'll be living here from now on."

"Well, it's a fine house," Leo admitted, feeling weirdly conscious of the uncommon length of their conversation.

"Yes, it is a fine house," Bergmann acknowledged, "or at least it will be once it no longer smells like a gas station. Enjoy your ski tour, boys."

Bidding Bergmann goodbye, Leo and Günter continued their tour in silence. Once they were safely out of earshot Günter quipped, "Nice to see he found a personality along with the bones of his dead sister."

It could have sounded mean under the circumstances, but Leo laughed because his friend was only telling the truth.

Turning off the gravel road, they headed for the trees. Although the snow had settled, the snaking indentation left by the previous day's skiers was still visible and Leo moved ahead of Günter, taking the lead. Some fifteen minutes later he paused to remove his Gor-Tex jacket, having warmed up enough to swap it for the lighter cagoule in his rucksack. As he changed, he noted the presence of the mountain's regular residents and his eyes briefly followed the tracks of foxes and deer beneath the sheltered white canopy of the trees.

"Interesting that Bergmann is using the old house again," Günter remarked after he'd swapped his own thick jacket.

"I guess so," Leo replied, although the move didn't strike him as particularly remarkable. A house was like land – it could possess a man more deeply than love. "And what about your situation, have you convinced Lisa to come home yet?"

"She returned last night," Günter informed him, and Leo looked up, finding no hint of victory in his friend's face. "Lisa and the kids are back in their bedrooms, I'm on the sofa. But it's OK, you know, it's going to take time. She's still pretty hurt, and I can't blame her. Baby steps and all that."

Leo nodded – glad to hear there had been a thaw in marital relations – and resumed his own baby steps up the face of the mountain.

As the two men traversed through the trees, they passed a small, abandoned hut, its one window scuffed with age, standing like a rotting monument to a bygone era. Over the years, Leo had passed the hut a dozen times or more, thinking little of it, but on this occasion he felt a strange sort of sadness as he considered the ravages of time and its relentless march forwards. Over the centuries man had achieved much – taking possession of the skies, harnessing the energy of the sun, landing on the moon – but perhaps the greatest prize of all remained as elusive as ever, the ability to go backwards, to return to past glories and amend past mistakes. Time was an honest if hard master of the moment. And once something was done there was no undoing it. A man could only hope that the future might bring something to take the edge off any error.

After an hour and thirty minutes the men cleared the forest, coming to rest at the foot of a steep incline, its pristine white coat broken only by a smattering of bushes and grey slabs of vertical rock. With their leg muscles burning, they both paused to drink after which they inspected the scene ahead of them.

"What do you reckon?" Günter asked.

"I'd say 30 centimetres," Leo replied, knowing he was being asked about the depth of fresh snow.

"We should keep a fair distance then."

"Do you want to go first?"

"No, you carry on. I feel like having it easy today."

Leo smiled, knowing Günter was being polite. He lifted the catch on his boots, effectively putting a block under the binding in order to scale the steeper parts of the slope. He then stepped forward, his skis sinking a fraction into the powder. As he turned to traverse, he saw Günter starting to follow, confident that there was enough space between them to distribute their weight on the slope and thereby lessen the chances of them both being taken out should an avalanche occur. When Günter reached him, Leo set off for the other side of the incline, avoiding the rocky outcrop where the mountain was too steep for the snow to gain a hold. As they climbed higher the air felt sharper in their lungs, but the snow fell ever lighter until eventually it stopped altogether. Thirty-five minutes later they saw the hulking, wooden mass of the *Wiesberghaus* loom into view, its roofs and walls wrapped in a white blanket, belching smoke from a chimney. A favourite on the ski tour trail, the hut was famous for its rustic hospitality and hot apple strudel, and by the time Leo and Günter reached the open door they were sweating profusely and ready for cake.

Stepping out of their skis, they both took a moment to catch their breath before detaching the skins and readjusting the binding ready for the coming descent. As Leo's body began to cool, he ambled over to a rock pile a few metres from the hut. Clambering up he looked south towards Dachstein's glaciers, enjoying the vast snow desert caught between the goliath peaks that pierced the low-lying cloud. The scene was as perfect as a film set, and it was the closest Leo had got to touching heaven for most of the winter. He loved the mountains – not with a romantic heart, but with a raw affection and a deep respect that came from a lifetime of knowledge and experience. And it pained him, physically pained him, to think that one day the mountain's wintery mantel might be lost. Swiss scientists had recently predicted an end to Europe's great Alpine glaciers within a century. It seemed inconceivable standing where he stood at that moment, but if summer temperatures rose by a mere three degrees Celsius, the Alps would lose up to 80 per cent of their glacier cover. Two degrees more and they might be completely ice-free. The staggering beauty of the Dachstein would be lost to the descendants of those who had enjoyed it. And adding to this pain was the undeniable truth that the daily drive to Linz, to work at a job he hated, made Leo complicit in the destruction of the very thing he loved. His carbon footprint might not count for much in the great sea of crap being pumped into the skies, but he had watched *The Meaning of Life* and it had taken only a wafer thin mint to explode the fat man. Everything counted. Every action had a consequence.

"Are you having another funny turn?"

Leo glanced down to see Günter staring up at him, already changed and hungry for cake. Taking a last look at the glacier before him – feeling sentimental, feeling annoyed at feeling sentimental and feeling increasingly chilly – Leo descended the rock pile to rejoin Günter. Stripping quickly out of his top he briefly embraced the slap of cold air on his chest before diving into a clean t-shirt. Five minutes later the two of them were in the *Wiesberghaus* enjoying coffee and strudel.

Following three cigarettes and 'one little beer', the two friends returned to their skis, feeling the minus temperature for the first time since dawn. Günter grinned as he put on his helmet and adjusted his shades and Leo felt his excitement. There was nothing greater than skiing through virgin snow. It was the closest a man got to flying, and with a 'whoop!' they set off – Günter going first, carving tight zigzags in the landscape, which Leo replicated a few metres further to the right. Racing for the forest, their knees taking the strain of the bumpy terrain, they barely paused to look as they sped into and through the trees, feeling gloriously alive.

On the drive home, Leo took a call from Harri who had heard via an old police colleague that the bones of Bergmann's sister had been finally and formally identified. Although the strange amulet discovered among the child's remains had been evidence enough to convince the majority, the authorities had required more forensic proof, which they received on Friday.

"Well, I guess that's an end to it," Leo said.

"Or a beginning," Harri replied, before quickly contradicting himself by admitting it was probably too late in the day for Bergmann to go far with a fresh start. It was an innocent observation that unwittingly rattled Leo, especially when he returned home to find his mother fussing in the kitchen – fixing his lunch like an apparition out of the twilight zone with the both of them having regressed twenty years. He then recalled having given her a key.

After pausing to kiss his mother's powdered cheek, Leo headed for the study, where he unpinned the list of the missing from the corkboard on the wall. Placing it on the desk he reached for a pen and with his index finger he traced the list of names; Andreas Riezinger, Albrecht Heschl, Bernd Meurers, Claudia Kimmes, Kurt Eisl, Waltraud Bergmann...

"Hello Waltraud," he said softly, the name sounding oddly adult for a little girl. Yet the facts had always been there, neatly written, if given little thought, on the sheet of lined paper before him – 'Waltraud Bergmann, born 1949, missing 1958'. It was sad to think that it had taken the discovery of bones, so evidently child size, to make a little girl of such a grown up name. Leo clicked his pen to add a new entry beside her details, 'found 2012'. Then, in a moment of recurring sentimentality, he also wrote the name she was more commonly called by those who remembered: 'Traudi'.

Leo's eyes ran down the list of the names seeing, perhaps for the first time, more than an inventory of the missing. The list was actually a record of grief, a register of lives lost in the truest sense possible. And beyond those names he knew there were many more names: the scores of bereaved who had been trapped by hope, unwilling or unable to mourn whilst the absence of a body kept possibility alive. Leo had devoted 18 years to the rescue team and in all that time he had closed the open circle only once – Markus Beck, born 1980, missing 1998, found 2002. Markus had disappeared whilst snowboarding. Leo remembered the search well because it was the first time he had experienced failure with the team. For three days they had looked for the teenager, but they had found no sign. He had disappeared. And though there was plentiful speculation, nobody could say for certain what had happened to him, not until almost four years later when a group of cavers discovered his body, deep inside the Dachstein. It was a chance discovery – the labyrinth of tunnels within the mountain is huge, carved by an aeon of water pushing through the limestone rock – but it had solved the mystery. Markus had fallen into one of the many holes or vertical caves that riddled the mountainside. It was more than possible that Traudi had suffered a similar fate, walking over a snow-covered opening, falling to her, hopefully quick, death. It would never be clear how or why the mountain finally released her bones, but the heavy snowfall this year followed by the extreme and very quick thaw could have raised the water level within the mountain, perhaps dislodging the child's bones from a shelf in the damp, dark cold where she had lain for more than five decades. Nobody would ever know for certain, but for some it was enough to simply have her found – admittedly too late for her traumatised mother, but in time to at least allow her brother some semblance of peace.

"Leo!"

He pinned the paper back on the board, wondering whether the Dachstein might release the rest of her secrets within his lifetime. He then wondered whether he should add the details of his latest ski tour to his journal while he could still feel its memory burning within his tired muscles.

"Leo!" his mother shouted again. "Your lunch is ready!"

"OK! I'm not deaf!"

"You soon will be if I have to come in there and box your ears!"

Smiling, Leo resisted pulling out the journal and went to the kitchen, finding his mother still fussing with a cloth on the work surfaces.

"Looks very clean," he acknowledged.

"You live like a student," she replied. She shut the fridge door on the bagful of shopping she had brought with her. After pouring two coffees from a cafetiere she led the way to the sitting room where Leo found a *Leberkäse* in a *semmel* bun waiting for him on a plate.

"No napkin?" he asked.

His mother replied with a withering look. Taking a seat opposite her son, a hand briefly fluttered over her hair before swooping down to her lap to smooth the fabric of her skirt. Leo recognised the signs, but he had a question of his own first.

"Why did you lie to me about visiting Bergmann?"

To her credit his mother barely flinched. "Did I lie?"

Leo stared at her and Margarethe raised her eyebrows. "Okay, perhaps I did," she conceded. She looked at her son's cigarettes. They almost looked appealing.

"We used to be close," she admitted, "a long time ago, when we were both young. I suppose I wanted to protect him somehow. Reinhardt was gibbering about seeing the dead and then you revealed you'd seen the two of them arguing in the square. I was concerned for him. I knew about his sister, we all did, at least those of us of the same generation, and you hang on to whatever you can find when something like that happens – even ghost stories. I felt sorry for Heinrich, nothing more than that. And so I went to his house to offer some kind of support and a few words of advice. He didn't listen, of course, but I didn't know he was also seeing ghosts at that time. And I didn't want to tell you because, to be frank, I didn't think it was any of your business."

"Well, that's put me in my place," Leo observed.

"You know what I mean."

Margarethe gazed at her son, scarcely able to believe that the baby she once held to her breast was the man now sitting before her. Even so, she still recognised the boy in her child and she worried about him. She always would.

"Have you decided what you're going to do with that suitcase?" she asked, tilting her head backwards, towards the front door.

Leo shook his head. "I'm still thinking."

"A person can think for too long you know. You've had weeks now."

"I know."

Margarethe placed a hand on his arm. "Then you might also know that there's a reason why Hallstatt men tend to marry local girls."

Leo sighed. He had heard it all before – Ana was lazy; Ana was hot-headed; Ana was moody and unpredictable – and he was about to shake off his mother's touch when she surprised him, revealing that she too could be unpredictable on occasion.

"I think Ana is a lovely girl," she said softly, "and for a while it seemed that she really did make you happy. But when all is said and done the two of you are very different people, with very different interests, who come from very different places. People have roots, Leo, and they reach deeper than you think. If you take a plant from its soil can it grow in the desert?"

"Possibly, if you water it."

"And did you water it?"

Leo frowned and his mother squeezed his arm. "Think about it, Leo. It's time you came to a decision. Whatever you choose to do, you are my son. All I want is your happiness."

Leo sat on the stairs, staring at the suitcase. It was fairly innocuous as far as luggage went – black, functional, leather trim with wheels and a handle – and yet it stood like a beacon of failure at his door. Ana had packed it, but the clothes inside belonged to him, as did the choice. He either stayed or he went. So, it was not only a suitcase – it was an end or a start – but with everything having happened so quickly his mind had yet to decide which.

When Ana had returned from her fortnight in Valencia, Leo had recognised things might not be going well. He tasted the apprehension in her kiss at the airport. He noted the careful conversation during the drive home and the conscious effort it took to keep the tone light. It was a forced camaraderie they shared, and once they walked into the house the pretence became that little bit harder to maintain. Ana looked inside the fridge to find it was empty. She inspected the coffee tin to discover it bare. And she had glanced at the Stubai Glacier fleece waiting for her on the dining table with something bordering contempt.

"Is that my Christmas present?" she asked.

"Do you like it?" he replied.

"You didn't even wrap it."

Ana then extracted a number of gifts from her suitcase, dressed in festive paper and bows, an inscription penned to each and every one of them. Among the assorted boxes and wrappings were little things such as lip balm and moisturiser 'to keep you pretty on the mountain'; an AWOLNATION CD 'to help you look cool in front of your students'; a new watch 'to help you count down the hours until you see me again'; and a traditional Spanish Navaja hunting knife 'because I know you like to kill things'.

Leo opened the gifts, appalled.

"You said we shouldn't spend much this year."

"I changed my mind."

"Well, thanks."

"You're welcome."

And though he bent to kiss her and she accepted his lips, the day never truly recovered and later that evening they went to bed at different times, both feigning different levels of fatigue.

The following day the mood was little better and it felt like winter had slipped under the door to settle in their house, with both of them living separate lives under the one roof. As the hunting season was drawing to an end, Leo left home early to reach the woods by dawn, returning to the house, and his bed, by mid-afternoon. Occasionally, they went skiing, but when the lifts closed Leo preferred to descend off-piste rather than join Ana in the cable car. When they were indoors, he naturally gravitated to his study whilst Ana wrapped herself in a blanket to stare out of the window, watching the snow fall. Even on New Year's Eve they failed to reignite their previous warmth, with Ana leaving Berni's shortly after midnight, claiming she could no longer cope with the 'relentless machismo'. Leo followed her six hours later and that afternoon, on the first day of the New Year Ana told him they 'needed to talk'. Unfortunately her timing was awful. Leo was hungover and horribly dehydrated. More than that, he was growing tired of feeling like the bad guy.

"We could move to Spain," she suggested.

"And what would I do in Spain?"

"Work in an olive oil shop?"

Leo held her stare, not totally convinced she was being facetious. Naturally, another night of cold shoulders and sleeping back-to-back followed, but to Leo's surprise Ana woke up the next day in a far more positive mood, and, foolishly, Leo believed the danger had passed. It was a belief helped by the fact that later that night they made love for the first time in a month. In every sense of the word, Leo was relieved and he naturally assumed that life was resuming its normal play. He started to relax again. He went hunting unhindered by guilt. He fitted in a couple more ski tours. And every evening he ran for an hour, whenever the falling snow would allow. Of course, it was only now, almost three months later, that he understood that the bounce in Ana's step during those days wasn't due to any thaw in their relations, but rather to a determination to take control.

In short, she was plotting.

When the new school term began, Leo suspected nothing. Every day he left their bed a fraction before dawn, returning home some twelve hours later to find Ana either reading a book or glued to the laptop. More often than not she was wrapped in a blanket and wearing two pairs of socks, and she would offer to heat up some noodles. He would have preferred lasagne or a meaty paella, but it was nothing he felt he could mention. Even so, he sensed nothing untoward, nothing overtly unusual. Ana continued to work at the salt shop, he continued to drive to Linz, they slept in the same bed and they chatted about whatever was worthy of comment from the day they had spent apart. There was nothing within their routine that gave him any reason to suspect that there was anything other than the cold of winter that was making his girlfriend act cooler than she used to. Then, on the Thursday night during that first week of the new term, she had insisted they make love – insisted, there was no other word for it – and as he buckled under the pressure to perform it was an unusually awkward and clumsy experience that brought them both to an ultimately unsatisfactory finish. Afterwards, as they lay side-by-side, both nursing their own respective disappointments, Ana had turned to him, her brown eyes huge and softened by kindness.

"I love you," she said.

Naturally, Leo had replied that he loved her too, before rolling away to set the alarm and turn off the light. The next day, when Leo returned from work, Ana was gone.

Every trace of her life with him had vanished: the few knick-knacks, the astonishing number of knickers, the creams and scented candles. She had cleaned the kitchen, the bathroom and changed the bed sheets. Even her smell had been eradicated by bleach. Nothing remained of the woman he had called his girlfriend for the past three years – nothing apart from a suitcase left by the door and a letter laid on the desk in his study.

All that Ana had to say had been inscribed on one side of a blank sheet of paper. Leo read the letter. He then read it again before heading for the shed. Under a rock by the door he found the key she had left. Removing the padlock, he opened the door, and immediately felt the weight of her loneliness land on his chest. Inside the shed, taking up most of the floor, was the trunk of wood he had carried from the lumber yard. Its centre had been hollowed and tiny, intricate flowers had been carved along one edge. It was nowhere near finished, yet it was quite clearly a cradle.

"*This was my gift to our baby. I never told you because I wasn't sure how you would react and I really wanted to enjoy the moment, fearing you wouldn't. Unfortunately, nine weeks into the pregnancy I miscarried. You were away with the rescue team. You never called. And when you returned home I was so unhappy, and so angry with you, I couldn't even share my grief.*"

Leo stared at the cradle, until it began to blur. Sitting in the dust – amongst the wood shavings of what had clearly been a labour of love – he lit a cigarette that his chest was too tight to inhale and it burned away in his fingers. For a long while he couldn't move, but when he finally forced himself to his feet, he went to the pub.

The next few weeks passed by in a monotonous haze of shame and disbelief. He drove to Linz every day, barely noticing the journey. He taught his classes with a distraction that confused his pupils. He hovered outside the principal's door, always on the verge of entering, but never quite making it. And he waited for the term to break, convincing himself that this would be the right time to make a decision. But a day into the vacation, the winter descended, trapping him in Hallstatt and closing the exit route. The suitcase waited in the hallway, and Ana's letter was an almost constant presence in his hands – not permitting any escape from the sorrow, the veiled accusations, and the dripping disappointment that permeated every line.

"*I love you, Leo, but being with you has only made me lonely. I have too little to do and you have too much. I have no sense of 'me' here. For a time I was the Spanish Girl. Then I was Leo's Spanish Girlfriend. I have no friends to call my own. I only had you, and I thought that would be enough. But it wasn't because I wasn't enough for you. You had so many other things to do.*"

Sat on the stairs, Leo lit a cigarette, flicking ash onto the floor whilst remembering how he had squandered their time. There was work, the commute, his sports, the occasional weekend away – held hostage by duty and responsibility – and then there were the beers he enjoyed at Berni's that allowed him to shake off the stress of chasing the clock. Of course, he recognised this had left little space for Ana, but they had spent most of their nights together, and he had believed this to be their time. According to the letter, this was a belief that was close to delusional.

"*On paper it might seem that I enjoy the lion's share of your day, being with you from night until dawn. But hours spent in bed are not a substitute for living them. Sleep brings a distortion of time, turning hours into minutes. The time you give me, Leo, feels not like the lion's share of your day, but rather like the carcass that remains after the feast. And gradually, this has turned me into someone I barely recognise: someone moody, uptight, and aggressive. It's hardly surprising you thought I was depressed. But I wasn't depressed. I was disappointed – in you, in me, in what we had become."*

Leo lit another cigarette. He looked into the packet, aware that it wouldn't be long until he would have to brave the cold and the attentions of Elsa in the corner store. Not that the cold unduly worried him, quite the contrary in fact. It reminded him he was still alive. In contrast, Ana was a woman who lived for the summer. She had spent a lifetime kissed by the Spanish sun and she missed the blue skies, the coarse grass and the sun-bleached stones of her home.

"I used to watch the clouds passing overhead as I waited for you to return to Hallstatt. Some days they would race across the sky at such a pace it seemed like they were running scared of the coming winter. I knew how they felt. And when winter arrived, I would look at the trees, at their branches dipping under a dragging weight of snow, and I would feel like we were all being buried in the same grave, interned alive under a relentless, merciless cold. Winter it seems is not for me. I think you know this already. It simply lasts too long here. But I walk into your study and I look at your photographs and I understand that winter is not only for you, it is a part of you. Those poor children that were found in the ice, you look at them and see something magical – as objects that have been preserved for an eternity by the wonder of ice. But I see them as the children they once were – children who died frightened and alone, killed by the cold."

Leo forced himself off the stairs and into the kitchen. He made himself a coffee and turned to look out of the window. The snow was falling again, but gently, descending like clumps of feathers upon the town. How could someone not see the beauty? He inspected the sky, finding a patchwork of grey and white cloud. It reminded him of a duvet, not a harbinger of death. On the ground, he watched people come and go, running about their business, knowing that unless they were students or visiting

Chinese he would know them all. And then he looked at the great walls of the Dachstein, created by layers of soluble bedrock, hiding some of Austria's largest caves, and supporting the glaciers of Hallstatt, Gosau and Schladming. It was a formidable presence hanging over the town, but it wasn't only a mountain, it was a mother to the people below, a mother who had opened her veins to feed her children with the blood of White Gold. Though she caused as much pain as she did joy she was no different to any other religion in that respect. And without the Dachstein, there would be no Hallstatt. Without the Dachstein, Leo might never have set eyes on a glacier. And there it was again, that familiar missed beat within his chest as he contemplated the loss of the region's great ice fields. In all honesty, Leo wasn't sure he could stand to witness such a passing.

"I have packed you a suitcase. Inside you'll find a pair of jeans, a couple of t-shirts and a jumper. There is also a toothbrush and a phone charger. Don't call me. Don't email. Just pick up the suitcase and come. I promise I will wait for you. And if you don't come, well, time will reveal your decision and I will wish you only the best. For me, there is nothing left to say, except I love you. Ana."

Leo lit a cigarette and leaned against the cooker, using the sink as an ashtray. He really was a pig, he thought, and things could only get worse. If he didn't do something to change his life he might very well end up drowning in a cesspit of indecision and faeces. He loved Ana. He wanted to be with her. He wanted to feel her soft arms about his neck. He wanted her to laugh at his jokes. Leo then glanced through the window at the mountain, at the immovable mass of grey rock that had entombed the old and the young, and the presence of which kept him anchored to the town, stopping him from drifting too far away. However, the Dachstein was made of limestone not blood and Leo recalled the crib in the shed: the unfinished evidence of another's broken dream. He thought of Ana and of her letter and of the promise she had made after all the accusations and regret. He thought of it all, and by the time he had smoked his last cigarette he knew what he would do.

Deep down, in the pit of his stomach, he guessed he had always known.

Flicking his cigarette end into the sink, Leo walked from the kitchen. For a second or two, he paused in the hallway, hardly believing he had come to a decision. Scratching roughly at his beard, he took two steps forward, picked up the suitcase by its handle and with a quick glance at the door, he took it upstairs.

Taking the steps, two at a time, he reached for the phone in his pocket and dialled.

"*Servus* Günter, fancy a little beer?"

Acknowledgements

As ever, my first thanks go to Mum, Dad and Louise for their eagle eyes, encouragement, love and support. After that, it's pretty much a free for all of gratitude.

Without doubt, the beautiful village of Hallstatt was a tremendous source of inspiration, as was the whole Salzkammergut region where I spent three happy years from 2009 to 2012. During that time, I also had the good fortune to make some hugely colourful and inspirational friends who all played a part in this book, sometimes unwittingly. So thanks to Ursula, Jackie, Elke, Janet, Annette, Celia, Doro, Günter, Georg, the real-life rescue heroes of the *Lawinen- und Suchhundestaffel Bergrettung Oberösterreich* and pretty much everyone I ever met at KuK in Bad Ischl. Also many thanks to Hélène and James who appear to have become my trusty go-to first-draft readers.

Special mentions also go to Christa and Marita who were a huge force not only in my life, but also in the beating heart of this book. However, the biggest debt of thanks is owed to Lorenz. This is his book from the very first page to the very last. Always special. So very, very special.

BORN UNDER A MILLION SHADOWS

(TRANSWORLD 2009/ HENRY HOLT AND COMPANY 2010)

The Taliban have disappeared from Kabul's streets, but the long shadows of their brutal regime remain. In his short life eleven-year-old Fawad has known more grief than most: his father and brother have been killed, his sister has been abducted, and Fawad and his mother, Mariya, must rely on the charity of family to eke out a hand-to-mouth existence.

Then Mariya finds a position as housekeeper for a charismatic western woman, Georgie, and Fawad dares to hope for an end to their struggle. He soon discovers that his beloved Georgie is caught up in a dangerous love affair with the powerful Afghan warlord Haji Khan, a legendary name on the streets of Kabul. At first resentful of Haji Khan's presence, Fawad learns that love can move a man to act in surprising ways, and an overwhelming act of generosity persuades him of the warlord's good intentions.

But even a man as influential as Haji Khan can't protect Fawad from the next tragedy to blight his young life, a tragedy so devastating that it threatens to destroy the one thing Fawad thought he could never lose: his love for his country.

APHRODITE'S WAR (TRANSWORLD 2011)

THE ISLAND IS DIVIDED, BUT ONE MAN'S LOVE WILL NEVER BE COMPROMISED...

Cyprus, 1955 - a guerrilla war is raging and four Greek brothers are growing up to the familiar sounds of exploding bombs and sniper fire.

Determined to avenge the death of his elder brother and to win the heart of his beloved Praxi, young Loukis joins a cell of schoolboy terrorists operating in the mountains. But when his cohorts blow themselves up in a freak accident, he returns home in shock, yearning for the warm embrace of his family - and of his sweetheart.

But his adored Praxi is now married to someone else, and playing at her feet is a young toddler...

CPSIA information can be obtained at www.ICGtesting.com
Printed in the USA
BVOW08s0709300616

454028BV00002B/19/P